PAYBACK

a Novel

Barbara A. Kiger

Tallahassee, Florida

Inquiries should be addressed to:
CyPress Publications
P.O. Box 2636
Tallahassee, Florida 32316-2636
http://cypress-starpublications.com

Cover photograph courtesy of Brenda Kiger

Cover design Juanita S. Raymond

Library of Congress Control Number: 2004112083

ISBN 0-9672585-6-1

First Edition

Dedication

To my family and friends, especially
Wayne, Dottie and Paula

Acknowledgements

As a book needs more than an author's sometimes overactive imagination, I was fortunate to have help from three of my sons, Chuck a truck driver, Pat a former policeman, and Jim a lawyer. I was fortunate, too, in that my editor, Lee Raymond, was a long-time friend who already knew my foibles and limitations. My writer's group, the Tallahassee Writers' Association, gave me support and encouragement whenever I needed it, and provided expert advice through their programs and speakers. What is right about *Payback* I share with all of them. What is wrong is exclusively mine.

Something given or demanded . . .

Payback

Chapter One

ADRIFT SOMEWHERE BETWEEN DREAM STATE AND NOT-QUITE-AWAKE STATE, I FUMBLED THE ringing telephone to my ear and answered its persistent clamor with a mumbled, "Hello?"

"Ginny! Leslie Parker's been shot," a voice answered. It was Steve's voice, sounding more like the doctor he was than my lover, which he also was.

I shook my head. I must have heard wrong. Leslie was a doctor, a surgeon like Steve, not a patient.

"She's on her way to surgery, and she's asking for you. Will you come?"

The urgency I heard in his voice made me a believer. I rolled from the bed naked, my preferred state of dress for sleep, and pulled bra and panties from a drawer where they nestled between Steve's jockey shorts and tee shirts. "I'm on my way," I said, and then asked, "Is Bryan there?"

"He's not here, Ginny."

"Dr. Brock," another voice interrupted.

"Got to go, Ginny. They're ready for me." The clatter of a receiver being hung up sounded in my ear.

Shot! I shivered, suddenly feeling cold. Where in hell was Bryan?

I dismissed Leslie's missing husband and wiggled into jeans and a long-sleeved turtleneck. How had it happened? A mugging?

The zipper on my jacket caught halfway up, its metal teeth biting into the facings. Holding the fronts together, I ran from the house to my Ford Ranger. Overnight, Michigan's lower peninsula had become a freezer. Still, my small truck started on the first try, and I headed out Valley Avenue toward the eastbound freeway. On the radio, easy listening jazz switched to an easy listening announcer who said it was four a.m. and twenty degrees.

Even at this hour, the lot set aside for Mercy Hospital's Emergency Room offered few empty spaces. All were far removed from the brightly lighted entrance. I pulled in between a Nissan Pathfinder and a Honda Civic, cut the engine, and braved the cold.

Shadows lurked beyond the pools of arched overhead lights, and I avoided their dark corners as I zigzagged my way through the rows of parked cars. Definitely a mugging, I decided.

A pair of mobile trauma units with wide, gaping doors blocked the hospital's entrance. Two bulky figures emerged from inside one of the orange and white vehicles and hurried a stretcher up the ramp. Marion City was having a busy night.

Inside, restless bodies with deadpan faces and deader looking eyes waited in molded plastic chairs. Ahead, a set of swinging doors denied admittance to all but authorized personnel. I pushed through anyway. A familiar figure wearing green hospital scrubs, Maggie Janko by name, the nurse half of a doctor-nurse couple with whom Steve and I often double-dated, freed herself from a similarly clad group.

"Have you seen Steve?" I called.

"He's still in Surgery, Ginny," Maggie answered. A uniformed police officer claimed her attention, cutting off further conversation.

Deflated by the prospect of a long wait, I headed for the staff lounge. Patience was not one of my virtues.

The chair was uncomfortable, and the feature article in a dog-eared nursing journal offered nothing but blood and gore. I flipped the magazine to its backside and shoved it to the far side of the table. Behind me the door opened.

"You looked like you could use this." Maggie handed me a mug of what smelled like freshly brewed coffee.

"I just checked with Surgery. Dr. Parker's holding her own."

I brought the cup to my lips, inhaled the fragrance, and took a sip, relishing the jolt of caffeine that came with it. "Steve said she was asking for me. Do you know why?"

Maggie sighed herself into a chair with, "Aren't you her lawyer?"

I nodded. Regina Marie Arthur, if that's who I was, it being too early in the morning for absolutes of any kind, law school graduate and head of the Arthur & Arthur Security Agency, was in fact Leslie Parker's lawyer.

"She hired me to find financing for a house," I admitted. I blew on the coffee and got to the heart of the matter, the reason I was sitting in a damnably uncomfortable chair in the nurse's lounge of Mercy Hospital's Emergency Room. "Steve said she'd been shot. Do you know what happened?"

Maggie shook her head. "We're just the repair shop."

"Is Bryan here yet?"

Maggie's attention reverted to her half-empty mug.

"What's wrong?"

"Let me see if the EMTs who brought Leslie in are still here. They can tell you more than I can."

Maggie was gone, leaving me with a legion of questions that needed answers. I was alone, sitting at a Formica table, its top dirtied by intertwined coffee rings and a litter of mugs. I drummed my fingers. Fortunately, the wait was short. The EMT was a no-nonsense guy, who swaggered into the room and with little urging got right to the point.

"There were three of them, two on the bed in the motel room and the doc. She was outside in a car, in the front seat behind the steering wheel." He settled into a chair, making it look almost comfortable. "The two on the bed were dead. The doc was still alive. It looked like an in-and-out gut shot, but she was bleeding like a stuck pig."

He paused. I waited. It was his show.

"She kept calling out, 'Bryan,' and pointing to the open door of the motel room."

Could it be? Was the man on the bed? . . . "You're sure he was dead?"

The EMT nodded his head. "I got a good look at him, besides which, the coroner wasn't in any hurry to move him."

"You said two." I took in a deep breath, steadying my unsteady voice. "Do you know who the other one was?"

The man shifted. His chair protested. "I was too busy to ask."

"Just tell me what you saw." I leaned forward, urging an answer.

"I didn't get a very good look at her—"

"Her?"

"Her," the man repeated. "She was on the far side of the bed."

The door to the lounge swung open. "We've got us another run," a second EMT, a slimmer version of the first, called.

"Did he tell you about Bryan?" Maggie had followed the second EMT into the room.

I nodded, though not really listening, and pushed away from the table.

"Where are you going, Ginny?"

"To get some answers."

The voice on the other end of the city's EMT system told me the location of the shooting. It was the information I needed, and I headed for the parking lot. Maybe it was the news I'd just received rather than the weather, but it seemed colder out now than before. I worked free my formerly recalcitrant zipper on the run, and as before, the dependable Ranger started without urging.

Police cars and uniformed officers blocked the front entrance to the Riverside Motel, the location to which the EMT dispatcher had directed me, but I chose an unguarded side entrance and slipped the Ford into the back of the lot. A crowd had gathered in front of the second unit. I headed for it, staying behind a row of parked cars as I did. Leslie Parker's gray Mazda, circled in crime scene tape, was among them. I pulled in beside it, killed the engine, and once again braved the cold.

"What's going on?" I asked a man who stood close by.

"Don't know," he said. He hunched his shoulders and stuffed his hands deeper into his pockets.

"I heard a doctor was killed," a shrill voice volunteered.

"No, they took him away in the ambulance," another countered.

I tuned out their voices and worked my way towards a policeman.

"My name's Ginny Arthur," I said to the officer who guarded the door and a midnight-blue Jaguar that was parked in front. Both were cordoned off with yellow tape.

"Tom Blakely." He offered a warm smile and a wave with a hand that held a clipboard. "You probably don't remember me, but I met you a couple of summers ago, Miss Arthur. I drove you home after that shooting in the woods north of town."

Memory tugged. I remembered the shooting, the bodies in the boathouse, even the fear. But not the man. "That was a long time ago," I said with an apologetic smile.

The policeman nodded agreement. "So, what brings you here tonight? Another case?"

I nodded yes as my eyes wandered over the car. Bryan's, I wondered? He drove one like it.

"If your client's in there, you might have a problem." Blakely indicated a door numbered 14B. "There's two of them inside, and they're both dead."

"Do you know who they are?"

Blakely shook his head. "Sorry, can't help you there. I'm just the gatekeeper." He proffered the clipboard, which I could see held a list of names. "Whoever comes or goes has to sign in and out with me."

I nodded politely and stepped forward. How far would Blakely let me go?

I was never to know. The door to 14B flew open, stopping my forward progress. Back-lighted in the opening stood a redheaded man who looked remarkably like . . . "David Arthur." Uncle David's name escaped my lips and with it a rush of emotion, anger mostly, for the man who had betrayed, then deserted me.

"Hello, Red," the man in the doorway said. His bottom lip curved into a smile, the corners disappearing into an overgrown, even-redder mustache.

My anger, unreasonable though it was, needed an outlet, and I fixed on this unknown someone. Only before I could speak, he banged the door shut.

The crash of the door closing in my face opened another in my mind. I was back in time, back to the night Blakely had so recently mentioned. Blakely was there, opening the rear door of a cruiser, and that man. The man who was Uncle David's look-alike. My eyes opened wide as if seeing again those long ago images.

"Are you satisfied? People get killed, crooks escape, and you crawl back into your safe haven." His blue eyes under bushy red brows, red as my own red hair, bore into me. "When will people like you learn to leave police work to the police."

"But—"

"But nothing, shit!" He grabbed the door from Blakely's hand and shoved me none too gently into the back of the cruiser. "Go home and stay home, Red."

I blinked my eyes, fearful that the remembered tears might make a comeback.

"Who was that?" I demanded.

"That's Douglas MacPhearson, Miss Arthur, one of the homicide detectives."

A gust of wind blew the yellow tape upwards. Allowing myself no time to think, or rather change my mind, I ducked beneath it and turned the doorknob. "Detective MacPhearson?" I called as the door opened.

"Here," a voice from across the room answered.

My eyes sought the man but found the bed.

"Who are you, and what are you doing here?" growled a nearby voice.

"Ginny Arthur," I managed. My eyes fixed on the man in the bed, moved up his legs and stopped at his head. Naked, obscenely dead, the body screamed violence.

"Are you okay, Red?"

A hand touched my arm. It was MacPhearson. Uncle David's look-alike, an antagonist, a nemesis from the past returned to haunt me.

He had separated himself from the crime scene specialist, the criminalists garbed in disposable coveralls, head and foot protectors and latex gloves who were brushing, dusting, and vacuuming the room and its contents.

I felt my mouth move, but my mind refused to engage. The blood-splattered form of a woman, whose chest wore layers of congealed blood, had my full attention.

MacPhearson shuffled closer, moved between me and them. A wall, he cut off my view of the dead.

"You did say Ginny Arthur?"

It was a question. I nodded and leaned against the door. There are some things law school didn't prepare you for.

"Mind telling me what you're doing here?"

I took a steadying breath. He'd emphasized *me*, but I ignored it. "Leslie and Bryan Parker are my clients. She was shot here tonight."

I moved, tried for a second look at the bed, but MacPhearson and his muscular six-foot-plus frame moved with me.

"They call me Mac," he said.

A bump from behind pushed me closer, and I tipped my head to look at him. His slightly curled red hair—it was redder than mine—touched his ears and brushed the top of his collar. His eyes were blue, and his face the color of fresh sunburn. Seen this close, his resemblance to David Arthur faded.

He touched my arm again. "The same Ginny Arthur who was involved with the murders of those Marion State students a couple of summers ago?" His brows, bushy like his mustache, came together as he talked. Had he always had a mustache?

My mind shifted from then to now. "It's that man on the bed I'm interested in. Is it Bryan Parker?"

I'd seen enough to know it was, but I didn't want him asking questions about Uncle David or, for that matter, me.

MacPhearson turned sideways, allowing me an unobstructed view. "You tell me. He isn't carrying any identification."

Anger still too close to the surface threatened, and I brushed past the detective. Bryan's body lay with his face to the room. Splattered blood, bone, and brain from a hole in the middle of his forehead and an even bigger hole in the back of his head formed a macabre patchwork pattern.

I mentally filled in the hole in his forehead. "It's Bryan Parker," I said.

"That's what this says, too." The detective held up a clear plastic bag in his latex-gloved hand, holding what appeared to be a man's wallet.

I pulled open the door. "Thanks for your help."

"Any time, Red."

"The name's Arthur, Miss Arthur," I corrected.

"Any time, Miss Arthur," he countered.

I heard him laugh, heard him say, "I heard you not only found the killers, you also broke up a twenty-year-old burglary ring. Is it too late for an apology?"

His words followed me into the cold and the crowd that still waited.

"Asshole!" I muttered through clenched teeth.

"Did you get what you came for?" Blakely called as I headed toward the Ranger.

"I did," I said, and a lot more besides, I thought.

I offered Blakely a wave, but he was gone, his face lost in a sea of other faces.

An ambulance arrived as I pulled onto Ann Street. I slowed and let it pass. Was it only last summer that Steve had introduced me to the surgical resident and her dark-haired husband? Only last summer that I'd rented Uncle David's apartment to the couple?

Though I still thought of the apartment as belonging to David Arthur, in reality it was mine. Uncle David had transferred ownership of the Michigan Street building as well as his interest in the Arthur & Arthur Security Agency to me before leaving, before going to wherever in hell he had gone.

Uncle David . . . My thoughts wandered even farther. MacPhearson. That redheaded detective . . . The lights of the emergency wing brightened the winter dawn and chased away my thoughts. This time only one trauma unit guarded the hospital's entrance. Inside, however, things had not changed. Blank faces still stared from plastic chairs, and a harried Maggie still talked to uniformed policemen.

Chapter Two

MAGGIE TURNED AWAY FROM THE POLICEMAN. "STEVE'S IN THE LOUNGE, GINNY." HER EYES found mine. "Bad news?" she asked.

"Bad news," I agreed.

Maggie's expression changed to one of concern. She reached to touch me.

"Later," I said. All I wanted now was Steve. Pushing the horror of what I had seen in the motel room as deeply into my mind as possible, I hurried down the hall to the nurse's lounge.

His face wore a day's stubble, and a hank of unruly brown hair fell across his forehead. He looked tired, exhausted, beat. I resisted the impulse to push the hair aside and instead settled for a smile of hello.

"How's Leslie?" I asked. I pulled a chair close and sat beside him.

"She's in the Surgical Intensive Care Unit. The surgery went fine, and if everything else goes as well, she should be on her way home in a few days." He squeezed my hand. "Where did you go?"

"I went to the motel and checked out Leslie's story."

"And?"

"Bryan's dead."

Steve massaged his bloodshot eyes with thumb and forefinger. "She kept calling for him, said he was dead, and mumbled something about a gun."

I thought of Bryan's bed partner. "Nothing else?"

"She asked for you." Steve slid down in his chair, rested the end of his spine on the edge of the seat.

The door opened. Maggie, her arms filled with charts, backed into the lounge. "I hear Dr. Parker's going to be okay."

"So far so good." Steve pulled himself from the chair. "And it's time I checked on her."

"Can I see her, Steve?" I hesitated. "That is, if you think it's okay."

Steve looked down at me. "Let me have a look-see first. Wait here. I'll give you a call."

The door swooshed shut behind him, hiding Steve's bulky frame and the slight limp caused by a long-ago leg fracture that had ended a promising football career. Though the limp usually went unnoticed, the day's, or rather, the night's long hours had exacerbated the condition.

My leg twinged in sympathy. "He looks so tired," I said.

Maggie laughed. "Occupational hazard, Ginny. Residents are always tired." She turned serious, as if a light had been turned off inside her. "Did they really find a woman in bed with Bryan?"

I nodded.

"Poor Leslie." Maggie's face was a mix of emotions. "But I guess she was lucky she wasn't killed, too."

Maggie closed the chart in which she was writing. She picked up another. I stayed with the scene in the motel room. Tried to imagine how it must have played.

The door opened. A head, topped by an untidy mop of bleached hair, popped in and called my name. "Dr. Brock would like you to come to SICU," it said.

"Tell him I'm on my way," I said.

The doors across from the elevators on the fourth floor bore the legend, SURGICAL INTENSIVE CARE UNIT—AUTHORIZED PERSONNEL ONLY. As before, I ignored the warning. Steve was inside Room Number 2. His eyes were fixed on the monitors above the bed, and as if needing to reaffirm what they saw, his fingers rested on her wrist.

I hung back. Steve saw me and smiled. I took it as an invitation to enter.

Leslie Parker's face, framed by her almost-black, brown hair, looked as white as the pillow that supported her head. Plastic tubes ran from her nose, while others snaked from overhead containers and dripped blood and clear fluids into the veins of her arms. Surrounded by the medical paraphernalia, her petite frame had shrunk to doll size.

Overwhelmed by the technology, I asked, "Can she talk?"

"I can talk, Ginny," the still figure whispered. "You saw Bryan?" Leslie's free hand picked at the sheet.

I nodded, then realized her eyes were closed. "I saw him," I said.

Her eyes flew open. Darkening from blue to violet, they locked on mine. "Is he dead?"

"He's dead." I covered her pale fingers with my tanned ones, stilling their agitation.

"Two minutes more. That's all," Steve warned, his eyes still fixed on the monitors, his fingers still on her wrist.

"Ginny?"

I leaned closer.

"Will you take care of Zeus and Hera for me, the cars and . . ." her voice faltered, "Bryan?"

Not trusting myself to answer, I gave her hand a reassuring squeeze.

Steve motioned me away. He bent over his patient and after what seemed like hours said, "She's asleep."

I stared at the motionless girl. Was she really going to be okay? Steve said she would be, but like Leslie's words, my thoughts faltered.

Steve took me into the SICU lounge and, over yet another cup of coffee, did his best to assuage my fears.

"It was an in-and-out gunshot wound fired at close range," he explained. "The bullet just nicked the bowel and caught only a few small bleeders."

"All that and you still think she's going to be okay?" I asked in typical lay-man fashion. I brought the strong brew to my lips, felt my stomach recoil, and pulled it away.

Steve laughed. "We've stitched up the bowel, tied off the bleeders, replaced the blood and started her on antibiotics."

I threw up my hands, acknowledging defeat.

"We'll probably move her out of SICU tomorrow." His fingers brushed my cheek. "I miss you."

I smiled, warmed by his caress.

"Are you going home?" he asked.

I looked at my Mickey Mouse watch. Steve had given it to me to replace the one I'd broken in the woods that same summer as the shootings, as the dead college students, the fear, and the redheaded detective. It showed after nine, and I shook my head. "Too much to do."

I gave in then, and pushed back the hair that lay over Steve's forehead. "Will you be home tonight, Doctor?"

His "I'll be there" was music to my ears.

Dr. Steven Brock had come into my life three years ago. The only good re-sult of an appendectomy, he was as much a part of my life now as the scar that marked my belly. Steve had been the surgeon on call the night I went to the hospital doubled over with pain and more afraid than I wanted to admit. The ex-football player, then a first-year surgical resident, had held my hand both before and after surgery.

Filled with thoughts of the man who for the last year had found a place in my bed and a home in my heart, I passed back through the Emergency Room. The shift had changed and Maggie was no longer there, but another nurse, one as round as she was tall, called me over.

"Maggie said to give this to you."

She handed me a tan purse. It was zippered shut, with a thin leather shoulder strap that swung freely between us.

"It's Dr. Parker's," the roly-poly nurse added. "The police took her clothes but said they didn't need this."

Three forms later, including one that needed two signatures, I had freed the purse from hospital bureaucracy and was in the Ranger headed for the Michigan Street offices of the Arthur & Arthur Security Agency.

Founded over twenty-five years ago by my father Daniel and his twin David, the agency provided alarm systems for residential and commercial properties in and around the Marion City area. A business which by its very nature had allowed David Arthur to successfully plan and execute the many robberies that had plagued the city for over two decades. The scandal had brought the firm to near ruin. I'd been advised to call it quits, to close the agency. It was advice I'd chosen not to follow.

I made another time check as I pulled into the building's parking lot. Nearly ten. Thelma would be wondering what happened to me. Uncle David's former secretary and now, since his hasty departure two years ago, my mentor, met me with a smile and a shake of her head at my casual attire.

"I just came from the hospital," I explained. While known for my assortment of slacks and button-down oxford shirts, jeans and rumpled turtlenecks were a bit too informal for business wear even for me.

"Leslie Parker and her husband were shot last night," I said, using the news as both an excuse and an explanation.

"Shot?" Thelma's jaw dropped. I'd caught the usually unflappable, large-boned, dark-skinned woman off guard.

"Shot," I repeated. "Leslie's in the hospital, and Bryan's in the morgue."

"Bryan's dead?"

"He's dead," I affirmed, "and before you ask, I don't know how it happened."

"Is Leslie going to be okay?" Thelma's fingers tightened over the edge of the desk.

"Relax, Thelma. Steve says she'll be fine."

"Have you seen her, talked to her?"

I nodded. "I talked to her this morning. She's in Intensive Care, but she'll be out of there tomorrow and home in a few days."

Thelma loosened her grip on the desk and took a deep breath. "How about some coffee? It's fresh."

My taste buds threatened rebellion and I heeded their warning. "No time. I promised Leslie I'd take care of the cats."

"Need any help?" Thelma stood, demonstrating her willingness.

I said I didn't, readjusted the straps of my bag and of Leslie's purse and headed for the stairs that led to the tenth floor penthouse apartment.

I fished out my key ring and, with the key I still kept on the ring, unlocked the door to what had once been Uncle David's home. An Ansel Adams print hung on the wall in the hallway. A black and white view of the Grand Canyon, it hid the alarm system. I slid the picture aside and switched the signals from green to red, ON to OFF.

In the living room, I pushed the button that opened the drapes. Light flooded in, giving life to the earth-tone colors of carpet, couch and chairs. Leslie and Bryan had changed little since moving in, and the room still bore the stamp of its former owner. Lord knows the firm could have used the money the furnishings alone would have brought, but I hadn't been able to part with them.

I leaned my forehead against the large, floor-to-ceiling thermopane window. In the distance, the Oswago River, bright in the late morning light, wound its way between the buildings that marked Marion City's downtown. "Why did you do it, Uncle David?"

Though the question went unanswered, the words evoked painful memories of the tall, handsome redhead who had been a father to me since the accident that had taken my real father, Uncle David's twin, from us.

Why did you do it? Only a thought now, but still the question demanded an answer. Was it the money? Did you relish the thrill of outwitting the police?

I pressed my palms against the window pane, stared at the sky, then the river, and smiled ruefully. If it was excitement Uncle David sought, he now had plenty. Not only did the local police still have an open warrant for his arrest, the FBI was looking for him, and, if rumors were to be believed, Interpol as well.

"Meow."

I turned around, my reverie broken by the authoritative cry. Zeus sat on the arm of the couch. God-like, he surveyed his kingdom. Hera, the female half of the neutered pair, sat on an orange cushion beside him. In regal splendor, reminiscent of the Greek gods for whom they were named, the Siamese cats watched my every move.

"I'm here to take you home with me."

I walked towards them. Zeus remained immobile, but Hera, always friendly, met me halfway. Purring hello, she rubbed her sleek brown body against my pant leg.

I ran my hand over her arched back. "Do you know where your travel cage is?" I asked the pliant female.

Hera headed for the kitchen, and I followed. Zeus, not wanting to be up-staged, bounded ahead. Our search ended just inside the pantry door.

I pulled the wire cage into the middle of the kitchen floor and stepped back to watch. Zeus led the way inside, made several circles around the center and settled down. With a conspiratorial wink in my direction, Hera scampered in after him.

I left the cats to settle and freed a chair from beneath the kitchen table. Like the cats, I too had my share of curiosity. Sliding the strap of Leslie's purse from my shoulder, I emptied the contents onto the table's polished surface. The resultant clatter was met with a loud "meow."

I ignored my furry companions' attempt at conversation and rescued a rollaway tube of lipstick and set it beside a ring of keys, a comb, and blush. A pin-on identification badge showed Leslie's picture. Would she ever smile like that again? I wondered.

My fingers probed the inside of the bag. A hospital receipt for valuables loosed itself from a corner.

Why didn't that woman give this to me when I was at the hospital? I shook my head at what I considered to be the roly-poly nurse's ineptness and shoved the receipt into my jeans pocket.

Leslie's keys went into my shoulder bag, and the lipstick, comb, and blush back into the tan purse. I fingered each item before dropping it inside. If they could talk, what would they tell me? I zippered the purse shut and set it on the table, then picked it up again. Where was her wallet? Did the police have it, or was it the reason for the receipt?

I'd think about that later. Today I had the cats, Leslie's and Bryan's cars, and Bryan's body. I shuddered, the last being something I didn't want to think about now either.

"How long will you be keeping them?" Thelma asked when I returned to the office. She inserted a finger through the wire cage and rubbed Hera's neck.

"Only until Leslie gets on her feet."

I thumbed through the stack of mail. Thelma exchanged meows with the caged pair and handed me a list of the day's appointments.

"Anything important?" I asked over the chorus of catcalls.

"Nothing I can't handle," she said.

I looked up. "Still quiet?" I asked.

Thelma shrugged her shoulders. "Several of the old clients have come back, and we're getting more telephone calls every day." She smiled, not the wide smile that said everything was okay, but wide enough.

I smiled back. "Are you saying we're out of the woods?"

"The trees are still thicker than I like, but we're getting there. Now, get out of here before I decide I can't handle things by myself."

I did. The morning, already long, showed promise of becoming an even longer day.

After a stop for food, cat litter, and a pan to hold the litter, I introduced the Siamese pair to their temporary home. At least I tried to, but Zeus refused to leave the cage, and Hera would not leave her boyfriend.

A shower and lunch left me feeling much better. Thinking food would also benefit my houseguests, I set out water and a bowl of canned, liver-flavored cat food. Hera purred thanks, and Zeus meowed, a raucous sound I took to mean, "What took you so long?"

The park across the street invited a run, but I refused. Mickey said there wasn't time, and the sun, now high overhead, agreed with the watch's smiling face.

The noon hour traffic was in full swing when I nosed the Ford into Marion City's municipal parking lot. Inside the building, which numbered the police department among its many tenants, the hallways were filled with pedestrian traffic in a rush to get wherever it was they wanted to be. I entered the flow and followed it to Lieutenant Larry Rhodes's office.

Chapter Three

THE DOOR WAS AJAR, AND I PUSHED IT OPEN. LIEUTENANT LARRY RHODES, THE MAN WHO HAD been a boyhood friend to both my father and his twin, looked up.

"Ginny," he said, seeing me. A welcoming smile lit his face. "What brings you here?" The stocky, blue-eyed man, who even in street clothes looked like a cop, pushed a hand through the salted black hair that framed his temples.

"A couple of shootings. Have you heard about them?"

"Which ones? We've had several." His laugh had a hollow ring.

"The pair at the Riverside Motel on Ann Street, a man and woman," I answered.

"That the one where the doctor was shot?" Rhodes's smile faded as his brow furrowed. "Do I sense a special interest here?"

I nodded. "The doctor is Leslie Parker, a surgical resident at Mercy Hospital. She and her husband are the couple who rented Uncle David's apartment."

A shadow darkened Rhodes's eyes. David Arthur's treachery had left its mark on his friend, too.

"Is this lawyer business or detective business?" he asked.

"Lawyer business. Dr. Parker asked me to handle things for her while she's in the hospital."

"What sort of 'things'?" Rhodes sounded suspicious.

I selected one of the pair of straight-backed chairs that fronted his city-issue desk and explained about the Siamese pair, Leslie's Mazda, the Jaguar, and Bryan's body.

Rhodes relaxed into his chair. "So, what do you want me to do?"

"For starters, how about finding out when the coroner will release Bryan Parker's body."

"It'll have to be identified first. If his wife's in the hospital, that might take a while."

"It's already been identified," I said.

Rhodes came away from the back of the chair. "Who did the honors, or shouldn't I ask?"

"I identified the body at the motel last night." Knowing I'd gain nothing by hedging, I brazened it out.

"You never learn, do you?"

"You sound like Thelma, always worrying about me." Unlike the police lieutenant, whose tone of voice had become decidedly unfriendly, I kept my tone light.

"With good cause." He aimed a finger at my nose.

I waved his hand aside. "I know you feel responsible for me now that Uncle David is gone, but I can take care of myself. So get off my back."

Rhodes was ready to argue.

"God, Larry! Look at me!" I leaned towards him. "I'm not a kid anymore."

"Okay! Okay!" Rhodes pulled back, as if he expected our verbal exchange to become physical. "You win. From now on I'll stay out of your business." He turned his face away, attempting, but failing, to hide the mix of emotion that showed there.

"How about we start this conversation over," I suggested.

Rhodes sighed. "Okay . . . Tell me why you went to the motel last night."

I started with Steve's early-morning telephone call and ended where I had begun, with Leslie's request that I take care of the cats, the cars, and Bryan's body.

"Did you identify both bodies?" Rhodes asked when I finished.

"Only Parker's, I didn't know the woman." I hesitated. "Do you know who she is?"

Rhodes said nothing. I interpreted his silence to mean he either didn't know or wouldn't say and changed the subject.

"I met a homicide detective last night by the name of MacPhearson. Do you know him?"

"Came to us from the upper peninsular about ten years ago, ex-army, military police, intelligence," Rhodes recited as if reading from MacPhearson's personnel folder. He stopped. "I thought you were interested in Parker's body."

"Just curious," I said.

"That's what I was afraid of," Rhodes muttered.

I held up my hand. "Relax. I only want to know when the coroner plans to release Parker's body. Nothing more."

Rhodes's eyes held mine as he grabbed the telephone. "Okay, I'll see what I can do," he grumbled.

I listened as he bantered names, dates, and times with an unknown someone on the other end. He looked first serious, then humorous, as if sharing an insider joke. I stopped listening.

Picnics and birthday parties, ball games, ice skating, Christmas trees with presents, good memories of times spent with the hard-headed policeman filled my mind. You are a part of my past, you are my family, Larry Rhodes, and I love you, but damn it all, I can't let you smother me.

"The coroner will release Parker's body as soon as he finishes the autopsy." Rhodes's words interrupted my thoughts.

"When will that be? Two days? Three?"

"They didn't say." He held up a cautionary hand. "Maybe this afternoon or tonight. Tell you what. Give me a call in the morning. I'll see if I can get you something definite by then. Now, how about lunch?"

Diplomacy dictated I accept the policeman's offer and I did.

Lunch was a tuna salad sandwich on whole wheat eaten in the building's cafeteria, and even though I'd eaten only a short time before, I found I was still hungry.

"How's Marianne?" I asked Rhodes about his wife after we'd seated ourselves at a table for two along the room's back wall.

"She's doing just great. Her last check-up was negative, and her hair's grown in enough that she doesn't need a wig anymore." Rhodes's face mirrored the joy his words conveyed.

"Is she getting out much?" I pictured the slender brunette whose driving energy had made her one of the city's leading real estate agents.

"She's not back in the office yet, but she's sure burning up the computer at home."

"I saw the article in the paper telling about the work she's doing with Reach To Recovery."

Rhodes's grin spoke of happiness and promised hope. "You can't keep a good woman down, Ginny, and Marianne's the best."

Rhodes walked me to the building's front entrance when we finished, and after settling on a time for me to call him the next morning, I jogged across the parking lot to the Ranger. A finger search of my shoulder bag assured the presence of Leslie's keys. Cats and husband taken care of, it was time to tackle cars.

The cross-town freeway brought me to the Riverside Motel. Last night's police cars were gone, the front entrance clear. I pulled in and headed toward the rear of the parking lot. Leslie's Mazda was still there, still parked where it had been the night before, and still ringed with yellow tape.

Unlike last night, today I had my choice of parking places, including an empty spot in front of 14B where last night the Jaguar had been parked. As did Leslie's gray sedan, the door too still wore its ribbon of crime scene tape.

I drove past where Bryan's Jaguar had been, parked now in the municipal lot I was sure, and slid in beside the Mazda. Bright sunshine flooded my windshield, but a swirl of dry leaves suggested a cold wind, and I pulled on my jacket before sliding from the truck.

I circled the gray sedan and wondered what my next move would be. When I'd made the promise to Leslie, I had forgotten the Mazda was part of a crime scene. Picking it up was not going to be as easy as I had thought.

"Do you have the key?" A voice behind me asked.

I whirled around, my hip making painful contact with the side of the Mazda as I did.

"What business is it of yours?" I demanded. My hip hurt like hell, but I resisted the impulse to check for damage.

"More my business than yours, I think," said last night's redheaded detective.

In the bright sunlight, he looked even less like Uncle David. Still, there was something about him . . . "Leslie Parker asked me to take care of her car. Did she ask you to do the same?" I let irritation hide my momentary confusion.

His eyes twinkled. A trick of the sun on contact lenses, I wondered, or was he laughing?

"No, she didn't ask me."

I gave a triumphant snort.

"I'm just doing my job, Red, and in case you've forgotten, the name's MacPhearson."

"And my name's Arthur, in case you've forgotten."

MacPhearson's grin widened. "No, Ginny Arthur, I haven't forgotten, and since we're both here, how about we look at the car together?"

I pulled Leslie's key ring from my shoulder bag and walked to the driver's door. As luck would have it, bad luck, the ring held three similar looking keys. I felt his eyes on me as I reached across the tape and inserted the first in the lock. It slid part way but no farther. Damn. I tried the next and then the next. It fit, and the lock clicked open.

A brawny hand closed over mine. Red hair and freckles covered its backside, and the attached arm pushed me aside. "I'll get it," MacPhearson said.

"I can do it," I said. Only I couldn't. He already had.

MacPhearson's shoulder blocked my view, forcing me to look over his arm. The light gray fabric on the driver's seat was spattered with dark, irregularly shaped patches that looked both wet and dry. A musty metallic smell permeated the air around us, and a jelly-like substance covered the carpet in front of the seat. A bug, species unknown, lay trapped near the outer edge.

"Blood?" I asked.

MacPhearson looked at me over his shoulder. The twinkle was back, and the sun had nothing to do with it.

"What makes you think so?" he asked.

I drew away, disdaining an answer, and banged my other hip into the Ranger. MacPhearson stepped back, pushing into me.

The locks clicked and the car door slammed. My fingers tightened around the key ring as I pulled away, dusting the truck's length with the seat of my pants as I did.

"Dr. Parker asked me to take care of the car," I reminded him, but MacPhearson wasn't listening.

I looked where he looked. A speckled red-brown trail led from the driver's side of the Mazda, across the paved lot to a cement walkway, and from there to the door of 14B.

"More blood?" I asked.

MacPhearson shrugged. "Good guess, but I'll wait until the lab boys have a go at it." He smiled a let's-be-friends smile and looked at his watch. "They should be here in about ten minutes. In the meantime, how about a cup of coffee?"

I started to shake my head, but made it a nod. He'd make a better friend than an enemy.

"Name's Douglas." MacPhearson talked as we walked, stopping when we reached a walkway that separated a pair of motel units. "Sugar and cream?" he asked.

My eyes swept the row of vending machines. "Coke," I answered.

"Are you going to continue to run the security agency?" His voice sounded over the clink of coins.

My mouth shaped itself into a nearly perfect circle, which I hastily reshaped into a straight line.

"Don't look so surprised. It wasn't that long ago your uncle's exploits were front page news."

"I didn't know the case was that famous." Though I should have known. The case had been front page news for several weeks, and for several more weeks again following Uncle David's disappearance. I brought the Coke to my mouth and hid behind the aluminum can.

"Infamous is more like it. He had half the police force hopping."

A squeal of tires and a screech of brakes announced the arrival of the forensic unit.

"Hotrodders." MacPhearson took a final swallow and crumpled the cup.

"I'll need the keys." He held out his hand.

I ignored his wiggling fingers and licked away the overflow from the top of the Coke can. "Who was the woman in bed with Bryan Parker?"

"You her lawyer, too?"

I shook my head.

"Curious?"

"Asshole," I muttered. The epithet fit him well.

Ignoring or perhaps not hearing me, MacPhearson nodded towards the Mazda. "I still need the keys."

I handed them over. The hoped-for trade had been a long shot.

Palming the keys, MacPhearson gave me an inquiring look.

"Curious," I admitted.

His grin reappeared, and with a call of "See you later, Red," he joined the men from the mobile unit.

"Ginny Arthur," I called after him.

I watched the criminalists disappear and reappear around and in Leslie's gray Mazda, saw them scrape bits of the brownish red spots that led to 14B, and was still propped against the side of the motel when they climbed back into their mobile unit.

MacPhearson made a show of laying Leslie's keys on the sedan's hood. With a called "It's all yours" he crossed to his car and followed the van out of the parking lot.

I watched him go, walking slowly towards the Mazda as I did. Had I just blundered into this particular crime scene investigation or had MacPhearson somehow engineered it? But if so, how? I shook my head. It was a question I couldn't answer, at least not now, that is.

I picked up the keys. Using the cellular phone from the Ranger, I called the office and asked Thelma to send a driver for the truck.

Yellow tape no longer circled the Mazda, but a look through the window told me the "blood" was still there. I needed something, anything . . .

A stack of discarded newspapers caught my eye. Not what I would have ordered, but it would do the job. Several minutes later I settled myself over the headlines and had the seat pushed back to accommodate my long legs.

"Damn!"

A second pool of congealed "blood" lay hidden under the seat. With a frustrated sigh—it was a lo-o-ng day—I covered it over with more papers and headed for the office.

"Finish your errands?" Thelma asked when I came through the door.

"The Mazda's in the parking lot, and the cats are at home."

Her eyebrow lifted. "What about Mr. Parker?"

"I talked to Rhodes." The couch that marked the office's reception area invited me over, and I sank gratefully into its overstuffed cushions. "The coroner will release the body after he finishes the autopsy. Larry said—"

The door to the office flew open. A figure dressed in flowing white robes rushed in, followed by a gloved hand wielding a wide-barreled gun.

Chapter Four

"**G**RANDMA!" SHOUTED A WHITE-ROBED GIRL AND A BOY DRESSED IN A SILVER JUMP SUIT. Thelma opened her arms wide and caught the children to her. "This is a surprise." She kissed the wiggling pair, then turned her attention to the woman who stood in the open doorway behind them. "What brings you here?"

"They wanted to show you their costumes," the woman said. Tall and big-boned, she bore a striking resemblance to the dark-skinned secretary.

Thelma smiled, a smile that told me she was not buying her daughter's explanation. "But I'll be seeing you at the Halloween party tonight," she said. "Couldn't you have waited until then?"

The larger of the two children, whose clear plastic headgear resembled a football helmet with a hinged face guard, pulled free of his grandmother. "I'm an astra—"

"Astronaut," his mother corrected.

"Spaceman," the little boy shouted. He shoved the visor in place, grinning as it snapped shut. His gun at the ready, he crouched beside the couch and shot pinpoints of light at Thelma's desk.

"Slow down, Scooter," his mother commanded.

The silver astronaut chose not to hear, and with another spin made me his target.

"Hey, Spaceman, I'm a friend."

I caught the small boy as he lunged forward, but couldn't hold him. He sprang free. The office was his battlefield, the books, desks, and chairs his enemies.

Thelma gave the astronaut a dismissive headshake and stooped to the little girl's level. "You're a beautiful angel, Peanut."

She planted a gentle kiss on the child's cheek while her fingers traveled the length of the cardboard wings that graced her granddaughter's back. "And I hear you painted these yourself."

Peanut nodded. "I did, but Mama and Daddy helped me."

With a groan and an almost audible click of knee joints, Thelma stood. Her eyes left the upturned face of the small girl and fixed on the woman who still stood in the open doorway. "Okay, Carol, what gives?"

"Pete was called out of town."

"Why should that be a problem? You know I planned on helping you with the kids tonight."

Thelma rescued a book from the charging spaceman and handed him a throw pillow. I watched the scene unfold before me. Something was afoot. Thelma knew it, and I sensed it.

"Pete volunteered me to do his job." Carol paused, "And I volunteered you to do mine."

"Which means?" Thelma crossed her arms over her breasts.

Safe on the couch, I waited for the older woman's foot to start tapping.

"I have to set up and run the games, and you have to help with the food."

"And who's going to watch these two and take all those pictures you wanted me to take?" As expected, Thelma's foot started tapping.

"I thought maybe . . ." Carol looked at me.

"Oh no." I knew what her next words would be. I came off the couch, prepared to defend myself.

"But it's too late to get anyone else," Carol wailed. "And we've just got to have pictures. Pete's mother gave us the camera just so she could have a video-tape of the party."

I dodged the angel and the astronaut and argued no. Close on my heels, Carol pleaded yes. I'd almost won when Peanut put her hand in mine.

"I'll be real good if you'll take my picture tonight, Ginny," she said in her little girl voice.

I was hooked, and Carol knew it.

"I'll get the camera," she said.

Thelma shook her head sympathetically. "They say there's one born every minute—"

"They shouldn't be too much trouble." I looked from the docile Peanut, who stood with her wings pressed against Thelma's legs, to the rampaging Scooter. My heart sank. What in hell had I let myself in for?

Carol gave me an abbreviated lesson in camera techniques, and I promised to be at Marfield Park by seven. The women, mother and grandmother, each with a small hand held securely in their own, left the office. I followed them out. Maybe I could persuade a certain doctor I knew to go with me.

Rejecting plan A for plan B and returning to plan A, which was really no plan at all, I headed for the Ranger and set out for Mercy Hospital.

My first stop was the switchboard. Though Steve carried a beeper and I knew the number, experience had taught me that when in the hospital voice paging was the quickest way to find a busy doctor in a busy hospital.

"Dr. Brock will call you on the house phone." The operator indicated a pair of wall-mounted phones. One rang, and I answered it.

"Leslie's awake, and she'd like to talk to you," Steve said after we said hello.

"I'll be right up." I hesitated, then said good-bye. Convincing him to spend his off-duty time with a cardboard-winged angel and a silver-suited spaceman was something best done in person. It was, as I had known it would be, no plan at all. But as the saying goes, fools rush in where angels fear to tread, and hadn't Thelma already labeled me a fool?

Leslie lay propped against a pair of pillows. The earlier array of plastic tubes was gone but the monitor wires still snaked from beneath her hospital gown, and her alarmingly pale skin still blended with the white bed sheets.

"How are you feeling?" I spoke in hushed tones, cowed by the atmosphere and her waif-like appearance.

Leslie attempted a smile. "Better than you sound."

I moved closer. "Convince me," I said.

Her lips broadened into a grin. "They're letting me have visitors now."

Oh?" I anchored my foot to the rung of a chair and pulled it beneath me.

"A policeman came to see me this afternoon."

MacPhearson? I wondered, but Leslie didn't say, and I didn't ask.

"He wanted to know if I saw who shot me."

"Did you?"

She nodded, her dark hair brushing the tops of her shoulders. "I saw him. He had a scar on his face, a terrible scar." She rubbed the side of her own face.

"Had you ever seen him before?"

Again Leslie shook her head. "And believe me, I would have remembered if I had. He had a face you couldn't forget."

Leslie's breathing grew rapid. Steve moved closer, but she waved him back. "The policeman wanted to know why I went there."

"Why did you go there?" I prodded. If MacPhearson could ask—intuition told me he was Leslie's afternoon visitor—I could ask.

Leslie smoothed the sheet that covered her. "Someone called while I was making late rounds. A man, his voice wasn't one I recognized, said Bryan would be there."

"Did he say why Bryan would be there?" Did she know about the girl?

"He didn't have to." Leslie looked from me to Steve. Surprise showed on her face. "Don't tell me you don't know."

Even though we did, hospital grapevines being what they are, we both shook our heads, telling her we didn't.

"You tell us," I said quietly.

"He had a date with his latest slut."

Leslie's voice was a mix of anger and pain. I moved to offer comfort, but she waved me back. "You don't have to feel sorry for me. This wasn't the first time." Leslie bit her lip, and the color, what little was left, drained from her face.

"Take it easy," Steve cautioned.

Leslie nodded, took a quivering breath. "You would have found out sooner or later. It's better you hear it from me."

"Then you'd better make it quick, because I'm about to end this conversation," Steve threatened.

"Start at the beginning, Leslie," I said.

The bedridden girl laughed derisively. "Bryan started having girlfriends in kindergarten."

I waited, making silence an ally.

"But then, you don't really mean the beginning," Leslie said flatly. "What you mean is the beginning here, or should I say the end."

"Just tell us about the telephone call and the motel, Leslie," Steve said.

"The call came while I was making late rounds." She reached for a glass of water. Steve held it for her, and I watched her drink, watched the swallowing motion move the muscles along the slim column of her neck. How defenseless she looked.

"I didn't recognize the man's voice," Leslie repeated, "but he told me if I was interested in knowing how Bryan spent his nights, I could go to room 14B at the Riverside Motel any time after midnight."

"And you went," I finished for her.

"I went." She looked at me. "You can understand, can't you?"

"I can understand," I said.

Relief flooded Leslie's face. "I knocked, but there was no answer," she said. "So I tried the knob. The door was unlocked. I opened it." She reached again for the water, and again Steve held the glass for her.

"I opened the door. He was on the bed, Bryan and his little slut."

I was staring in the room with her, seeing what she saw.

"Even with all the blood I knew I should go to him. God! There was so much blood! Yet I knew I should try to help him." Leslie rushed her words, as if seeking escape from the scene they painted. Her voice grew shrill. "He was there. A man with the terrible scar on his face. I don't know where he came from." Her eyes darkened, fastened on my face. "The bathroom maybe, or the closet." Her eyes left mine, flew around the room. "He was just there." Leslie's pupils constricted as though pinpointing the memory. "He had a gun," she whispered, "a big gun, and it was pointed at me."

"Time to go," Steve said, his eyes were on the monitors that lined the wall.

"Please, let me finish," Leslie pleaded. "The policeman, MacPhearson, he said his name was MacPhearson—"

So my intuition had been right. It was MacPhearson, and he knows about the telephone call and the man with the scarred face. He knows Leslie can identify the man who shot her, and I'll just bet she told him I'd be picking up the Mazda this afternoon, too. My thoughts overrode her words, forcing me to play a rapid game of catch-up.

"Oh God! I was so afraid. I tried to get away, out of the room, but—"

Leslie grimaced. Was she seeing the gun, feeling the pain from the bullet that struck her abdomen? I was back with her now, hearing her words, feeling her fear, hurting when she hurt.

"MacPhearson said they found me in my car." Leslie moved restlessly under the covers, the movements jerky, her breathing ragged as if pursued by unseen demons. "Was I going for help, Ginny?" Her voice became a whisper. "Was I running away?"

"If that's where they found you, then . . ." I left the sentence hanging.

"I can't remember." Tears filled Leslie's eyes.

"That's it, ladies."

"Did you know the woman?" I asked hurriedly. It was an insensitive question for such a sensitive time, but curiosity wanted an answer.

Leslie shook her head. "I rarely knew who they were," she choked.

Steve pointed a finger at Leslie. "You need to rest, Leslie, and Ginny, you need to go. Now!"

He took my arm and pulled me from the room. My long legs pumping to keep up with his longer ones, I followed behind him down the hall.

Steve stopped and pushed me into another room, his office. It was small, a desk and two chairs shoe-horned between four walls, but it offered what we wanted—privacy.

"I'm off call tonight, Ginny."

"Will Leslie be all right without you, Doctor?" I teased.

"I'm sure she will be. In case you've forgotten, this is a hospital."

He kissed me. I kissed him and our tongues touched. I forgot about Leslie, MacPhearson, and the man with the scarred face.

Steve pulled me tighter against him. "God, I can't wait to get you home."

The feel of him against me argued against babysitting spacemen and angels, but a promise was a promise. I planted my hands on his chest and pushed back.

"How about we talk about Halloween parties first, Doctor Brock?"

Chapter Five

STEVE WAS NOT INCLINED TO TALK ABOUT HALLOWEEN PARTIES, BUT AFTER MUCH PERSUASION OF the verbal and, well, physical variety, along with assurances of much better things to come, I managed to convince him that a promise was a promise, and he finally, though I must confess reluctantly, agreed to accompany me to Marfield Park.

Costumes were the next item on my agenda. Kissing, touching, and heavy breathing kept getting in the way, however, and we were unable to come up with anything more creative than hospital scrubs.

The surgeon's lounge provided everything we needed. Better still, it was empty, and we pulled pants and tops over our street clothes. Facemasks, head covers, rubber gloves, and paper shoe protectors went into a plastic sack. Then, like the thieves we were—borrowing hospital supplies for personal use was frowned upon—the two of us stole quietly into the night.

The glow of headlights and streetlights turned night into day, and not until we reached the park did the darkness threaten. There it slipped from hiding and pooled outside the patches of artificial light.

The setting was perfect and I shivered in the forgotten anticipation of childhood. A man, shadowed behind the glow of a flashlight, waved us to a parking place, and after adding facemasks and head covers to our costumes, we left the Ranger and joined the crowd.

"This is some party," Steve said, dodging a group of space invaders.

"The city sponsors it and foots most of the bill, but several churches and civic groups help. The only charge is a costume."

I moved forward and trained Carol's camera on Steve. There wasn't even the hint of a limp now, I noted with satisfaction. Somewhere along the line the busy resident must have managed a few hours of sleep.

"Hey, you're supposed to be taking pictures of the kids."

"Then start acting like one."

Steve grabbed my arm and pulled me alongside him. "How long has the city been throwing these parties?"

"It started in the sixties, when tricks began showing up in treats."

"I know all about that. I had to put a couple of stitches in a kid's mouth last year."

I made another threatening move with the camera, and Steve pulled me closer.

We passed tables where toothy jack-o-lanterns guarded popcorn balls, candied apples, cookies, doughnuts, and brownies. I put the camera to my eye as we came to a group of assorted bums, ghosts, and pirates. All held long forks, and busied themselves over charcoal grills.

"Smells like hot dogs and hamburgers are on the menu," Steve said. He swiped a cookie from under the nose of a grinning pumpkin.

"You're supposed to have your mask on," I protested.

"Want a bite?" He lifted my paper mask and filled my mouth with a doughy mixture of chocolate chips and nuts.

"Ginny, Ginny," a small voice called from inside a shadow.

I swung the camera into place and started filming. Looking every inch an angel, Peanut fluttered toward us. Her wings swayed behind, and her white and gold robes flowed around her. Only her footfalls, skipping across the trampled grass, testified to the small girl's corporeal nature.

She wrapped her arms around my legs, and I dropped to her level. "Where's everybody?" I asked.

"I'm here, and Grandma's over there." Peanut danced free and led the way "over there."

I caught her hand, afraid of losing her in the crowd. "Do you remember Steve, Peanut? He's a doctor."

Peanut gave him an up-and-down look. "I know," she said. She gave me the same scrutiny. "And you're a doctor, too." She hid a giggle behind chubby little-girl fingers. "But you're really not, because you work in an office with Grandma."

"So, you did come." Thelma moved from behind a table groaning under its load of goodies.

"Was there ever any doubt?" I helped myself to a paper plate and piled it with baked beans, potato salad, and coleslaw.

"Want the truth?" Thelma wrinkled her red-painted nose and sneered through randomly blackened teeth.

"You two at it again?" Steve asked. He followed me down the table's length, choosing green bean casserole and lasagna.

"And she managed to persuade you, too, did she?"

"I'm easily persuaded." Steve laughed.

"Where are Carol and Scooter?" I asked between mouthfuls.

"She's helping with the games, but I don't know which one." Thelma tucked a napkin into the neck of Peanut's costume and handed her a plate. "It's baked beans, honey, just like Ginny's eating." Peanut took the plate and spooned the brown beans into her mouth.

"You should try some green beans, Peanut," Steve urged. "They have mushrooms and French fried onion rings in them."

"Ugh!" The little girl wrinkled her nose as she continued to eat the baked beans.

I licked my fork clean. "Where are they holding the games?"

"Behind the bonfire. Here, give me that." Thelma pushed up the sleeves of her patchwork shirt and took my empty plate. "You can't miss them. They're near the big tent."

"It's not a tent. It's a house, a h-haunted house," Peanut corrected solemnly. "Can we go see it?" The angel looked from me to Steve.

"What does your Grandma say?" Steve ruffled the child's curly hair.

"She says it's okay. Don't you, Grandma?"

Thelma handed her granddaughter a cup of apple juice and a peanut butter cookie. "If you drink this first."

The brown-faced angel downed the juice, and the three of us went in search of the haunted house. I videotaped our progress, and caught a cookie-fisted, winged creature pursuing a hulking, green-garbed surgeon.

Besides our own angel, there were enough others to form a celestial chorus. If caught acting too ethereal though, red-suited figures with three-tined forks persuaded them to forgo such behavior. Ghosts booed us, and bums panhandled for treats. Ballerinas danced around us, and fluffy-eared rabbits hopped across our path.

"Do they give prizes for the best costume?" Steve asked.

"Are you volunteering to be a judge?"

"Good Lord, no!"

The fire crackled, called us closer. Just beyond the leaping flames, the tent stood silhouetted in their light.

"The house, the h-haunted house," Peanut cried.

"Let's find your mom and Scooter first," I said, but the usually docile Peanut was already running toward the tent's brightly lighted entrance.

"Peanut, wait," I called but she was gone. "Steve—" Only, he, too, was gone. Both had disappeared behind the flapping tent flaps of the haunted house.

I ran to follow, but my feet tangled in the scrub suit's rolled pant legs. Slowed to a stop, I thought of misshapen mirrors, lowered ceilings, falling walls, and dead-end passages.

"No sense the three of us getting lost in there." I spoke the thought out loud, but nobody paid me any attention.

I wandered between horseshoes, pin-the-tail-on-the-donkey and musical chairs. Louder music pulled me to a roped-off section where teenage ghosts, bums, space creatures, angels, and ballerinas danced together. I moved slowly, capturing the festivities on film as I went.

Lured by the sound of splashing water and what sounded like several Scooters, I found another roped-off area. This one had tubs filled with water, bobbing apples, and dripping kids. Carol, her pointed witch's hat stabbing the night sky, stood among them. She had traded her broomstick for a roll of paper towels, and her booming voice cautioned the more energetic against drowning.

I caught her attention and mouthed an exaggerated, "Where is Scooter?"

She pointed to a nearby tub where a silver-suited spaceman hovered along its edge. As I watched, a helmeted head floated to the surface. Before a surge of adrenalin could move me, a brown face appeared, a red apple filling the space where his mouth should be.

"Take him, please," Carol pleaded.

I captured the small boy and with a handful of paper towels mopped the astronaut's wet face and silver suit. His gauntlets were beyond help, and I knotted them to the strap of my shoulder bag.

"Are you hungry?" Fearful of experiencing another disappearing act, I took a firm hold of Scooter's hand.

"Can I eat my apples?" He pointed to a pile of the red-skinned fruit. All bore evidence of having been caught by small teeth. No wonder Carol wanted to be rid of the boy.

"Later, Scooter. Let's get some warm food inside you first."

I pulled off my surgical head cover, improvised a knapsack for the fruit, and added it to my collection of camera, shoulder bag, and wet gloves.

The aroma of cooking meat lured us forward. Hot dogs were the order of the day, and soon a spaceman and his green-suited doctor companion were stuffing their faces with a pair of the mustard-and-ketchup-lathered frankfurters.

"Have you been in the haunted house?" I asked. We had finished eating and were circling around the bonfire.

"No." The boy shook his head. "I don't want to go in there."

I sensed his reluctance, but wanting to see inside I stepped closer.

"No!" Scooter shrieked. "I don't like it in there!"

I gathered his trembling body into my arms. "Scooter," I crooned his name. "You don't have to go inside."

As we backed away, my eyes did what I had wanted my feet to do, but neither Steve nor Peanut were anywhere to be seen.

"Let's go find Grandma," I said, it being the only rallying point I knew. One where I hoped Peanut and Steve would be.

We stopped to watch some revelers roast marshmallows, and as we passed the food tables, Scooter squealed with delight at the grinning pumpkins. Along the way, I continued to play cameraman.

Flashing lights near the parking lot caught Scooter's attention. I recognized it as another place where Steve might hide out and headed for the trauma unit. A police car and a uniformed officer, Tom Blakely, captured Scooter's attention.

We exchanged greetings, at least Blakely and I did, Scooter being too awestruck by the uniformed officer to do anything but stare.

"I've got a little boy like you." Blakely grinned down at the rapt face that grinned up at his. "And you know what?"

"What?" Scooter's eyes grew big.

"He wants to be a spaceman, too."

The two climbed into the police car. I saw my chance and took it, but Steve wasn't at the ambulance, nor had the EMTs seen him. Still, my luck wasn't all bad. The EMTs were the two who had made the run to the Riverside Motel. Now if MacPhearson shows up, I thought, we can have a reunion. A prickle ran up my spine as if someone was staring at me or, given tonight's atmosphere, had walked across my grave. I chanced a cautious look over my shoulder, half expecting to see the redheaded detective make an appearance. He didn't.

"How's Doc Parker doing?" the sturdier of the two techs asked. It was the one I'd talked to in the Emergency Room. His words rapidly dispelled my momentary feeling of unease.

"Doing fine," I said.

"She sure wasn't fine last night," the second EMT said. "Or I should say this morning," he amended. "We had a hell of a time getting her to stop bleeding."

"Ginny, Ginny," Scooter sing-songed.

"What Scooter?" I sing-songed back.

"Can I have an apple now?"

"Go ahead. They're by the curb." I called this last to Blakely who was holding fast to Scooter's hand.

I turned back to the EMTs. "Dr. Parker was in a car when you got there?"

"In the front seat behind the steering wheel," said the first.

"A gray Mazda," said the second.

Close by, a child wailed.

Chapter Six

Fear drove me to the small, astronaut huddled in the grass beside Blakely. "My God, what happened?" I grabbed the handkerchief the policeman held and mopped Scooter's tear-stained face.

"All of a sudden he started throwing up." Blakely held out a half-eaten apple. "He took two, three bites, and that was it."

"Make it stop hurting, Ginny." Scooter groaned, his arms tight against his stomach.

Help came in the form of rough hands that shouldered me aside and lifted the felled spaceman onto a stretcher.

"Was something wrong with the apple?" I looked at Blakely for confirmation.

The young policeman shook his head. "I don't think so. It happened too fast." His voice registered frustration.

He turned to leave. I caught his arm, unwilling to let him go. "What are you going to do?"

"For starters, I'm keeping the apples. They're evidence. I've already called for backup, and until they get here, I'm going to see that every damn bit of food in this park is confiscated." The formerly friendly face had turned decidedly unfriendly.

Sirens wailed in the distance. Growling like wounded animals, they came closer and closer.

"Did the EMTs call for backup?" I asked.

Blakely nodded. "Scooter's getting sick may be an isolated incident, but we can't take any chances."

His words harbingered the cries of children and the excited shouts of adults—all seeming to converge on the two of us and the parking lot that lay beyond.

My stomach gave a sudden lurch. I felt sick, and holding my abdomen didn't help. My hands covering my mouth, I ran for the curb. Beans, coleslaw, and then potato salad along with a hot dog spewed out.

"Are you okay, Miss Arthur?" An ashen-faced Blakely knelt beside me.

My outraged "hell no" became a weak "no."

"I'll get help. Will you be okay if I leave you?"

I said I would, but it was a lie. I was dying.

The EMT Blakely sent over came and went. He could do nothing for me. I was still at it, spewing out whatever it was my stomach found disagreeable, when Steve found me.

"You, too?" he asked. His voice was kind, his manner professional.

I pushed away his probing fingers and asked about Scooter.

"He's doing fine, Ginny. I just left him."

"Thank God."

Steve slid his arm around my shoulders. "How about you?" he asked.

"I don't feel a bit fine," I moaned, dropping my head on my bent knees.

"You will," he promised.

My stomach refused to believe him. I waved him away and closed my eyes, but a silver-suited spaceman waited inside my head.

I was sick again, then hoping for sleep, closed my eyes.

Thelma found me, offered a cloth to wipe my face, and wrapped me in a comforting hug. I felt an urge to kiss her painted nose as she led me to a patch of grass where a small boy lay sleeping. I looked around. "Where's Peanut?"

"She's with her mother."

"Is she—"

"She has what everyone else around here has." Thelma licked her lips, showing her blackened teeth.

"Damn!" I pulled in what should have been a calming breath and smelled the stench of sickness around us.

Scooter stirred. "Bad apple," he whimpered.

Bad people, I thought.

"Stomach hurts." His small fingers rubbed his belly.

Misery showed in Thelma's eyes. "If I ever get my hands on the son-of—" Her eyes swept the crowd as if searching for the culprit.

Scooter repeated his complaint. She gathered him close and crooned words of love into his ear. I rolled away from the pair and pushed to a sitting position.

Groans filled the air around me. Many, like me, were victims, while others did what they could to offer comfort.

"Ginny." Steve's voice sounded above the moaning crowd and wailing sirens. He touched my cheek. "Feeling any better?"

I wrapped my arms around my middle.

"That bad?" He slid my sleeve up and bared my upper arm. "I have something for you."

The rush of cold air and an alcohol swab caused a rash of goose bumps. I felt the prick of a needle.

"I don't know if this will help, but if it does, you should feel better in about fifteen minutes." Steve pulled my sleeve down and turned to Scooter. "Okay, Mr. Spaceman, let's have a look at you."

I rolled to my side. A condemned woman, I counted out what I was certain were my last minutes. Behind me, Steve and Thelma talked in whispers about . . .

My eyes flew open. Had I been asleep? Around me a field of others moaned discordantly, their cries a chorus from Dante's Inferno. I raised my head, heard nothing from my stomach, and sat up.

"Feeling better?" Thelma asked.

I smiled a wobbly smile. God, but it felt good to feel good . . . well, better.

I took another look around. "How many would you guess there are?"

"Here, about fifty, but Steve said they sent more than that to the hospital." She hoisted her grandson to her shoulder. "I think it's time I took this astronaut home."

"Did Carol take Peanut home?"

Thelma's dark eyes grew darker. "Peanut's in the hospital. She just wouldn't stop vomiting."

I watched them go, then picked my way through the prostrated leftovers from this year's Halloween party. I looked for Steve as I went, but found Larry Rhodes instead.

"You look like hell," he said.

I said I felt like hell, and asked if there had been a robbery. "None that I know of, just a few drug busts. Tonight I'm part of the disaster team."

"A good pick-pocket could make a killing," I said.

Rhodes looked around. "You're probably right." His gaze steadied. A grin spread over his face. "Hey, Doc, over here."

"I think we've about reached the end," Steve said in answer to Rhodes's question. He gave me a quick hug, leaving his arm to lie across my shoulders.

"The lab boys will be glad to hear that. They've been collecting samples from everything that hasn't been eaten and a lot of what already has."

"How long before you'll know anything?" Steve asked.

"If it is nothing too exotic, we should know something in a few hours."

"Give me a call when you find out?"

"Will do," Rhodes promised. He cocked an eyebrow at Steve. "Any ideas?"

"A bug, doctored food," Steve offered.

"We were lucky Blakely was here. He stopped the apple bobbing and pulled what food was left from the tables."

Rhodes looked to where the younger officer stood.

Blakely saw us and waved. "Miss Arthur," he called, starting towards us. "Your camera and shoulder bag are in the squad car, but I kept the apples. Scooter might ask about them when he gets to feeling better."

I had my doubts, but thanked the policeman for his thoughtfulness. Steve linked his arm through mine. Together we headed for the parking lot. The day was finally over. Wanting to catch the end, I fitted the viewfinder to my eye and started filming.

Chapter Seven

THE CAMERA CAUGHT A PAIR OF EMTS LOADING A STRETCHER INTO THE REAR OF A TRAUMA unit. "This is the last, Doc," one of the two called. He waved good-bye and climbed inside. His partner, his humorless face filling the lens of the camera, slammed the door shut. It had been a bad night for everyone.

Halogen lamps and a lowering moon lighted our way. A few sad looking witches and sadder bums passed by, but the clowns had disappeared, as had most of the outer space creatures, angels, and ballerinas. We walked on, leaving behind trampled grass and crumpled litter, debris from the crowd that had gone before us.

I made a final sweep of the area with Carol's camera. Was there anything worse than the end of a party? Only the party wasn't over, at least not for us.

"Damn!" Hands fisted on hips, I stared at the green truck.

Steve ran his finger over the windshield. "Soap," he said.

We cursed the pranksters for this latest insult, but a liberal application of elbow grease and a scraper removed the worst.

When Steve offered to drive, I didn't argue. On a how-do-you-feel quiz, my score was zero.

My Valley Avenue bungalow never looked so good. I ignored the furry pair who twined themselves around my legs and was under the shower before Steve had the front door locked.

"Want some company?" he asked. His head popped through the shower curtain.

My how-do-I-feel score headed north, I opened my arms and invited him inside.

Later, feeling more refreshed than was usual from my shower, I fell asleep with my head on Steve's shoulder. His strong, steady heartbeat, a lullaby, sang in my ear.

The telephone rang, bringing with it the memory of the last middle-of-the-night telephone call I'd received.

"Not again," I moaned.

I forced my eyes open and looked at the illuminated face on the bedside clock.

"Eight." So it wasn't the middle of the night. I added an expletive.

Another ring, "Okay, okay!" I shouted. I was getting angry—hell, mad.

"How are you feeling?" Thelma asked.

"Fine." It wasn't true, just the standard reply. My voice dropped to nearer normal. Thelma had that effect on me.

"Good, because I won't be in today," she said. "Carol and Pete are still at the hospital with Peanut, and I'm babysitting Scooter."

I swung my legs over the side of the bed, checking to see how fine I was.

"The surveillance room supervisor will send someone up to give you a hand," Thelma continued, "and I should be back on Monday."

A list of instructions followed. Despite the late night and my abrupt entry into wakefulness, I smiled at the voice in my ear and waited for Thelma to take a breath.

"I'll take care of the office," I said when she did. "You take care of Scooter."

We said our good-byes and hung up. Wishful thinking drew my eyes to the far side of the bed, but as I had known it would be, it was empty. Surgical rounds started at seven.

An assortment of costumed figures barfing into shrubs and trashcans joined me in the shower. I didn't linger, and the face that met me in the bathroom mirror took more than its usual application of makeup to rid itself of the ravages of last night's ill-fated party.

Zeus and Hera greeted me with a series of Siamese catcalls as I entered the kitchen. I answered in people talk, and we continued the conversation while they breakfasted on canned turkey and I on oatmeal raisin crisp.

Under their watchful gaze, I gathered up my shoulder bag, jacket, and Carol's video camera and slipped through the front door.

The air was crisp, and the sun had started its climb into the sky. Like me, November had put on its best face.

I stopped by the sixth floor where the monitoring equipment, the watching eyes of the Arthur & Arthur security systems, was located to thank the supervisor for lending her help. Surveillance being the agency's primary business, it was not often that I borrowed staff. The supervisor called a greeting as I entered, her face changing from stern to concerned as we talked.

"Everything should be back to normal by Monday," I promised, stemming the flow of her sympathetic murmurings.

"The mail is on your desk, Miss Arthur," Thelma's temporary replacement called as I entered the agency's office.

Her hair was blond, her eyes blue, and her name Beth. She smiled. I liked her immediately.

As Beth had said, the mail lay in a neat pile in the center of the desk. Hidden behind a circular advertising the merits of a "state-of-the-art" pressure-sensitive device was a gun registration form. I shook my head. Despite all my arguments, Rhodes had actually done it.

"There'll come a time when you'll need a gun." I could hear the dark-haired lieutenant's words.

"Never!"

I shoved the form back inside the envelope. What I needed was less interference in my life.

"Men!" I swiveled around and stared out the window. Clouds scudded across the sky, darkening the surface of the Oswago River.

"Did you call me, Miss Arthur?" Beth asked from the doorway.

"No!" I snapped. I felt guilty and followed with an apologetic smile. Rhodes's shortcomings, rather my reaction to them, were no fault of hers.

I widened my smile. "But since you're here—"

We ran through Thelma's canceled-this-and-rescheduled-that list. Beth caught on quickly. The Arthur & Arthur office was in capable hands.

We finished. I picked up the phone to call Rhodes, but decided against it. He might be able to tell me when Bryan's body would be released, but he couldn't tell me what to do with it. Only Leslie could, and like so many other tasks, this was another one better done in person.

Styrofoam and plastic cups, some crumpled, others half full, littered the hospital lot. Torn paper napkins brushed my legs and nodded hello before the wind pulled them away. Except for the absence of trampled grass, the parking lot looked much the same as Marfield Park had the night before.

It was no better inside. Only here, a crew of blue-clad figures with brooms and trashcans busied themselves removing the evidence of the past evening's upset stomachs.

I decided to rid myself of the video camera first, and took the stairs to the second floor. There a nurse, whose uniform was blue jeans and a tee shirt that read MERCY NURSES CARE, pointed out Peanut's room.

"Hi, angel," I called as I poked my head through the door.

Peanut sat cross-legged in bed wearing a hospital gown covered with teddy bears and a grin that spread from ear to ear. A happy face, it contrasted sharply with her parents' tired faces and down-turned mouths.

"Long night?" I asked.

"It sure was." Pete answered for the two of them. "But you're looking good. Mind telling us your secret?"

"A competent doctor and a good night's sleep," I said. I didn't say how much of each I'd enjoyed.

Peanut's bright eyes invited me close, and I planted a kiss on her upturned face. "Anyone know yet what made her so sick?"

"They said it was ipecac. It causes nausea and vomiting," Carol said as if reading from a drug circular.

"Ipecac! Isn't that what they give to people who have been poisoned?"

Pete nodded agreement. "Apparently someone laced the food at the Halloween party with it. Steve said Peanut got a walloping dose."

"They can't stop it from working once it's ingested," Carol added. "It just has to run its course."

"It usually lasts about an hour, but Peanut kept throwing up," Pete said.

Carol rubbed the small band-aid on her daughter's arm. "They've been giving her IV fluids most of the night."

"How are we doing this morning?" a nurse wearing blue jeans and the NURSES CARE tee shirt called as she entered the room.

"Can I go home?" Peanut asked.

"You sure can." The nurse's grin said she was used to having her questions answered with questions. "Just as soon as your mom and dad sign these papers."

I laid the video camera on the bedside table and waved good-bye. Busy with the business of going home, the four ignored my exit.

I walked up the couple of flights of stairs to the fourth floor only to find that Leslie was no longer in SICU. She had, the staff told me, been moved to the surgical wing on the second floor.

I retraced my steps. Another nurse, this one in traditional white, directed me to the nurses' station.

"Dr. Parker's in 224," the unit secretary said, "but you'll have to check with the gentleman over there first."

The gentleman, a police detective named Hightower, took my name and, after learning I was Leslie's lawyer, waved me inside. So, MacPhearson did consider the scar-faced man a threat.

Like Peanut, Leslie, too, wore a hospital gown. Unlike Peanut's gown, however, Leslie's had no teddy bears, nor did she wear a happy face. She was, in fact, crying.

"Leslie, what's wrong? Are you in pain? Do you want me to get the nurse?" I babbled in a hand-wringing voice. Hospitals and sick people always intimidated me.

"I'm okay, Ginny." She sniffled loudly. "It's this." Leslie waved a folded newspaper between us.

COUPLE FOUND SLAIN IN MOTEL ROOM. I read the headline, and then the article below it. It named no names and told me nothing I didn't already know.

"Quite an epitaph, wouldn't you say?" Leslie said when I finished.

Say? What could I say? Leslie sighed and, as I had seen her do before, arranged then rearranged the sheets that covered her.

"I'm not going to have a funeral," she said finally.

It was the subject I'd come to discuss, and I ran with it. "If not a funeral, then what? The coroner will be releasing Bryan's body in a day or two."

"I know . . ." Her dark eyes fastened on mine, their blue depths mirroring the sorrow I knew was inside. "Please, Ginny, you mustn't think I don't care. I really did hope things would be better when we came here."

"You were in Detroit?" I asked, fueling the conversation.

She nodded. "Bryan was transferred to Marion City. It was really a promotion, and I was accepted into the residency program here at Mercy Hospital." Tears washed down Leslie's face as she sank into the pillows.

Was talking too much for her? Feeling guilty, I looked around, expecting to see Steve. He wasn't there.

"I thought all our troubles were over."

I handed her the box of tissues from the bedside table, and she dabbed her eyes and mopped her runny nose.

"I'm going to have him cremated. It's what he wanted."

I nodded, and one by one I asked the questions that had to be asked, and one by one Leslie labored through the answers.

We finished and I moved toward the door, escape uppermost on my mind. She looked better, and Steve hadn't put in an appearance. The gods were on my side, and I had no intention of pressing my luck.

It was Leslie who did.

"Did you take care of the cats, Ginny?"

My hand closed over the door handle, leaving escape a tug away. "I picked them up yesterday and took them home with me."

A smile tilted the corners of her mouth. "Are they driving you crazy?"

I pictured Hera with her beguiling personality and Zeus with his haughty disdain for anything human. "Not yet."

"Give them time, they will." She sobered. "What about the cars? Are they still at the motel?"

I shook my head. "I moved the Mazda. It's in the lot behind your apartment. Is that okay?"

"I just wanted to know where they were." Leslie took a deep breath. "And Bryan's car? What about the Jaguar?"

"It wasn't there when I went back yesterday. I suspect the police have impounded it, but I haven't checked it out yet." I felt my face redden with the guilt of omission. I took in a quick breath and breathed the air out slowly. "Anything else?"

Leslie shook her head. It was my cue to exit.

Chapter Eight

I PUT THE PARKERS ON HOLD AND HEADED FOR THE HOSPITAL'S COMMUNICATION CENTER, BETTER known as the switchboard. In this sprawling haystack, the one most likely to find a missing needle was the switchboard operator. With a little luck, I might catch Steve between what he did all day and sometimes all night.

The center was located just off the first floor's main corridor, in a room that seemed too small to hold the operator and the electronic equipment she tended. Not that the board itself was large, for it wasn't. It had been updated during the last round of renovations five years ago. The wall-sized board with its many mouths and wired plugs was gone.

There were those who had wanted to gut the system completely, to start over again with one of the newer computerized models. But, thwarted by the older hangers-on on the hospital's board of directors, these changes had never come about. When people call Mercy Hospital, we want them to hear a real person, a real-live person answering, not a recorded voice offering a list of options, they'd argued—and they'd won.

I watched the operator's fingers move deftly across the lighted panels. Gray-haired and gray-eyed, she smiled "hello" when she saw me.

"Will you page Dr. Brock?" I asked at the first quiet moment.

"Dr. Brock, please call the operator." Her businesslike voice sounded over the hospital-wide intercom system.

Several minutes passed. Steve didn't answer, and she repeated the page.

A flurry of lights turned the switchboard into a kaleidoscope of color and commanded the operator's attention. I waited. The board quieted, but still Steve did not answer.

"Would you like me to beep him, Miss Arthur?"

I nodded, and she tapped in Steve's beeper number on what looked like a telephone keypad.

"Do you have to do that often?" I asked.

Behind her wire-rimmed glasses the operator's gray eyes looked puzzled.

"Use the voice pager and the beeper," I explained.

"If they don't answer one, we usually try the other."

"And if they don't answer either?"

Her eyes twinkled. "We leave them a note, but that doesn't happen too often."

I laughed. "Are you saying the doctors are a responsible lot?"

The operator joined in my laughter. "As responsible as most, but if they don't answer, there's usually someone else around who will answer for them."

A red light glowed above the telephone keypad, and a gentle hum sounded from a hidden speaker.

"That should be Dr. Brock," the operator said. She pushed a button, listened, then shook her head. "Sorry. It's not him. It's the Operating Room secretary. He's scrubbed."

The switchboard operator looked up inquiringly. "Do you want to leave a message?"

I shook my head, and she recited a "no message" into the mouthpiece.

"What made you think it was Dr. Brock?" I asked when she finished.

The operator pointed to the lighted board and the digital display above it. "That's his beeper number."

"But there are so many doctors. How do you know whose number is whose?" She was good, I knew, but that good?

"The house staffs' numbers are easy to remember. They get beeped the most because they're around the most. A good memory helps, too." She grinned a sly grin and handed me a leather-bound ledger that contained a list of names and numbers. "Here, Miss Arthur, meet my memory."

She swiveled around and pointed to a bank of miniature mailboxes. "And if we take a message, that's where it goes."

I found Steve's name in the ledger. The number beside it matched his beeper number as well as the number on one of the boxes.

I scribbled "I love you, Steve" on a pad that lay beside the switchboard, tore off the sheet, and handed it to the operator. She read it, laughed, and slipped it into Steve's box. It felt good to leave a part of me behind for him to see. The old-timers on the hospital board knew what they were doing after all. No system, no matter how sophisticated, beat the human touch.

"Do you keep track of all incoming calls?" I asked, shaking off my philosophical mood.

"Just emergency calls, bomb threats, disasters, things like that. But we don't have to write them down, they're recorded automatically." The switchboard hummed loudly and several lights flashed. With a dismissive wave, the gray-eyed operator bowed to the demands of the bright-eyed monster.

Bumper-to-bumper noonday traffic met me outside. The changing signals and flashing brake lights reminded me of the hospital switchboard. Which one of the operators had talked to Leslie's late-night caller? Might they remember something about him? I worried the question over in my mind, letting it go when I reached the municipal building.

Rhodes's nose was buried in the *Marion City Press*. He waved me to a seat and pointed to a double-size headline. HALLOWEEN TRICKS FELL CITY RESIDENTS.

"Have you seen this?"

"No, but I don't need any reminders. I was there. Remember?"

Rhodes dropped the paper on his desk and stared up at me. "Feeling any better?" he asked after a long moment.

"I'm here, aren't I?" my sarcasm softened by a smile. I hitched a chair closer to his desk. "Do you know who did it yet?"

Rhodes shook his head. "Lots of guesses, but no hard facts."

"Carol and Pete told me it was ipecac."

"Yeah, I heard that, too." Rhodes snorted. "Anyone who'd use that stuff has a mighty warped sense of humor." He leaned into his chair and propped his foot on the bottom drawer. "How is Peanut?"

I made a mental comparison of last night's fleet-footed angel with the smiling imp I'd seen earlier that morning. "As good as she was when I started videotaping her last night."

Rhodes's brows knitted together. "I didn't know you had a video camera."

"I don't. It was Carol's. She needed a cameraman, and I was drafted."

"Blakely talked about a camera . . ." Rhodes's words dangled between us, making them a question.

"Same one," I answered. "I dropped it off with Carol and Pete at the hospital this morning."

Rhodes's elbows hit the desk. Though he bore little resemblance to Rodin's Thinker, I could see the wheels turning inside his head.

"Tell me," I said.

"It's a long shot," he said slowly, "but it's worth a try."

"What's worth a try?" I tried to guess what he was thinking, but the wheels inside my head were rusty.

He handed me the phone. "Call Carol. Tell her a car's on the way to pick up her camera."

Rhodes walked to the door and barked an order into the squad room. It took several rings before Carol answered the phone. When she did, I barked Rhodes's message into the receiver. Being a smaller dog, my bark was more a yap.

I wasn't before and was still no good at waiting. Activities such as foot tapping and finger strumming helped, but with each passing minute, the tension in the small office grew more unpalatable.

"Relax, Ginny," Rhodes chided. "Even after the tape gets here, it'll be a while before we know anything. That is, if there is anything to know."

I didn't like the pessimistic note in Rhodes's voice. I wanted optimism. Still, I stopped the finger strumming but not the foot tapping. There was little left of the original enthusiasm that had brought me to Rhodes's office. "Did you find out when the coroner will release Bryan Parker's body?" I asked, hoping the change of subject matter might improve my mental outlook.

Rhodes checked his watch. "The coroner's probably at lunch. Why don't we grab something and go by the morgue afterwards?"

"The camera?" I reverted to the original subject matter. Mental gymnastics be damned, that was uppermost in my mind.

"If it gets here before we get back, they'll give me a call, Ginny." Rhodes's tone was conciliatory. Knowing I was acting more child-like than adult-like, I stopped the foot tapping and offered an apologetic smile.

The something we had for lunch was another tuna sandwich, the eating of which we stretched to fill the noon hour. At one we headed for the city's forensic department. The strong antiseptic smell that met us reminded me of another visit, and of Julie Sinclair's missing boyfriend. A case whose many twists and turns had led to the discovery of David Arthur's double life—respected Marion City businessman and international art thief.

Rhodes stopped in front of a closed door. Was it the same door, I wondered? He turned the knob and pushed the door open. I shoved the old thoughts aside and walked in ahead of him.

"This is Ginny Arthur, Martha." Rhodes introduced me to a plumpish, middle-aged woman, a most decidedly live-not-dead, plumpish, middle-aged woman, whose desk guarded the door to an inner office. I smiled, and she smiled back.

"Miss Arthur's here to claim the Parker body. Is it ready to go?"

A book slammed shut inside the inner office, and a voice boomed over the sound of scraping chair legs. "It is if Martha's finished with the paperwork."

Martha freed a paper from the pile on her desk. "Everything's ready, Dr. Beller."

A large-bellied, round-faced man rolled out of the inner office. "Do I need to sign anything?" asked Marion City's chief forensic pathologist.

Martha checked the form. "You do," she said.

He gave Rhodes a nod of recognition, then looked at me over his half-moon glasses. "Are you a relative?"

He stopped beside Martha's desk and hooked fat thumbs through his belt loops.

I watched his pants slide over his round belly. "I'm his wife's, Leslie Parker's lawyer." I freed my eyes from his slipping trousers and fixed them on his face.

"A lawyer, are you?" He pulled his breath in and his pants up. "In that case, maybe I should tell you a couple of things about Mr. Parker." He took the pen Martha offered, and wrote where she pointed.

"The cause of death was a thirty-eight hollow-point bullet. He was shot through the head, front to back, but if that hadn't finished him, his cocaine habit would have."

Dr. Beller tossed Martha's pen on the desk and started back to his office. "Fill out a requisition. When the lab sends me their reports, I'll send you a copy of the autopsy."

I nudged Rhodes as the pathologist disappeared into his office. "Ask him about the woman," I whispered.

"Are you her lawyer, too?" Dr. Beller boomed from behind his half-open door.

I felt my face grow hot. "No, sir."

"Then I don't know anything about her," he said.

A grin tugged the corners of Rhodes's mouth as my face turned from pink to red.

"Sign here, dear." Martha gave my arm a motherly pat.

I signed, not one but two forms. She tore the bottom half from one, and handed it back to me. "This is the release for Mr. Parker's body. Give it to the funeral director. He'll know what to do with it." She tucked the other form into her desk. "I'll keep this one. It's your request for the autopsy report."

I scanned the form I held in my hand. "This covers the body, but what about his clothes and the car?"

Martha shuffled more papers. "His personal effects should be in the Evidence Room," she said. "Now, let's see." She thumbed through another pile, found another form, and handed it to me. "This will get you the car. Forensics has finished with it and it's been released."

I signed where she pointed. "Do you have an inventory list for Mr. Parker's clothes?" I asked.

Martha's smile brightened. "Detective MacPhearson has that, but I'm sure he'll let you see it."

I stifled a "damn right he will" and followed Rhodes back through the corridors and up the stairs.

"Take a right when you get to the end of the hall," he said when we reached the squad room. "MacPhearson's office is two doors down on the left."

A phone rang, interrupted by a voice calling, "It's for you, Lieu."

With a promise to call when he had the videotape (the policeman had read my foot-shuffling performance correctly), Rhodes entered his office. I followed the hall to the end, turned right and counted two. The second door on the left was open, and as if sensing my presence, MacPhearson looked up.

"Well, hello, Red." A smile slid from beneath his mustache.

I moved forward, stopping at the front edge of his desk.

"Coffee? Seat?" The detective waved at a steaming Mr. Coffee and a straight-backed wooden chair.

I waved away the coffee and took the chair, which proved as uncomfortable as the one in Rhodes's office. "I'd like to see the inventory list for Bryan Parker's personal effects. I was told you had it."

MacPhearson swiveled his chair sideways and ruffled through a stack of folders. "I can do better than that."

"The list will do," I snapped.

He gave me an innocent stare. "Why, Miss Arthur, are you refusing my offer?" He opened the folder and picked up a sheet of paper.

"Look—" I began.

"No, you listen." MacPhearson read from the list, pausing after each item as he did.

"Black jockey briefs, navy socks, navy slacks, light-blue dress shirt, medium-blue alpaca crew neck sweater, hand-tooled black leather-like belt, hand-sewn black leather-like tasseled loafers, yellow metal Rolex wristwatch, black leather-like wallet with—"

"What's your point?" I asked when he finished.

"I didn't want you to think we were hiding something."

I rolled the forms Martha had given me into a tight tube and snapped them impatiently against the edge of MacPhearson's desk.

"Is one of those for the Jaguar?" MacPhearson indicated the pair of mistreated forms.

"Why?" I asked, not from curiosity but rather from caution.

"Just wondered if you knew where it was."

"And if I don't?"

The twinkle was back. I shrugged, hoping he would think it indifference and not irritation—hell, anger. What was there about MacPhearson that made me so angry?

"It's in the police lot, but you'll have to pay the towing charge before they'll release it."

I stood up. "Thank you, you've been most helpful. Now, if you'll give me the keys."

He handed them to me. "Anything else?"

"I still want a copy of the inventory list." I propped a hip on the corner of his desk. If Leslie asked, though I doubted she would, I wanted something to show her.

"Can do." Wearing his usual infuriating grin, MacPhearson disappeared through the door. "Don't go away," he called over his shoulder.

I shot his retreating back a withering look, realizing what it was about him that I so disliked. Everything!

I reveled in the revelation, but strangely got little satisfaction. The minutes dragged. I thought of Bryan's underwear, his socks and shoes, pants and shirt, belt, watch . . . Something was wrong. Something . . .

Chapter Nine

MACPHEARSON PUSHED THROUGH THE DOOR AND REENTERED THE OFFICE, HIS MALE PRESENCE filling the small space. The "something" which had never quite been in my mind fled.

I slid off the corner of the desk and held out my hand. "I'll take the list."

"Can we talk first, Ginny?" MacPhearson ignored my outstretched hand and settled into his chair.

I waggled my fingers. "Hand it over."

"Please, Ginny, sit down."

I shook my head.

"Okay, okay." He slid the inventory list across the desk.

I picked up the paper, folded it together with the forms which by now were beginning to look somewhat the worse for wear, and placed them carefully in my shoulder bag. "Did you have a specific subject in mind?" Once again curiosity won over discretion. I had, after all, accomplished what I'd set out to do.

"Just wanted to share some background information on Bryan Parker." He grinned. "I've got this notion that knowing the past helps one understand the future, or in this case the present."

He flipped open a folder. "Interested?"

I eyed the folder.

"Don't worry. I won't ask you to compromise any principles."

Don't trust him, a voice inside my head warned. I ignored the warning and reclaimed the uncomfortable chair. "Anything interesting? Like a police record maybe?"

MacPhearson thumbed the pages before him. "His record's cleaner than mine. Only a couple of minor traffic violations."

"Are you saying you have a record?" I deadpanned, picturing a lanky, freckle-faced teenager running from a uniformed police officer.

"Just the usual kid stuff." His blue eyes twinkled. "How about you, Red? How's your record?"

I said nothing, and MacPhearson rolled backwards and picked up Mr. Coffee. "Change your mind?"

What the heck. In for a penny . . . I nodded, and MacPhearson filled a pair of mugs.

"Parker would have been forty next month." MacPhearson read from the file on his desk. "He was born in Detroit, educated in parochial schools, and graduated from Wayne State at age twenty with a degree in biology. Stayed an extra year and left with an MBA."

My lifted eyebrow posed the next question.

"You're right. Mr. Parker was a very bright boy. He graduated with a 4.0."

"I'm impressed," I said. I hadn't realized how little I'd known about Leslie's husband. "Did his family have money?"

MacPhearson shook his head. "Parker was raised by a spinster aunt who mostly lived off welfare. The money came from grants and academic scholarships."

"Did he do as well professionally?"

MacPhearson fitted his hands to the back of his head and leaned into his chair. It was obviously more comfortable than mine. "From all indications Upchurch Chemicals considered him one of their golden boys," MacPhearson said. "Parker went with them right after college, was made a district manager after only a year and promoted to regional director when he came here."

Was this the life of a drug addict? I blew the steam from my coffee and took a sip. What I was hearing didn't fit with what Dr. Beller had told me.

"Is something wrong?" MacPhearson asked.

I shook my head. "Just thinking—"

"Murder makes you think, Ginny."

"What else have you got in that folder?" I asked. I wasn't about to pursue any philosophical issues with the man behind the desk.

MacPhearson made a have-it-your-way shrug. "Parker married Leslie five years ago. He met her when he was working on a research project with her father, who is also a doctor, a surgeon. But I suppose you already know that."

I sensed dangerous ground ahead and straightened against the slats of the chair. Talking about Bryan was one thing, talking about Leslie quite another.

"Leslie Parker also went to Wayne State," MacPhearson continued. "She interned at Providence Hospital in Detroit before coming here for her surgical residency."

"Which brings us up to date." I allowed myself a smile. The information he'd chosen to share with me was available to any six-year-old with half a brain and a computer.

"Not quite," MacPhearson corrected. "There's still the little matter of murder."

"Murder?"

He grinned. "Interesting enough, Parker's playmate was also a doctor's daughter." His grin widened. "Her name's Nancy Webber, but then I suppose you already know that, too."

I ran my tongue along the rim of the cup. The name meant nothing to me, but damned if I'd let MacPhearson know. I hid my ignorance behind another question. "Any idea who the killer might be?"

"I was hoping you could tell me," MacPhearson said. He moved, settling deeper into the chair. "You're the one who's been talking to the widow."

The voice inside my head issued another warning. This time I listened. "And so have you, Mac. I've met Detective Hightower."

MacPhearson shrugged. "She's our only witness." He laid crossed forearms on his desk and leaned forward. "Does she have any idea who the scar-faced man is?"

"She didn't say and I didn't ask," I lied. No tongue in cheek or crossed fingers, even with Leslie's voice whispering in my ear, "he had a face you couldn't forget."

"Care to guess?" MacPhearson invited.

"A jealous boyfriend?" I offered.

"Or maybe a late-night telephone caller?" MacPhearson countered.

"Now who's guessing?" I stood, picked up my shoulder bag, and slid the strap over my arm.

"Got to start someplace." He grinned. "But thanks for hearing me out, Red." MacPhearson stood. He moved closer and touched a curl that lay near my ear. "I bet it looks like fire in the sun."

"Like yours?" My smile was casual, intended to brush off his parting gesture as meaningless. Yet . . .

Pursued by doubts that said it wasn't, I hurried down the hall to Larry Rhodes's office. It was empty. Damn! The videotape would have to wait. It was late, and I still had to spring the Jaguar.

"You need the bill from the police garage," a bored clerk in the City Treasurer's office told me.

Her delivery implied it was information any fool would know. I left in a huff. Unfortunately, I neglected to ask where the garage was. Several wrong turns later, I found it.

"I need the towing bill for a Jaguar," I explained to a sixtyish man wearing greasy overalls and a Detroit Tigers baseball cap. "It's midnight blue with a leather interior."

He pointed to a yard overgrown with wheeled vehicles. "It's out there."

He turned the page of a ledger that lay open on the desk before him and ran his finger down the list of entries. "Came in Thursday just before noon." He dropped his finger from the page. "If you want it, it'll cost you seventy bucks."

"Isn't that a bit steep?" The distance between the Ann Street motel and the municipal building was less than five miles.

"Could be," the man agreed. "But maybe you can find someone cheaper to do the tow if you decide to take it."

"I have the keys," I said. I pawed through my shoulder bag.

"Keys won't do you much good." The man chuckled. "It's dead. Killed by a thirty-eight slug."

"Hell!" Surely MacPhearson knew?

My outburst went unanswered, and I followed the man into the field of discarded vehicles. He stopped before the midnight-blue sports car.

"Even standing still, she's something." His greasy hand caressed the Jaguar's bonnet.

"Where was it shot?" I asked, wishing it was MacPhearson.

The man sidled to the front of the car and pointed to the grill. "The bullet went in there and through the radiator."

"Can it be fixed?"

"Most anything can be fixed." He pulled at the brim of his cap. "But if you think the towing bill's high . . ." He paused, giving me time to reconsider. "You still want it?"

"I still want it." A trip back to the Treasurer's office along with a check payable to Marion City made it mine.

The funeral director Leslie had selected was on Marion City's west side. A painted sign, discreetly located to the left of the front entrance, read GABENSKI AND SON. Inside, somber organ music and air scented with hothouse flowers assailed both ears and nose.

"May I help you?" asked a man who could have been either Gabenski or son.

I handed the man, whose wavy gray hair was cut to show both his ears and the back of his neck, the last of the two forms Martha had given me.

He smiled, told me he was familiar with the procedure. We discussed cremation and urns. They could, he said, take care of everything.

I shook off the somber effects of Gabenski and Son with deep drafts of cold November air. The Ranger waited curbside, and I headed back to the freeway and Euro-Imports, the city's only authorized Jaguar dealer, where I discussed the need of a tow and left the receipt from the city's Treasurer's office.

The cost of repairs wasn't discussed.

It was nearing four before I finally made it back to the offices of the Arthur & Arthur Security Agency.

Beth met me with a smile. "Today's newspaper and your telephone messages are on your desk." Her smile deepened. "And your two afternoon appointments will be here in about an hour."

Starred on Thelma's list, they had been neither cancelled nor rescheduled. The sparsity of clients since Uncle David's disappearance didn't allow such luxuries.

I settled behind the desk in the inner office. The first telephone message was from Steve, asking me to meet him at the hospital for dinner. I returned his call. We agreed on seven. I said I'd bring a pizza.

The newspaper caught my eye as I hung up. A picture of Bryan's smiling face and that of a young, good-looking woman stared at me from center front. The caption read: BODIES OF MOTEL MURDER VICTIMS IDENTIFIED.

"Shit!" I finished the article, then aimed the paper at the wastebasket. The heavy breathing was mine.

I needed to move and pushed away from the desk. Blue skies and the even bluer Oswago River lay outside the office window. A peaceful scene, it made me feel even more restless. MacPhearson knew that Nancy Webber's identity had been released to the paper. Knew that it would be in the afternoon edition. Yet he'd insinuated it was privileged information.

Why?

Because he's an asshole, the now familiar voice inside my head answered.

"A damn fucking asshole!" I corrected. It was an overused expletive, but it fit my sentiments so well it would have to do.

I forced myself back to work. Rhodes hadn't called by the time I finished the last of my telephone calls, and I was considering calling him when Beth announced the arrival of the first appointment.

It was a new client, and as befitted his status, he received the royal treatment, a smile and coffee from Beth and a stand-up handshake from me. He suspected personal injury insurance fraud and wanted to discuss surveillance. This, as well as the electronic security systems that were the agency's bread and butter, was among the services we offered, and I was able to promise a team of watchers for the following day.

A husband and wife pair was the afternoon's second appointment. Old clients, they wanted to review the latest state-of-the-art pressure-sensitive devices.

They greeted me with hugs and suggested Beth have some of the cookies they'd brought with them. Beth went for more coffee, and I handed them a new catalog. We spent the next thirty minutes discussing the relative merits of new versus old equipment.

I promised to send a technician to do an on-site evaluation, and walked the pair to the door.

"Time to go," I said when the hall door closed behind the portly couple.

"Where did they park their sleigh?" Beth's blue eyes sparkled above her wide smile.

I laughed. "So you recognized them."

"Mr. and Mrs. Santa Claus."

Beth named the pair who, besides having the largest display of Christmas decorations in western Michigan, were the long-time stars of Marion City's annual Christmas parade. The couple, Mr. and Mrs. Roundtree, came in every year at this time to review the latest in surveillance equipment and to sign their annual contract.

We parted company at the stairs. Beth went down to the sixth floor. Leslie and Bryan Parker's mail in hand, the Arthur & Arthur Security office being the mail drop for the penthouse apartment, I climbed up to the tenth floor.

Chapter Ten

THOUGHTS OF MURDER AND THE DEAD JAGUAR FILLED MY MIND AS I CLIMBED, THE PAIR ON the bed vying for equal time with the blue sports car.

Below me, a door clanged open. I stopped to listen. Noisy feet clamored over metal treads, and another door opened and closed, reassuring sounds in this vertical concrete tunnel where sound often played tricks on one's ears.

Beth sure moves fast. I pictured the three flights of stairs that separated the offices of Arthur & Arthur from the surveillance rooms. Pictured my fleet-footed friend as a winged Mercury, not a mere mortal like me.

I smiled at the thought, and felt the smile broaden as I thought of Steve and our seven o'clock date. Seeing him would be good, but pizza? Maybe Chinese . . .

My foot hit a riser. In the distance, Sir Echo answered. Accompanied by a repeating bang-bang-bang, I pulled open the tenth floor fire door.

Three sets of keys nestled in the bottom of my shoulder bag, Leslie's, Bryan's and mine, each with a key to the apartment. I chose the first one that found its way into my fingers, inserted it into each of the two locks, and let myself inside.

A long-standing habit drew me to the Ansel Adams print. The alarm that hid behind it said ON. I entered the set of numbers on the digital pad that turned it OFF.

My footsteps, loud against the entryway's parquet floor, grew quiet when I reached the carpeted living room. The button that controlled the drapes was near at hand. I pushed it. The drapes flew apart to reveal a panoramic view of the city. The soft glow of artificial light from street lamps and office buildings competed with the dying light of the late afternoon.

The window called, and as I had so many times before, I answered the siren call and leaned my forehead against the cool pane. Only then he . . . my eyes misted, making the view fuzzy. Where was he? What was he doing?

"Why, Uncle David, why?" The cry became a moan as it escaped my lips.

The question had no answer, and I turned away, turned my back on the man who had turned his back on me. Outside the man-made lights grew brighter as night settled over the city.

Like other homes, the apartment had its set of special noises. Usually friendly, tonight, without the raucous cries of the Siamese pair, the creaks and groans made me strangely uneasy. I reached for the light switch before setting my shoulder bag and the pile of mail, my excuse but not the reason for me being in the apartment, on the kitchen table.

The glow from the fluorescent tubes challenged my jitters, and I chided myself for my foolishness. Still, a little music wouldn't hurt. Might, in fact, even help. I headed for the library, flicking on more lights as I went.

Bookcases and a brick-framed fireplace covered the right-hand wall, and to the right of that oak panels hid a built-in stereo system. It was Uncle David's desk that dominated the room, however. I'd rented the apartment furnished, and even though Leslie and Bryan had lived there for almost six months, their presence had made little impact. Still, it wasn't the tables and chairs or the desk that made it Uncle David's. It was the essence of the man himself, the feeling that at any moment his head would pop through a door or his voice call my name, that made the apartment uniquely his.

I crossed to the shelves that held the CDs, and loaded some easy listening rock, classics, jazz, and even a Willie Nelson into the trays. I hit random select. Dave Brubeck's "Take Five" filled the room.

I switched the desk lamp to its dimmest setting and gave the room a final sweep. Wyeth's Helga print still hid the wall safe and oak paneling the fire escape door. Someday this would all have to go, perhaps sooner rather than later because of Bryan's death, but . . .

I turned off the hall lights as I made my way to the master bedroom suite, and turned on thoughts of the Jaguar, or more precisely, the dead Jaguar.

Beethoven played on the stereo as I pushed open the door to a mirrored dressing room. Shadows lurked in the corners. I flipped on the light. All but one shadow vanished in the sudden brightness. A tease, it played in the mirror before joining the others. A trick of the light, I thought, but the thought that had brought me to this room with its opposing mirrors was a thorn, a sharp thorn that drove away the other.

Followed by my reflected image, I hurried across the dressing room. Behind me, a thump sounded. I listened. Willie Nelson's "You're Always On My Mind" convinced me it was his guitar.

The bathroom medicine cabinet had what I needed. With a tube of lipstick and a black eyebrow pencil in hand, I returned to the dressing room and began to draw on one of its mirrored walls.

Several minutes of furrowed-brow concentration passed before I stepped back and gave my handiwork a critical appraisal. It needed more black on the headlights and rounder lines near the bonnet where it met the grill. Another appraisal rated a satisfied smile. To my prejudiced eye, it looked just like Bryan Parker's prize sports car.

I closed my eyes and visualized the police lot, focused on the Jaguar's grill, and lipsticked a bullet hole on the mirror. I stepped back for another look. It looked right, just right.

A thump-thump interrupted. The throbbing bass of a jazz quartet swelled in volume. I ignored the foot-tapping rhythm and turned away from the car and faced the opposing wall of mirrors.

Knees bent, I made myself small, approximated Leslie's shorter stature, and poked my left index finger into my right side. Eyes fixed on the black and red car behind me, I jockeyed into position.

Bang! My finger pulled the trigger of the imaginary gun.

"That's how it happened," I told the smiling girl who watched me. "The scar-faced man killed the Jaguar when he shot Leslie."

Behind me, a shadow moved. My imagination took flight. Was something, someone there? A burglar?

"Don't be silly," I told my look-alike friend. We exchanged encouraging smiles and I turned out the light.

Thump!

The door? Had I locked it? And the alarm? I had turned it off, of that I was sure. My muscles tensed. I listened, but heard nothing.

My eyes, slow in adjusting to the dark, sensed movement. I pressed against the wall.

Thump!

Close? Far away? I couldn't place the sound. My ears were as worthless as my eyes.

Pop!

Glass showered my face. I ducked my head and slid down the wall. Movement filled the bedroom door, followed by a succession of thumps, first loud, then soft as they faded away.

I touched my face. Shards of glass pricked my fingers and cut my cheek. I shut my mind to the reality I refused to consider and freed myself from the shattered wall.

Noises, louder than the thumps, sounded somewhere in the distance. Braver now, knowing "it" wasn't near, I crawled to the door.

Grunts, groans, a crash, loud, then louder, sounded somewhere down the hall. Under cover of the noise, I pulled myself up.

Who? I had no answer.

Hugging the wall, I side-stepped down the hall. A crash from the living room warned of imminent danger. Afraid of being seen, I lowered myself to the floor.

The city's lights, reflected off the cloudy sky, shot through the windows and filled the room with irregularly shaped patterns of light and dark. I could see no one, yet I knew someone was there.

Ahead the thumping sound repeated itself, then again and again.

A man's shadowed form thumped across the room. He stopped. Turned. Back-lighted by the city's lights, he pointed a . . .

A pop, a sound like bubble gum bubbles popping, popped once—twice.

The man hesitated. Dropped his hand, made another half turn as if heading for the front door, then fell. Another man walked into the window's changing light patterns. Too scared not to watch, I watched.

The second man bent over the first man. Another bubble gum bubble popped. In the library, the stereo played Aaron Copland's "Rodeo." My muscles were like jelly, and my lungs ached from the strain of not breathing.

Fear became terror and threatened reason, but not enough to stop my thinking. I had witnessed a murder, and the popping noises were gunshots—silenced gunshots.

I turned to creep back down the hall. My way to the library and the fire escape was barred by a splash of light from the kitchen.

I weighed the merits of a sudden rush over a slow crawl. The debate stopped when a man came through the door and into the hall.

He turned from side to side, showing the gun and the brightly colored ski mask that covered his head. I made myself small and sank into a shadow beside a hall table. Seemingly satisfied with what he either saw or, more hopefully, did not see, he reached a gloved hand behind him and flipped off the kitchen light. It was a moment's distraction, a chance, and I took it.

The man moved above and behind me. He cursed. I kept low. Only not low enough, for his hand brushed my shoulder, and the gun touched my neck. Another forward lunge brought me upright. The library was only steps away. Three, two, and . . .

Pop!

Wooden splinters from the doorframe splattered across my arm. I fell into the room, swung my arm wide and slammed the door shut. Another shot followed, the bullet blasting a large hole in the door.

My shoulder hit the desk. I hugged its side and worked my way to the paneled wall that hid the fire escape. The door behind me banged open. The man loomed large in the lamp's light and moved toward me.

I grabbed the cord and yanked the lamp to the floor. The bulb broke, bringing back the darkness.

Another bullet hit where the lamp lay, and sent me behind the desk. Footsteps followed, and then a hand and a gun. The hand shoved the swivel chair into the wall. I grabbed the spinning seat and sent it back.

"Bitch!" the man cursed.

Froglike, I leaped forward. My way to the fire escape barred, I headed for the hall. Copland's "Rodeo" still played on the stereo, the fun-loving cowboys urging me on.

A pop sounded as I ran into the hall and another when I entered the kitchen. The half-open pantry door caught me as I ran past.

A push sent it swinging, and I forged ahead. Light coming through the front windows, the same light that had earlier provided a lighted stage for a murder, now showed an obstacle course for foot and eye.

Bypassing the living room, I angled toward the front hall but cut the corner too fast and was unable to negotiate the turn. I fell, hitting my head against the leg of an overturned table.

Close behind me, a giant bubble gum bubble popped.

Chapter Eleven

THE SOUND OF A POUNDING JACKHAMMER WOKE ME. I LIFTED MY HEAD AND LOOKED FOR THE source, but despite the awful racket, couldn't find it. I groaned as the realization hit me: The pounding was inside my head. I remembered the man with a gun. Fear, nauseating in its intensity, washed over me and I dropped close to the floor. Silence pressed in on me. Minutes passed. A worse thought struck. Was I dead?

Needing to know, I raised my hand and ran fingertips across my face in search of an answer. Another groan, then an "ouch" followed a quickly suppressed "damn." A painful bump had given my forehead an irregular shape, and several cuts criss-crossed my cheeks. Convinced I was still among the living, I continued my search. I discovered a large furrow over my ear that oozed when I touched it.

Afraid of what else I might find, I quit the search. Sleep beckoned. I fought the pull, but was dragged into the darkness.

Light tugged at my eyelids. I denied it admittance and again strained to listen. I heard nothing. Had sound ceased to exist? Was I isolated in a vacuum?

I threw caution away, pushed to all fours and sank back on my heels. The room was flooded with daylight. Where had the night gone?

More importantly, where was the man with the gun?

I listened for the creak of floorboards or the sound of breathing. The floorboards were silent, and the only breathing was my own labored gulps. The silence deepened. Was I alone?

Alone! My eyes swept the room. Where was the murdered man?

I looked to where I had seen him fall, to where a jumble of upended tables, chairs, and couches screamed "look at me." I ignored their mute cries, my attention caught by the shattered lamps with twisted shades. Could a burglar have done all this?

I cursed what I could not understand.

The epithet lent strength, and I pulled upright. A drunken two-step marked the effort. My wobbly legs steadied, and I took another look around. Stuffing from upholstered furniture and throw pillows blanketed the room like new-fallen snow.

I targeted the window and made my way toward it, but met an overturned dining room chair whose slashed cushion had burst like the flesh of a baked potato.

Snow? Baked potatoes? Besides my cuts and bruises, had I lost my mind?

I righted the chair and looked for the table. It lay on its side, with its top facing the window.

The man lay between its outthrust legs. There was a hole in his chest surrounded by a reddish-brown stain. I needed no one to tell me that the stain was blood, the hole a bullet wound.

An involuntary shudder passed through me. I stepped back, wanting distance between us, wanting to be anywhere but here.

The disgorged innards of the grandfather clock littered my escape route. Its cracked face grinned a welcome, but I refused the invitation to stay.

My pounding head impeded my progress, forced me to take the stairs to the ninth floor one at a time. Still, I was out of breath when I reached the office door.

I turned the knob. The door was locked. I pounded hard, and yelled louder. Thelma would be there. Thelma was always there. Only Thelma was not there.

It took a while before I found the answer. It was Saturday and, worse yet, the keys to the office were in my shoulder bag. Reluctantly, I reclimbed the stairs.

The dead man was still there. I tried to ignore him, but like a moth to the flame, my eyes were drawn to the table that marked where he lay.

The grandfather clock and his cracked face rescued me. Forced to maneuver carefully through its scattered works, I had little time for the man in the living room. Help was a set of keys away. The keys were in my shoulder bag, and my shoulder bag was in the kitchen . . . I hoped.

The kitchen had fared no better than had the rest of the apartment, its drawers emptied, its shelves cleared of everything including the shelf paper. As bad as it was, this wasn't what caught my attention. The telephone was still attached to the wall.

Forgetting the shoulder bag and keys and my cell phone which should also have been there, I pressed the receiver to my ear. I listened, and kept on listening. It wasn't wishful thinking. The dial tone was there.

My finger hesitated over the keypad. Thelma? She was busy with grandchildren. 911? I took a look around. Strangers weren't the answer either. I punched in Larry Rhodes's home number.

"Uncle David's apartment's been broken into," I said when he answered.

"Where are you?" he asked.

"Here, in the apartment, and everything in it's been trashed."

"Don't touch anything," he cautioned. "I'll be right there."

I looked at the telephone handset which I still held in my hand. So much for preserving the integrity of a crime scene I thought, replacing the receiver in its cradle.

I waited for Rhodes in the hallway outside the apartment. The floor and the wall I leaned against were not comfortable, but neither was the company of a dead man.

I took some calming breaths that didn't calm and finger-combed my hair. Should I start with the man lying between the legs of an overturned table, or tell him about the door I'd neglected to lock, the alarm I'd forgotten to reset?

The three thoughts were still chasing each other inside my head when the elevator door slid open.

Rhodes looked at me with darkening eyes. "You said the apartment was trashed, not you."

I wondered if 911 might have been the better choice.

He crouched beside me. His face wore a scowl, and he looked decidedly unhappy. "What in hell happened to you, Ginny?" He leaned closer, pointed to the matted furrow above my ear. "This looks like a gunshot wound."

The open elevator door tempted. I debated making a run for it, but it sighed closed. I sighed with it.

"You should be in the hospital."

"Not now. Maybe later." I pulled upright and led the way inside.

Rhodes's eyes swept the room. "Were you here when this happened?"

"It was like this when I woke up." I waved aside further questions and led the way to the overturned table.

"Any more surprises?" Rhodes deadpanned.

I didn't answer. I was looking at the dead man's face, which, in my haste to escape, I hadn't really looked at before. A scar at the corner of his mouth gave him a lopsided smirk, and his eye, the one that was still there, stared dully into space. Leslie was right. It was a face you couldn't forget.

"Do you know him?" Rhodes asked.

I shook my head. "I don't, but Leslie might. She said the man who shot her had a scar on his face."

Rhodes's brow knitted. "I've seen him somewhere, and not too long ago, either . . ." He bent for a closer look. "Did Leslie say anything about a walking cast?"

"No, but it explains the thumping noises I heard last night."

Rhodes's attention shifted from the casted foot to my face. "I think it's time you told me more about last night, Ginny. Obviously this guy didn't shoot himself."

"Well it certainly wasn't me," I protested. "I don't even own a gun."

"A situation that will soon be remedied," Rhodes muttered.

I said nothing. It was an old argument.

Rhodes led me to the chair I'd righted earlier. Away from the staring eye and scar-induced smirk, I told him about the unlocked door, the bubble gum pops and about the second man who had pursued me through the apartment.

Rhodes walked back to the body, and then circled it once and once again. The second time he stopped beside the man's outstretched arm. A gun lay close by, partially hidden by a gutted cushion.

"It looks like a forty-five, and it has a silencer." Rhodes reached into his jacket pocket. "Time to call homicide. Robbery's my thing, not murder."

I watched Rhodes speed-dial a number into his cell phone, my eyes locking with his as he lifted the instrument to his ear. Would MacPhearson, whose thing was murder, answer the call, I wondered? If he did, what would the redheaded detective have to say when he saw the scar-faced man?

While we waited for what Rhodes called the official police to arrive, we each slipped into a pair of latex gloves, mine coming from what seemed an endless supply Rhodes carried in another of his pockets, and toured the apartment, stopping to admire such landmarks as the hand-drawn black and red Jaguar and the library that had become a shooting gallery. Rhodes asked about the open safe, but I knew nothing of its contents. The tour ended where it had begun, in the living room.

"What do you think they were looking for?" I asked.

"Judging from the damage, it had to be something small, but not too small." Rhodes pointed to the pictures that hung on the wall. Most were askew, but none were damaged. "Something that would fit inside a cushion or under a piece of furniture."

Before I could ask more, the front door opened. MacPhearson, his red hair flying and his red face smiling, rushed in.

"Hello, Red," he said.

Rhodes called a welcome. I ignored him.

"Did Rhodes tell you that you look like hell?" MacPhearson asked. He stood in front of me.

I backed away from his critical stare, from words that sounded all too familiar. My foot caught on a piece of the clock's innards, and I staggered sideways.

MacPhearson's hand shot forward. "Careful. You're already in bad enough shape."

I pushed his hand away and side-stepped what looked like a giant spring. Again, MacPhearson offered help. Again, I refused.

His smile broadened. "Tell me, how does the other guy look?"

"Dead," I snapped.

"So I've heard, but then that's why I'm here." Like Rhodes before, MacPhearson fingered the hair beside my ear. "If you let it grow, the scar won't show."

My fingers found the matted wound.

"Better leave it alone." He pulled my hand down. "I suggest you get that doctor friend of yours to look at it. Only before you do, mind giving me a rundown on what happened here?"

I did mind, but knew I had no choice and gave him an abridged version.

"Are you suggesting vandalism rather than burglary?" MacPhearson asked when I finished.

I waved my hand, circling the room. "Take your choice, but as far as I can tell nothing of value is missing."

"Is this the place?" a voice from the hall outside the apartment interrupted.

"You got it, Doc." Rhodes called Dr. Beller inside. "The body's over there, between those table legs."

The coroner's round belly led him around and over the fallen grandfather clock. He jiggled to an abrupt stop when he reached me.

"You don't look near as good as when I last saw you, Miss Arthur," he said.

I gave him a half grin, a you-don't-say kind of look, and he continued on toward the body. Behind him came what seemed like an army of technicians. As I had seen them do in the motel, each began to dust, tweeze, vacuum, and collect their way through the debris.

"Beller should have sent you to the hospital," Rhodes complained, watching the doctor and the swarming criminalists.

My eyes remained fixed on MacPhearson. "He uses people," I said.

"Who?" Rhodes asked.

"MacPhearson," I answered.

Rhodes laughed. "That's his job, Ginny."

"He doesn't have to be so damned cocky about it."

Rhodes took my arm, turning me towards the front door. "I think it's time we got out of here."

I agreed, and we went in search of my shoulder bag. It was back again where I had left it, on the kitchen table.

"You'll have to clear it with Detective MacPhearson first," a technician said when I went to grab it.

"But it's mine," I argued.

The door swung open, and MacPhearson came into the kitchen.

"She won't give me my purse," I complained.

MacPhearson looked at the tech. "You finished with it?"

She nodded, and he slid the purse across the table towards me.

I fisted my fingers around the shoulder strap and fought the urge to swing the bag at him. "And are you through with me, too?" Enough was enough, and I'd had enough.

"I'll need a signed statement from you," MacPhearson said. He leaned against the counter. "But it can wait until tomorrow. You should feel better by then."

I shrugged off the tomorrow and feeling better, and turned my attention to the shoulder bag. Comb, lipstick, wallet, Palm Pilot—somehow knowing it was important that I do so, my eyes and fingers inventoried the contents. I stopped, withdrew my hand and gave MacPhearson an accusing look.

"Something wrong?" he asked.

Chapter Twelve

"Give them to me." For the second time in as many days, I held out my hand to the brash homicide detective. "You have my cell phone and Bryan Parker's keys, and I want them back."

MacPhearson shook his head. "The keys yes, the cell phone no."

I stirred the contents of my shoulder bag. "My cell phone is not here," I complained.

MacPhearson shrugged. "How about your pocket?"

I ran my hands around my hips, feeling the outline of abdomen and thighs, and came up empty-handed. I readied myself for another angry retort, but the vague memory of my cell phone, sitting in my office in its charger, surfaced above the jackhammer that still pounded inside my head.

"The keys then." I wiggled the fingers on my extended hand and gave the redheaded detective what I hoped was a scathing look.

MacPhearson dangled the keys between us. "And you can have them."

The movement caught my eyes. I swayed with it. I shook my head. It was a big mistake.

"I just wanted to know what they fit."

I grabbed the ring, stopping the motion. "These two are for the Jaguar." I separated them from the others. "This one's for the apartment, and this one is probably for his office."

"Office?" MacPhearson stared at the key.

"He has an office in the Professional Building across from Mercy Hospital." I made no attempt to hide my rapidly growing impatience.

"Have you been there recently?"

"Why?"

MacPhearson shrugged. "Just wondered if it looked anything like this place." He waved his hand indicating the chaos that surrounded us.

"Don't you know?"

He shook his head. "Hell, I didn't even know Bryan Parker had an office until you told me about it."

Should I believe him? I thought of Nancy Webber, of the bullet hole in the Jaguar, and decided to hedge my bets. "Tell you what. I'll have a look and let you know."

"How about we go together?"

"Get a search warrant." I was tired, and the jackhammer had decided to pick up the tempo. Rhodes was right. It was time I was out of here.

MacPhearson grinned a wide grin. "That takes a lot of time and effort."

"Spend it." I started for the door.

I'll call you later," I muttered.

"You still here?" Dr. Beller boomed into the kitchen. He stopped before me, hiding the homicide detective from view.

"That cut over your eye needs stitches." He lifted the hair over my ear. "And this needs a good cleaning."

"That's exactly what I've been telling you, Ginny," Rhodes cut in.

I scowled at my overzealous protector. "Okay, you win, but I'll drive myself. The Ranger's in the parking lot."

"I don't think so," Dr. Beller said.

It was all Rhodes needed to hear.

I got the shakes in the elevator. Rhodes blamed it on the cold and draped his coat over my shoulders. Only it wasn't the cold, and the coat didn't help.

Shivering, I thought of the man with the scarred face and of the other who had hidden his face beneath a ski mask. I pulled Rhodes's coat tighter around me. This wasn't a simple break-in, or a case of one burglar surprising another, of this I was sure despite the bump on my head. I shook my head for emphasis, fool that I am, and leaned against the side of the elevator until the nausea passed. But if not that, what?

With the heater on high and the gas pedal on the floor, Rhodes made it to the hospital in record time. The usual cache of customers waited in the Emergency Room, but Rhodes's badge sped up the admitting process.

"What happened to you?" a nurse asked. Her gentle eyes and gentler fingers probed my face.

"A bullet made the hole over her ear, and she got the bump and the cut over her eye when she fell against a table leg," Rhodes answered.

The nurse wrote on a clipboard as Rhodes talked. Then, with a face that told me nothing, wrapped a blood pressure cuff around my arm and stuck a thermometer in my ear.

Hurting?" she asked.

I nodded.

An electronic buzz sounded and she pulled the probe from my ear. "The doctor will be right in." Clipboard in hand, she left the room.

"Do you want me to call Steve?" Rhodes asked.

"I'll do it."

I slid off the exam table, walked to the house phone that hung beside the door, and punched in Steve's beeper number. As usual, it wasn't Steve who answered, and I gave the nurse who did my message. I hung up. Tears threatened, escaped, and slid down my cheek. I felt alone, so alone.

"Ginny?" Rhodes asked softly.

I blinked away the tears. Unable to answer, I concentrated on climbing on the table.

"What have we here?" The door opened abruptly, and a skinny, black-skinned, white-coated man came into the room.

"A headache," I mumbled through tight lips.

Rhodes rolled his eyes.

The skinny doctor read from the clipboard, then pumped up the blood pressure cuff. He added his own scribbles to the nurse's notes and then switched off the overhead light.

"I'm Dr. Canfield." He played a beam of light into each of my eyes. "And you can relax, because I'm in charge of headaches today."

After several seconds of nose-to-nose togetherness, he mumbled, "When did this happen?"

I told him.

"Did you lose consciousness, get sick to your stomach?" he asked.

I answered, "Yes and no."

"Hum," he said. He flipped the small light off and the overhead fixture on. "You have quite a bump." He smiled. "I know it hurts, but how much does it hurt?"

"It started out feeling like jackhammers, but now it feels like a hangover."

Dr. Canfield snapped on a pair of gloves and explored the knot over my eye and the bullet wound on the side of my head.

I winced. "Take it easy."

No longer able to hide his concern, Rhodes asked, "How bad is it, Doc?"

"It doesn't look too bad, but I'll need some skull films to be sure." The doctor looked at me as he answered Rhodes's question. "But let's sew you up first."

He started for the door, but Rhodes stopped him. "Will she have to stay the night?"

"All depends on what the X-rays show, but I don't think so." Dr. Canfield looked at the police lieutenant, whose caring expression belied his daily brush with life's vicissitudes. "Look, why don't you wait in the lounge. Have some coffee, and I'll call you when we get through here."

The doctor took hold of Rhodes's arm, leading the policeman from the room as he talked. Canfield paused just before the door closed behind them and gave me an over-the-shoulder wink.

The nurse's return followed quickly upon their departure. Along with assorted paraphernalia, she brought a wagging tongue. "This won't take long, then Dr. Canfield can get started."

She touched the side of my head. "Not much he can do with this one, but he can fix the cut over your eye so that you'll hardly see the scar."

She continued to prattle as her gloved fingers moved swiftly from the tray to my face. "I'm just washing you off." She moved from forehead to cheeks. "Boy, are you ever going to have a shiner."

Finding little comfort in this latest bulletin, I said nothing.

Soon afterwards, I was wheeled into X-ray wearing several black stitches and a hospital gown over my bloodstained shirt. Here, along with having my head filmed from every angle, I suffered the curious stares of the staff. Some I knew, but they didn't ask and I didn't say.

"My God!" Rhodes said when I was wheeled back into the white and chrome examining room. "You look terrible."

I glowered. My self-esteem took another nosedive.

Steve, tired-looking but smiling, pushed through the door.

"And what have you got to say?" I challenged.

"You missed our pizza date last night."

"I mean this." I pointed to my face.

"What's to say? I can see everything I need to know."

"You probably read my chart," I accused.

"Never did," Steve denied.

"Spies?"

Steve shrugged. His smile faded, replaced by his doctor look.

Spies, in the form of Police Lieutenant Larry Rhodes no doubt, I decided, but I didn't feel like arguing. "So how about getting me a mirror? I want to see what everyone's talking about."

Wordlessly, Steve retrieved a mirror from a corner cabinet and handed it to me. I guess he didn't feel like arguing, either.

Both Rhodes and Steve remained quiet as I studied my reflection. "If I'd had this face a couple of nights ago, I wouldn't have needed a mask," I quipped, choosing levity over tears.

"You don't look that bad." Dr. Canfield's thin face broadened into a smile as he walked into the treatment room. He pointed to the crease over my right ear. "Grow your hair a little longer, and nobody will know it's there."

"Will I have a black eye?" I wanted to confirm the nurse's prediction.

Dr. Canfield nodded. "But you won't have much of a scar when these come out." His black finger indicated the row of equally black stitches.

I handed Steve the mirror. "Are you going to let me go home?"

Dr. Canfield nodded. "Your X-rays are fine, but you'll need to come back in a couple of days to get those stitches out."

"Can't Steve do it?"

Canfield winked at Steve. "You willing to take over, Doc?"

Steve grinned. "Okay by me."

Canfield added a note to the chart then pulled a sheet of paper from the clipboard. "Read it over. It'll tell you how to take care of your face." His smile was bright, his eyes dark pools of merriment. "And since I've been fired, I'll see if I can't find someone else who needs me."

Rhodes stood and stretched. "I guess that means we can all go home."

"I'd like to talk to Leslie first." I looked at Steve. "She needs to know about last night, and I want to be the one to tell her." Not MacPhearson, I thought, but didn't mention his name.

Yes and no flickered across Steve's face.

"I promise to make it quick."

Yes won, but I knew his heart wasn't in it.

Rhodes, who said he needed to make a telephone call, stayed behind.

"The news might upset her." We were alone in the elevator headed for Leslie's room.

"I'm sure it will," Steve said, his tone of voice noncommittal.

Sensing he was not an ally, I fell silent.

Hightower still guarded Leslie's room, but recognized us both and waved us inside. He stared a little long at me, but to his credit said nothing. Leslie, however, had no such reticence.

"If you need the bed, I'll get out," she offered.

"You should see the other guy," I said.

Leslie didn't laugh. "What happened, Ginny?"

I touched the bump on my forehead and the row of black stitches. "I hit my head on a table leg, and this," I pointed to the furrow over my ear, "is a gunshot wound."

Leslie's eyes widened, and Steve moved closer to the bed.

"Your apartment was broken into last night, and I was there when it happened."

"No!" she gasped.

"Your apartment was broken into," I repeated. "There were two of them. One shot the other, and then shot me before he got away."

Leslie's pale face grew paler. "One was—"

Steve stepped closer to the bed as if preparing to stop the conversation.

"One was killed," I finished for her. I took a deep breath. "He had a scar on his face."

Leslie fingered the bed sheet. "A scar?"

Steve made more doctor noises, but Leslie waved him aside.

"Was it the man who shot Bryan?" she asked.

"The police don't know yet, but they're working on it."

Her fingers smoothed the sheet. I pushed away from the bed. I had done what I had come to do.

"Ginny?" Her eyes caught mine. "Why did they break into the apartment?"

I thought of the overturned furniture, the slashed upholstery, of the total and wanton destruction. "I don't know," I answered truthfully.

"Bryan and I don't have anything worth stealing." Her fingers went back to work, pleated one row along the top of the bed sheet and then below that another. "They must have been after something of your uncle's."

The quick inventory I'd taken earlier suggested otherwise, but—

"It has to be," she argued as if reading my mind. "He knew the apartment was empty."

I opened my mouth, ready to speak, but Leslie rushed on. "Just think about it, Ginny. Your uncle had all those paintings, that sculpture on the mantle and—"

"I don't know what they were looking for, Leslie, or why one killed the other." I took a steadying breath. I sounded like a broken record.

"But you will find out, won't you?"

The question caught me by surprise.

"He killed my husband, shot me, and broke into my apartment, Ginny. I have a right to know."

"I'll find out," I said. I would probably have done so anyway, but her asking legitimized my presence in the case.

Steve put his arm around my shoulder. "Not today," he said.

"Steve's right, Ginny." Now even Leslie sounded like a doctor. "Everything can wait until tomorrow. Today you need to go home and get into bed."

Though outnumbered, I held my ground. I had one more thing to do, the thing being MacPhearson's request to see Bryan's office.

We discussed the matter, after which Leslie gave her permission.

"I'll take care of it," I said. I didn't say when.

Chapter Thirteen

STEVE HEADED FOR THE STAIRS. I HAD HOPED FOR HIS OFFICE, BUT THE DETERMINED SET OF his jaw suggested I not ask. It started out not too bad, however, for Steve stopped at the first landing for a quick hug and a somewhat longer kiss.

"I've been wanting you to do that all night." I moved closer and deepened the kiss.

Steve was the first to break free. He touched my face, his gentle surgeon's fingers moving over the bump on my forehead and the stitches above my eye. "Do you know how badly you could have been hurt?"

I snuggled against him, anticipating another round of hugs and kisses. "I know, but I wasn't."

Steve stiffened, but being unwilling to relinquish the moment of intimacy, I silenced further protest with another kiss.

"Ginny!" Steve's voice was harsh, his hands rough. He pushed me from him.

My heart quickened. I was hot then cold. "How about dinner tonight? I promise I'll be there." I heard the wheedling note in the plea, but I couldn't face Steve's anger—especially tonight.

"Dinner, be damned. I want to know what's going on."

My humor had fallen on deaf ears, but now and in this place, even if the stairwell was still empty, was not the time to discuss murder or murderers.

"Tonight, Steve." It was not a request. Softening their potential impact, I held tightly to his hand as I pulled him down the last flight of stairs. I had seldom been on the receiving end of Steve's anger, and no matter how justified, and I knew it was, it was a position I didn't particularly relish.

Rhodes was waiting, pacing the hall outside the Emergency Department.

"They gave me your purse." He held up my shoulder bag. With a "See you around, Doc,"—Rhodes either didn't see or more likely chose to ignore Steve's belligerent mood—the police lieutenant pushed open the exit door.

"Chinese at six," I called to Steve backing after the policeman.

I waved. Steve waved back, but he wasn't smiling. Why was it the men in my life were always so . . . male?

Rhodes gunned his unmarked police car away from the hospital lot. "MacPhearson's waiting for us at headquarters," he said. "He's set up the videotape you shot at the Halloween party. Wants you to have a look at it."

Ahead of us a traffic light changed to red. Rhodes slowed. "I think your dead man is on that tape."

I opened my mouth, but Rhodes shook his head. "Don't ask any questions now. Wait until you've seen the film."

Calls of "How's it going, Lieu?" met us as Rhodes led the way through an almost empty squad room to a much smaller anteroom.

"I see they got you patched up." MacPhearson unfolded his lanky frame from a chair that looked too small for him.

I ignored the remark and took a seat in front of a big screen TV. Behind me, I heard MacPhearson laugh, and though it rankled, I ignored this, too.

A switch clicked, and Steve, wearing green scrubs, stood in front of me, complaining once again of having his picture taken. Tables loaded with food took his place, and after that, a small, dark-skinned angel waved hello. Fascinated, I pushed aside the events of the past few hours and watched Thursday night's Halloween party come to life.

"You can almost feel the heat," I said when the leaping flames and crackling sounds of the bonfire roared into life.

"Watch!" Rhodes commanded.

I leaned forward and immediately saw what it was Rhodes wanted me to see.

"That's him!" I pointed to the screen. "That's him. Back it up."

Big and little ghosts, bums, and angels flew backwards, and the fire died as the action reversed. At my direction, MacPhearson rolled the tape forward.

"That's him."

MacPhearson slowed the tape, stopping it as a figure detached itself from the crowd and limped into the foreground.

"Are you sure?" Rhodes asked.

I stared at the image frozen on the monitor. A red kerchief covered his head, and a black patch hid the eye the bullet had removed. But there was no mistaking the scar that lifted the corner of his mouth or the casted leg that showed beneath his ragged jeans. Thursday's pirate was definitely Friday's dead man.

"I'm sure," I said. "Do you know who he is?" I looked from MacPhearson to Rhodes.

"He uses several names," MacPhearson said, "but lately he's been calling himself Tim Williams."

The detective rested his arm on the table that separated the two of us. "He's from Detroit originally, and he's accumulated quite a rap sheet over the years. Seems to fancy pushing drugs, extortion, and blackmail. He's only had one conviction, but it caused him hard time in Jackson."

"Is he the killer?" My attention focused on MacPhearson who was the obvious source of information for this party.

"He fits the description Leslie Parker gave me of the man who shot her at the motel, but we're going to need more than that."

MacPhearson restarted the tape. Several other costumed figures, clowns, bums, scarecrows, and witches moved forward and hid the pirate.

"Is that the only shot of Williams?" What I'd seen had whetted my appetite.

"Watch." Elbows on knees, Rhodes leaned forward.

Once again fire leaped from the screen, and once again, I saw the one-eyed pirate. A laughing clown with a red-painted nose and a mostly black beanie sidled up behind him.

"Watch their hands," MacPhearson said.

With a barely perceptible motion of hand and wrist, the pair exchanged folded bills and a small plastic sack of what appeared to be grayish-white stones.

"Crack?" I asked.

"Looks like it." MacPhearson reversed the film, giving us another look. "And it looks a lot like what we confiscated at the party that night. I'm having these frames blown-up. That should tell us more."

A group of dancers swayed under the colored lights to Randy Travis's "Forever and Ever Amen." The music gave way to the shouts and squeals of happy children. A witch's hat hid half of Carol's distraught face. With a roll of paper towels, she pointed to where a dripping spaceman bobbed for apples.

The scene changed. Emergency personnel worked over small figures. My stomach gave a decided lurch.

"I didn't shoot that."

"Blakely did," MacPhearson said.

Scooter's little boy face filled the screen. His astronaut's bravado was gone. In its place a forlorn figure with tear-streaked cheeks sat quietly sucking his thumb.

A field of felled partygoers took Scooter's place. Although their costumes differed, all wore expressions of abject misery. I swallowed hard, but still tasted the bile.

The moon, a sliver in the night sky, cast an eerie glow over the parking lot. Two figures moved to center front—one a pirate, the other a ghost.

"Who's that with Williams?" I asked. The pirate's awkward gait made him easy to recognize.

"We're working on that," MacPhearson said. He switched off the VCR.

I turned and faced the two policemen. "Was there anything on the film to show who laced the food with ipecac?"

"Afraid not." Rhodes sighed himself from his chair. "It was a long shot. We knew that going in. This time, it didn't pay off."

"We got a hell of a lot more than we expected," MacPhearson said quietly.

"Does that mean those sons-of-bitches will go free?" I was angry, and I wanted both of them to know it.

"Not necessarily. We've got a citywide call out for anyone with pictures of the party, and Channel Eight has offered to share the footage they shot for the eleven o'clock news. Who knows, we might get lucky yet." MacPhearson shoved back from the table.

"What about Leslie Parker?" I asked. "Have you shown her the tape?"

"Not yet, but I plan on showing it to her later today, and before you ask, stills of Williams and that red-nosed clown are being circulated." A smile tugged the corners of his mouth. "Just keep your shirt on, Red. We should know something soon."

Rhodes yawned. "Until then, I'm going home." He moved toward the door.
"Ready, Ginny?"

"Why don't we set a time now?" MacPhearson interrupted.

"You said my statement could wait until tomorrow," I said.

"And so it can, but I'm not talking about that." MacPhearson hitched a thigh
over the corner of the table.

"Then what are you talking about?" I asked, feigning ignorance.

"Playing hardball, are you?"

I felt the usual flush of anger. "Look, if you're that anxious to get into Parker's
office, get a search warrant." My conscience prickled, but I ignored it.

MacPhearson pulled an envelope from his pocket and laid it on the table
between us. "What time do you want me to pick you up, Miss Arthur, or do you
prefer I go alone?"

I looked at the envelope, and then the policeman. Anger threatened to es-
calate, but prudence intervened. "I'll meet you in the lobby at seven."

Rhodes's unmarked police car became another war zone. It was definitely
not my day, but after much arguing between the two of us and threats from me
to cab it downtown, he agreed to drop me at the office. He wasn't a gracious
loser, but neither was I.

It was a short drive from the Arthur & Arthur offices to my Valley Avenue
bungalow where a raucous chorus of meows greeted my homecoming. Zeus
displayed his usual poise and complained at a distance, while Hera voiced her
woes as she rubbed her sleek body against my pant leg. Knowing there would
be no peace until they were fed, I led the way into the kitchen. A can of tuna
and fresh water quieted the loud-mouthed pair. I chose milk and carried a glass
with me into the bedroom.

The mirror over the dresser caught my reflection. I stopped to look. The
swelling over my eye had lessened, and a blue bruise covered my upper lid. Dr.
Canfield's prediction had come true. I had a shiner, and it was a beauty.

Determined to ignore what I could do nothing about, I finished the milk
and swung tired legs over the tub's rim. A hot shower and some Tylenol eased
my pain. A couple of hours sleep did even more, and when I climbed back into
the Ranger, I was feeling considerably better.

Lighted streetlights held back the five o'clock gloom, but like the cats, the
dark was poised, ready to pounce. Overhead, thick clouds threatened snow, and
wind gusts buffeted the Ford. I shivered, turned the heater to high, and waited
for warmed air to fill the cab.

My first stop was the Peking Palace on Bridge Street where I loaded up with
carryout Chinese. Along with covered parking, the ramp across from the hospital
was also attached to the Professional Office Building. This being my ultimate
destination, I bypassed the open-air emergency lot and swung into an empty
spot on the ramp's ground floor. The snow, which earlier had only threatened,
began to fall as I headed up the walk to the hospital's front entrance.

The operator eyed me speculatively as I made my usual stop by the switchboard. A busy board diverted her attention. A question that needed answering claimed mine. While I waited for Steve to answer his beeper—tonight I'd gone the do-it-yourself route instead of having the operator voice page him—I picked up one of the house phones and punched in Leslie's room number.

"Just one question," I said when she answered. "What time did that man call you on Wednesday night?"

"Nine-fifteen, nine-thirty, I don't remember exactly. I had already started rounds and had seen at least two or three patients." Leslie sounded concerned. "Is it important you know the exact time?"

"Probably not, but I'm here at the switchboard and thought I'd ask the operator if she remembered taking the call."

Leslie sighed, her breath loud in my ears.

"Stop worrying," I reassured the dark-haired surgeon and hung up.

Tonight's henna-haired, frail-looking operator was not the operator I'd talked to before. Our curiosity was mutual, however, and hers was the first to find voice.

"What happened to you?" she asked. The switchboard had quieted, and I had her full attention.

"I fell and hit my head on a table," I answered.

The partial truth elicited a string of soothing sounds and a gentle head wagging.

"Were you on duty Wednesday night?" I asked, hoping her sympathy would extend to answering a few questions.

"I was." Her hair, though no match for my own red hair, glowed brightly in the switchboard's lights.

"Dr. Parker, Leslie Parker, one of the surgical residents, had an outside call sometime after nine that night. Do you remember taking it?"

"I know who Dr. Parker is." She sounded offended.

A light on the switchboard blinked and cut short my apology.

"It's Dr. Brock." She nodded to a nearby house phone.

Mindful of her listening ears, I kept the conversation short, and settled on dinner in his office in fifteen minutes.

"You asked about a telephone call on Wednesday night?" she asked when I finished.

I nodded. "Dr. Parker received a call about nine-fifteen or nine-thirty—" I stopped.

The operator was wagging her head. "There weren't any calls after nine on Wednesday night."

"Are you sure?"

"Of course I'm sure." She crossed thin arms over a meager bosom. "I wouldn't say so if I wasn't."

I said nothing. This was one woman I didn't want to antagonize.

"We had a disaster on Halloween," she continued, "and just before that call came in, I was thinking we might go two nights without any calls after nine."

"What's so special about nine?"

"That's when we turn the patients' phones off," she said with a self-satisfied smile. "Only direct calls to the nurses' stations go through. Everything else stops here." Her smile broadened. "That's a hospital rule."

Another of the old-timers' rules, I wondered? I didn't ask. "What about paging or beeping?" I asked instead.

"No paging, just beeping, but I didn't beep anyone, either. Wednesday was a very quiet night."

The switchboard lighted up, and the operator bent her henna head to answer. Convinced that the conversation had run its course, I picked up my bag of Chinese and started down the hall. If the operator hadn't taken the call, then Leslie's caller must have known where to find her.

I hit the elevator button. Or my redheaded friend had been on a break and someone else had been on the switchboard.

I turned back, wanting to check out this last thought, but a whiff of egg roll changed my mind.

Chapter Fourteen

WE BEGAN WITH A REPEATED CHORUS OF I'M SORRY, ADDED VOWS OF IT WOULDN'T HAPPEN again, promised to tell each other everything and progressed to a kiss which, given the privacy of Steve's office, a thing denied us in the stairwell, was a kiss I meant to enjoy.

With a sigh, reminiscent of Hera's response to Zeus's ardor, I moved my lips over his, tasted him. Passion flared hot between us. I pressed closer, felt him harden against me.

Steve was the first to pull away. "I smell egg roll," he said hoarsely.

"Complete with duck sauce." I handed him a paper sack and struggled to control my breathing as I pulled down my shirt and . . . .

Egg roll in hand, Steve bit off the corner of a packet of sauce. Having only a scrub suit to contend with, his clothing adjustment, rather readjustment, was more rapid than mine.

Searching further for order in a sea of emotional chaos, I mounded cashew chicken and beef with pea pods on paper plates and, in as casual a tone as I could muster, asked, "What time do you make late rounds?"

"After nine." Steve wiped duck sauce from the corner of his mouth with his index finger.

"And what's so special about nine?" I asked for the second time that evening.

I handed Steve a plate and added mustard sauce to my egg roll. We ate picnic style, using Steve's desk, where not too many minutes ago we had made love, for our table.

"That's when visiting hours end." Steve's lips moved over the edge of his cup, his tongue reaching to taste the hot tea.

My tongue, hesitant, nervous, circled my lips before asking, "Isn't that rather late to be bothering patients?"

"I only check the critical ones and that day's surgeries. They're usually anxious to see me." He sipped the tea. "Why so many questions?"

I moved my eyes away from the temptation of his lips. "Just wondering what you did around here at night," I teased.

He laughed.

"I'm serious. What if I want to reach you at night?"

"You can always call me."

"Only if I know where you are."

"Right, but if you didn't, you could always beep me. You have the number."

"Or leave a message at the switchboard."

Steve quirked an eyebrow. "To whom have you been talking?"

"Tonight, a redhaired, rather thin switchboard operator."

Steve grunted. "Should have known. That one's a stickler for rules."

Our eyes met.

"Ginny?" It was a question. "Ready to tell me what's going on?"

"There's not much to tell." I bothered a damp spot on his desk with a napkin.

"You get yourself shot, wind up in the Emergency Room looking like you look, and tell me there's not much to tell?" Steve shoved his empty plate into a paper sack. "I can be had once in a while, Ginny, but I'm not a sure thing." He rammed the sack into the wastebasket.

Intimacy fled. I cringed as if from a blow. "I didn't want you to worry." It was a lame excuse, and I knew it.

"Well I'm worrying, so tell me."

I speared a lonely pea pod. "You already know most of what's happened."

"Most isn't good enough." Steve folded his arms over his chest.

"I went up to the apartment last night to drop off the Parkers' mail." I rushed my words. A gentle giant at rest, Steve could be a bear when angered. "A couple of men broke in while I was there. One killed the other, then shot me." Though broke in wasn't exactly right, it seemed the perfect time for a white lie.

"Go on," Steve said.

"When I left here this morning, Rhodes took me to police headquarters. He wanted me to view the video I shot at the Halloween party. It seems I caught the dead man along with his scarred face and casted leg on film. He's an ex-con from Detroit who's currently using the name of Tim Williams. He's been in trouble with the law most of his life."

I fortified myself with a swallow of tea.

"The video showed Williams selling what looks like crack cocaine." I went on, telling Steve what Leslie had told me about seeing the scar-faced man in the motel room, and what Dr. Beller had told me about Bryan's drug habit.

Steve shifted in his chair. "Has Leslie seen the tape?"

"Probably, MacPhearson said he was going to show it to her today."

"I'd say that was part of his job . . ." Steve stared at me, his eyes narrowing.

I dug in mental heels. Was it my imagination, or had the conversation taken a wrong turn?

". . . So why are you making it yours?"

It wasn't my imagination. Steve wanted answers, and I knew they'd better be good. "Like Leslie, I have a vested interest in the case," I began. "I own the apartment, and whoever broke in and killed Tim Williams probably thought he'd killed me, too."

I raised my cup to my mouth, found it empty and tossed it away. "And before you ask, I didn't tell Leslie what Dr. Beller told me."

Steve's expression hardened. "About Bryan using drugs?"

I nodded. "And I think that's the reason for the break-in."

"Is there a connection between Williams and Parker?"

"That's my guess."

"And the police?"

"They're not saying."

Steve tilted back in his chair. "Do they think Williams killed Parker and shot Leslie?"

"They aren't talking about that, either." I shoved my plate into a sack and added it to the growing pile in the wastebasket. "And that's all I know." I grinned. "Scout's honor."

"If memory serves me right, you were never a scout, Ginny."

"I was a Camp Fire Girl."

"Doesn't count." Steve's expression softened. "You look tired."

"I am," I admitted. And sometimes I'm dizzy and nauseated, and sometimes I have a headache. Only I didn't tell him this, either, just added it to my lexicon of white lies.

The telephone rang. Steve answered, listened and hung up. "I have to go," he said. Reluctant as lovers are to part, one more reluctant than the other because of her guilty conscience, we left the egg-roll-and-tea-scented office.

The temperature had dropped by several degrees, and three or more inches of snow covered the ground. Gusty winds frolicked under the streetlights and threw great handfuls of snow into my face. I sensed the promise of much more to come.

Shoulders hunched, I crossed the street to the office building. Was Williams Bryan's supplier? Why had he broken into the apartment? Were drugs the common denominator? Had Williams killed Bryan Parker and Nancy Webber? Had he shot Leslie? My mind wrestled with murder and murderers, drugs and pushers as my tensely muscled body battled the wind.

A pair of glass doors loomed before me. I pulled one open and stepped inside. The ill-tempered wind slammed it shut behind me, its closing sounding like a thunderclap.

"Red," MacPhearson called. He stood in front of the building's directory.

"Parker's office is on the tenth floor," I said, remembering this bit of information from previous conversations I'd had with Bryan and Leslie. I stamped the snow from my feet and walked toward the elevators. "I trust you brought the warrant with you?"

MacPhearson patted his pocket. "Right here," he said. "Do you want it?"

I waved the offer away and punched the button that called one of the pair of elevators that, along with a stairwell, occupied the building's core.

The elevator arrived, and we rode the brightly lighted car to the tenth floor. The doors slid open, spilling light into a hall whose only other illumination was a few randomly scattered baseboard nightlights and a fire door topped with a red exit sign.

Humming a nameless tune, MacPhearson stepped from the elevator. I followed close behind, bumping hard against him when he came to a sudden stop at an intersecting hallway. His out-flung arm steadied me, and a raised finger cautioned silence.

"Look," he whispered. His finger, now a pointer, showed me where to look.

Two lines of black stenciled letters on a frosted background read UPCHURCH CHEMICALS Bryan Parker Regional Director. A glimmer of light showed beneath the door. Intermittently bright and then not so bright, it told of a third person.

Internal warning signs, honed to a razor's edge by last night's encounter with murderers and vandals, pulled me back from the corner.

"What are we going to do?" I asked.

"I'm going to wait and see who comes out of there," he said, "and you're going to take both elevators to the ground floor and get the hell out of here."

I didn't like his idea, but didn't think it was the time to argue. What was there about me that made everybody think they had to take care of me?

I pondered the question as I sent the empty pair of elevators to the first floor, waved them good-bye as the numbers marked their descent, and rejoined my would-be caretaker.

"What the hell?" MacPhearson asked.

He was about to say more when the door to Parker's office opened. A man, his features hidden in the dim light, moved shadowlike into the hall.

The door to Parker's office clicked shut, and the unknown man moved down the hall. Gun in hand, MacPhearson backed us around the corner. As we waited, the elevator started to rise.

MacPhearson hurried us toward the red exit sign. The door opened outward, and he pushed me through.

"Think we can beat it down?" he asked, his voice muffled by the noise of the ascending elevator.

I took a death's grip on the handrail and started down, hitting about every third step. Ahead of me, MacPhearson did the same. Behind us, the elevator reversed direction. A snarling tiger, it followed close on our heels.

MacPhearson stopped on the first floor landing. "Hold up," he said.

His rapid breathing made the words difficult to understand, but his restraining hand said what needed to be said.

I welcomed the wall that offered support and watched him ease the door open.

"What do you see?" The pain in my chest had reduced itself from knifepoints to pinpricks.

He said nothing, the silence broken only by the snarling elevator.

The realization hit, and I raced down the last flight of stairs. MacPhearson shouldered ahead. The elevator clanged to a stop on the ground floor, and a whooshing sound told us the door had opened.

MacPhearson cracked the door to the parking garage, and laid his eye to the slit that formed.

"Let me see."

He waved me back, but I wiggled forward and fixed my eye below his chin.

The shadowy figure, revealed by the lighted interior as a tall, broad-shouldered blond, stepped out of the elevator. With purposeful steps, the man headed for a row of parked cars. MacPhearson stiffened.

"Do you know him?" I hissed, following the blond man's progress.

"Shh!"

Obediently silent, I watched the man insert a key into the door of a dark-colored Grand Prix.

"Is that your truck?" MacPhearson pointed to the Ranger parked across from the exit door.

I nodded, but kept my eyes on the man and his car. As I watched, the Pontiac's engine roared to life, and its backup lights flashed white. MacPhearson pulled the fire exit door wide and started running. "Keys!" he called, not looking back.

I followed, rummaging through my bouncing shoulder bag as I ran.

"You're staying here." MacPhearson stopped beside the driver's door and held out his hand.

"It's my truck." I bumped him aside and unlocked the door. Faster than him, I scrambled in and slid across to the passenger's seat.

The Grand Prix's headlights arced across the parking garage's concrete interior, straightened and lurched toward the exit. MacPhearson twisted the key in the ignition. We hit the street in time to see the Pontiac make a right turn off Wealthy.

"Who is he?" I demanded.

We skidded around the corner.

"His name's Sammy Maxwell."

"And?" I sensed there was more to tell.

"He works for Victor Sands."

"The Crime Boss?" It was the name the papers had given the local restaurateur, who had recently been indicted for a variety of high-dollar white-collar crimes.

"That's the one."

The snow continued to fall. It made an already white world whiter and tried to swallow the Grand Prix. MacPhearson, however, was a persistent pursuer.

"But what was Sammy Maxwell doing in Bryan Parker's office?"

The man beside me laughed. "You'll be able to ask him yourself, Red, because we're going where he goes."

Having stated his intentions, MacPhearson followed the Grand Prix onto the cross-town freeway. The windblown snow lay carpet-like over the entrance ramp, causing the Ranger to skid sideways. I grabbed the dash. MacPhearson eased the brake and turned into the slide.

He grinned, the corners of his mouth disappearing under the curve of his mustache. "Don't worry, I'm not about to lose either him or your truck."

Believing him, I let out the breath I didn't realize I was holding.

MacPhearson maintained an even distance between truck and car, while in front of me the wipers worked in tandem to keep the windshield clear. Through the twin fans of cleaned glass, I watched the swirling snow pass through the Grand Prix's taillights.

"Why didn't you arrest him back there in the parking garage?" I stopped watching the snow and watched MacPhearson.

"I figured he'd be easier to talk to out of jail." MacPhearson switched to the middle lane behind the Pontiac.

"You practically had him red-handed," I protested.

" 'Practically' is the operative word. We wouldn't stand a snowball's chance in hell of tying him to a break-in."

"So why are we following him?"

"I like to keep the competition on their toes." MacPhearson grinned another of his wide grins.

"Competition?" Had I heard correctly? Had MacPhearson actually referred to the man who had broken into Bryan Parker's office as competition?

My head hurt. Fearing a return of the jackhammer chorus, I leaned back against the headrest and tried not to think. It was an exercise in futility.

"Tim Williams was mixed up with drugs," I said finally, giving words to my unwanted thoughts.

"And so are Maxwell and Sands," MacPhearson answered.

The Pontiac moved into the left-hand lane. MacPhearson followed, then braked and flipped on the Ranger's turn signal. "I should have known Sammy-boy was headed home," he said.

Chapter Fifteen

Home for Sammy Maxwell was the Sandcastle, a restaurant and lounge considered by those who wanted to be "seen" as the best nightspot in town in which to be "seen." Close behind, but not too close behind, MacPhearson followed the Grand Prix into the parking lot.

Despite the inclement weather the lot was crowded. A silent reminder that it was Saturday night.

MacPhearson stopped behind a row of parked cars. Ahead, the Pontiac slid into a reserved spot near the front door. The driver's door swung open, and the tall blond from the parking garage hurried into the brightly lit restaurant.

A place near the back of the lot was open. MacPhearson pulled in and cut the engine. Among the foreign and domestic vehicles that were its neighbors, the Ford truck looked sadly out of place. As out of place as my jeans and down jacket would look inside the posh nightclub. I suppressed a sigh. I knew without asking that my companion intended to do what he had said he would do. In a matter of minutes, I would be face to face with the notorious Sammy Maxwell. Fingering an imaginary crease in my blue denims, I stared at the Sandcastle's canopied entrance.

"Ready?" MacPhearson asked.

"Where you go, I go." The bravado was false, but since I had no hole to crawl into—

Determined to maintain the pretense, I fished in my shoulder bag for whatever help I could find. The only restoratives that came to hand were a comb and lipstick. The lipstick was easy, but my hair refused to cover either the stitches or the bullet path along the side of my head.

"Let me." MacPhearson took the comb from my unwieldy fingers and teased curls over my ears and forehead. I waited for the familiar rush of anger. Surprisingly, it did not come.

"I used to do this for my kid sister," he explained. "She had her arm in a cast one summer."

In that upper peninsula home Rhodes had told me about, I wondered? I pulled down the sun visor with its hidden mirror. Hiding a mix of emotion I could not explain, I frowned at the face that stared back.

"I'll ask for a dark booth," MacPhearson said sympathetically. The camaraderie lasted until we reached the front entrance.

"This could get sticky, Red," he said.

"Does that mean you've changed your mind about going inside?"

Like Rhodes, whose blue eyes turned black under stress, MacPhearson's cornflower eyes were as dark as sapphires. I had my answer.

A blast of hot air, amplified rock, and a black-gowned hostess met us at the door. "Do you have a reservation?" she purred, sounding more catlike than either Zeus or Hera. Cats again. Hell! The blow to my head had scrambled my brains.

The hiss of consonants became a thing of the past as she gave us a slit-eyed appraisal. MacPhearson with his suit and tie rated a half smile. Me? I didn't rate as much as an arched eyebrow.

"No reservation." MacPhearson favored the hostess with a grin that extended his luxuriant mustache to its fullest. "But we're not here for dinner."

"In that case . . ."

She led, and like sheep we followed to a place where the music was louder and the lights dimmer.

"Will you tell Sammy Maxwell that Doug MacPhearson is here and would like to see him?"

The detective palmed a bill which disappeared somewhere inside the hostess's skin-tight gown. With the slightest of nods, she slinked away. In her place a smiling, fresh-faced waiter waited to take our order.

MacPhearson reached into an inside pocket and pulled out a pack of Winstons. "Do you mind?"

I did, but didn't say so.

He lit up. "My only vice," he said, blowing the smoke into the room.

The arrival of our drinks, his a Chivas on the rocks and mine the house white in a stemmed wine glass, robbed me of the opportunity to argue the point.

"To you." He lifted his drink and gave me the same smile he'd just given the hostess.

I lifted my glass, but didn't return the smile.

MacPhearson ignored the rebuff and took a long swallow. He set his drink down, centering the glass carefully in the middle of the cocktail napkin. "If I'm not mistaken, we're about to get some company."

I sank into the depths of our semi-circular booth and watched a tall, dinner-jacketed man make his way across the room. He stopped beside our table and nodded a greeting.

"It's good to have you here, MacPhearson. Public servants, especially homicide detectives, are always welcome at the Sandcastle."

MacPhearson hefted his drink in acknowledgement. Sammy Maxwell produced a lips-only smile and sank into the leather cushion beside me.

"I don't think I've had the pleasure of meeting you." The smile touched his green eyes. "How about introducing us, Detective?"

"She's a friend of mine," MacPhearson said. "Who she is isn't important."

Not important! What was MacPhearson up to?

"At least not important to you," MacPhearson amended.

The explanation dropped my blood pressure back to normal, and I relaxed.

"Does that mean she's important to you?" Maxwell smiled, this time showing his dimples and perfect white teeth.

"She's important to me." MacPhearson took a long pull on his Winston and an even longer pull of scotch.

My blood pressure started up again. I sipped on my wine. What in hell was wrong with me? I took another sip of wine. It was, I realized, a surprisingly good Chardonnay. Beside me Maxwell continued his scrutiny, staring at me for what seemed like a very long time.

"I'd be interested in knowing how he treats less important people, Miss . . ."

My name wasn't offered, and Maxwell ran a forefinger over my stitches. "Was this a present from MacPhearson?"

I shook my head and pulled back but, squeezed between the two, found little room to pull.

"That's enough, Maxwell." MacPhearson sounded angry.

Maxwell hesitated, then laid his hands on the table. The light caught his onyx pinky ring and glittered off the diamonds that formed his initial. He chuckled. "Whatever you say, Detective."

MacPhearson rattled the ice in his glass. Almost immediately the fresh-faced waiter appeared with another. MacPhearson shook his head, and the full glass disappeared.

"You don't like our scotch?" Maxwell asked.

"Designated driver." MacPhearson lifted his glass and sucked an ice cube into his mouth.

"Since it isn't drinking, what brings you here?" Maxwell laid his arm across the booth's back and crowded closer.

"A few questions that need answers." MacPhearson shifted sideways away from me. It provided some empty space, which I was quick to fill.

"Official questions?" Maxwell asked.

MacPhearson shook loose another Winston. "Unofficial, of course." He lit the cigarette. "Like, what were you doing in Bryan Parker's office tonight?" He exhaled the question in a cloud of smoke. The words, like the smoke, hung between us.

Maxwell's smile faded, his face turned ugly. My mouth went dry, and I took a large swallow of Chardonnay.

"Don't bother denying it, Maxwell, I saw you there."

MacPhearson's words stopped my thoughts. His next made me wonder if he'd lost his mind.

"And what were you doing in Parker's apartment last night?"

I gulped the last of my wine.

"You saw me there, too?" Maxwell asked.

"Not me," MacPhearson said.

Maxwell gave me a curious stare, one I tried to avoid, and then slid from the booth. "Well, Detective MacPhearson, this has been a most interesting conversation."

"Oh, but I'm not through yet."

I held my breath. What more could MacPhearson say?

"What was your relationship with Tim Williams? Drugs?"

Maxwell's jaw tightened. The atmosphere chilled, plunging the temperature inside the Sandcastle to zero. MacPhearson reached across the table and snubbed out his cigarette. I wished I'd stayed in the Ranger. Five minutes later I was there, back again with MacPhearson in the green truck.

"Are you crazy?" I tried for calm, but got what sounded more like a screech.

"No," MacPhearson started the engine. "Just testing the water."

"It's hot," I muttered, tugging my seat belt tight.

"I had my reasons." He foraged under the seat and brought out a skinned knuckle.

"And just what did you hope to accomplish by accusing Sammy Maxwell of being a drug dealer and a second story man?"

MacPhearson sucked his bloody finger. "I told you it might get sticky."

I threw the window scraper at him. "Is this what you're looking for?"

He opened the door and climbed out. I shrank back from the cold. Asking Maxwell about the office, and even about Williams, was understandable, but the apartment?

I turned the heater on high. The air blew warm, but I stayed cold.

The truck door opened, letting in more cold and a shivering policeman. "There's over a foot of snow out there, and it's still coming down." He blew into his cupped hands.

I brushed his complaints aside. "Why did you ask Maxwell about the apartment?"

"Have a heart, Red. Can't you see I'm freezing to death?"

"You won't."

"Okay . . . okay, I asked because I think he's your mystery man, the shooter in the ski mask."

"Whatever gave you that idea?"

"He was in Parker's office, so why not his apartment?" MacPhearson's fingers touched mine. "Does that worry you?"

"Why should it?" I challenged.

"I saw the way he looked at you." He gave my hand a squeeze. "Trust me, Ginny. I won't let anything happen to you."

"That's certainly nice to know." I pulled my hand away. "The next time a might-be killer gets friendly, I'll give you a call."

"Do that," he said.

"Besides thinking Maxwell's the masked man, what other thoughts are running around inside your head?"

MacPhearson grinned. "Got your interest, have I?" He laughed, then quickly sobered. "Okay, here's the way I see it. We know Sands is the kingpin, that he controls just about everything that's illegal in Marion City. We also know, thanks to you, that Williams is a pusher. Now, people like Sands don't usually deal directly with losers like Williams."

"Which means he'd need an intermediary, someone like Maxwell," I interrupted, following where MacPhearson was leading.

"Or even someone lower down his chain of command."

I gnawed the inside of my cheek. "But what does that have to do with Maxwell being in Bryan's office?"

MacPhearson turned on the windshield wipers, sweeping away the new snow. "My guess is that he was looking for something. Drugs? Maybe a cash payoff? What's yours?"

I said nothing.

"Finish the thought, Ginny."

"They were looking for something, drugs, cash, whatever." I started slowly. "When they didn't find it in the apartment, Maxwell killed Williams, then went looking for it in Parker's office."

"I think they were looking for it in the motel room, too."

"Williams was looking for it," I corrected, "not Maxwell."

MacPhearson revved the idling engine. "I'd stake my life Maxwell was in on it. Neither Maxwell nor Sands would have trusted a flunky like Williams to do that kind of job."

"But if they did trust him and Williams botched the deal, wouldn't that give Maxwell a reason for killing Williams?"

"It could."

MacPhearson shifted into reverse and eased the Ford truck backwards.

A sudden roar shook the air, and bright lights filled the Ranger's cab.

"What the hell!" MacPhearson shifted gears and hit the accelerator.

The Ranger jumped forward, veered right then left. I hit the door, then the shoulder of the man beside me.

"What happened?"

My question went unanswered as the Ranger slowed, and MacPhearson gave the wheel another turn. His foot jammed the accelerator pedal to the floor. The truck bumped and lurched.

The roar sounded louder and louder, and the lights grew brighter and brighter.

"What's that fool trying to do?" I grabbed the dash.

"Kill us," MacPhearson answered flatly. He looked grim. "But it's not going to happen."

I looked at MacPhearson, then through the windshield to where he was looking. From out of the dark, a twin-beamed monster, a five-ton truck with an attached snowplow roared toward us.

"My God—" Words failed me, but my mind raced. MacPhearson was right. Whoever was out there meant to kill us.

I filled the air with a string of oaths, prayers really, as MacPhearson turned the Ranger into the path of the oncoming beast. Frozen into immobility, I could only stare at the approaching lights. Closer, closer . . . My eyes grew wide and a scream lost itself inside my head.

The monster's lights found their way through the windshield and grabbed us with long yellow fingers. The Ranger rushed on, defying the growling beast with its gentle hum. I waited for the grind of metal against metal, for the crunch of bone ripping through flesh. Nothing.

Nothing? I looked through the Ranger's rear window. The monster's brake lights showed red against the white snow. Fear loosened its hold on my tongue.

"It missed us!"

"Hell, Red! I missed it." His fist beat against the steering wheel, and he laughed.

MacPhearson headed across the parking lot, but the yellow-eyed monster pursued us, found us and stabbed us with beams of lights.

"It's in back of us," I cried.

MacPhearson's face had a determined look. "Well, then, I'll have to show him another trick."

He turned down an empty row and dodged between a BMW and a Saab. Gears ground behind us, but the twice-our-size beast was too big to follow. MacPhearson moved through the lot, sliding on the wet snow and fighting the drifts as he zigzagged from empty parking place to empty parking place.

"Make it! Make it!" I cheered, seeing the exit ahead.

MacPhearson shot the Ranger through the last opening and headed into the stretch. Only what should have been far behind was there waiting. It glared past the curtain of snow and gave a full-throttled roar. The roar grew louder, and rushed forward to meet us.

"Hold on," MacPhearson commanded.

I grabbed the dash and braced my feet against the floorboard. The Ranger shuddered, almost stopped, and then slid backwards into the hole it had just left. More grinds and shudders angled us forward. MacPhearson circled the row of cars and slid past the monster. We were on the run.

"Hurry, hurry," I pounded my fist against my knee.

Like a tornado, the truck swooped down on us. We bounced, hit and skidded. The beast growled and hit again.

The Ranger's rear end slid. We were turning, turning . . .

The monster lay ahead, behind it the Sandcastle. The mighty truck slowed, turned, and with a thunderous roar moved forward.

MacPhearson hit the accelerator. The four-wheel drive bit and pushed us forward. In the windshield, the restaurant grew larger and larger . . .

Chapter Sixteen

THE SANDCASTLE LOOMED LARGE IN THE WINDSHIELD, GROWING LARGER AS WE RUSHED TOWARD it. MacPhearson grunted. The beast roared. The Ranger shuddered, then skidded sideways. The popular nightspot became a collage of blurred lights, of bricks and staring windows. Wide-eyed, I braced for the crash.

I felt a jolt of deceleration, followed by the pull of rapid acceleration, saw an open space and a sign that read EXIT. MacPhearson floored the gas pedal and shot through.

He fought the wheel. The Ranger slid across the access road, and then straightened. We were on the highway.

"Are you okay?" MacPhearson asked.

"I—" I tried to speak, but the words would not come.

MacPhearson gave me a quick look. "You don't look too good," he said.

"D-d-damn you, MacPhearson, how do you expect me to look?"

I wrapped my arms around myself. Despite the heat from the heater, I couldn't stop shaking.

"Ginny—" He reached out his hand and touched my arm, offering comfort I did not want, would not accept.

I slapped his hand away. "Ginny, nothing! Your damn questions almost got us killed." The last two days had been too much—too much.

"It's part of the job," he said softly.

"Yours, not mine," I said. I waited for a response, but there was none.

We rounded a bend in the road and hit the edge of a large drift. The Ranger shuddered. The soft snow was not soft.

MacPhearson backed off, but more drifts blocked the way. He downshifted into low. His energy channeled into driving, he fell silent. Weary, I welcomed the silence.

The Ranger ate the miles slowly, and it seemed hours before we switched lanes and entered the interstate's ON ramp. Several cars, some spinning their wheels, others marooned at the bottom of the ramp, had tried but failed to negotiate the incline. The little truck made a valiant attempt, but it, too, seemed doomed to failure. MacPhearson fed the gas slowly. The wheels gripped, turned, kept on turning and eased us onto the freeway.

The plows had cleared a pair of lanes, and what little traffic there was moved at a snail's pace. It had stopped snowing, and the city slept under a high-riding moon. The peaceful scene outside belied the turmoil I felt inside.

"Do you think Maxwell was driving the truck?" I asked, when I'd had enough of the silence.

"That would be my guess," MacPhearson answered, inching his way around a stalled van.

"You guess? The next thing you'll be telling me is, you guess Bryan Parker shot his wife and killed his girlfriend before shooting himself." Hysteria, too near the surface, showed itself in sarcasm.

"A murder-suicide? It could have happened that way." He looked thoughtful.

I groaned. "My God—"

"Only, we didn't find a gun." He grinned then. Not the wide, lip-hiding-under-mustache grin I'd come to expect, just a softening of lips with a hint of a curve.

He swung the Ranger onto the Leonard Street exit and maneuvered around a small convoy of abandoned cars. "I'll take you home," he said. "If need be, a squad car can pick me up later."

The weather being what it was, I didn't argue.

The city's plows were out in force, promising a quick return to normal. Normal, however, did not include either my Valley Avenue driveway or the sidewalk that fronted the small bungalow.

"I hope you brought hip boots."

I pressed my face against the Ranger's side window and eyed the unbroken field of white that stretched between the front door and me. The snow was at least two feet deep on the level and three or four where it had drifted. Braced for the shock, I opened the door and climbed out. Cold, wet snow filled my Reeboks, climbed up my pant legs, and set my teeth to chattering.

The moon, which had earlier lighted the landscape, now hid behind a bank of clouds. The darkness prevented me from giving the truck more than a quick appraisal. With a promise to attend to my wounded friend tomorrow, I turned toward the house. An unexpectedly deep drift proved my undoing.

"Need a hand?" Concern showing on his face, MacPhearson loomed large above me.

I giggled childishly, ignored his outstretched hand, and swept my arms and legs in wide arcs.

MacPhearson's expression changed from concern to surprise, his mouth dropping open as it did.

"Chicken," I teased the seemingly dumbstruck policeman.

With a delighted whoop, MacPhearson joined me in the snow. Spread-eagled, we filled the yard with hosts of heavenly beings. Our laughter shattered the neighborhood quiet and released our stores of pent-up emotion.

Finally, as kids do when wet and cold from the snow, we sought the comfort of home. The front door, protected from the wind and snow by a porch and trellis that in summer supported a Don Juan climber, opened at the turn of the key.

A rush of warm air and a pair of complaining cats met us. MacPhearson shed his coat and shoes and lifted the friendly female into his arms.

Hera's cries changed quickly from protesting howls to contented purrs. Zeus, disdaining intimacy, sprang from couch to chair to table on his way to the kitchen.

"These two are quite a pair." MacPhearson stroked Hera with a practiced hand while he watched the antics of the cavorting male.

"They're hungry," I said.

I hung my coat beside MacPhearson's on the hall tree and left my Reeboks to puddle beneath it. In the kitchen, I spooned chicken into one bowl and ran fresh water into the other.

Zeus jumped from the countertop where he had been noisily supervising my efforts. Sniffing first one then the other, he chose the chicken.

Hera freed herself from MacPhearson's arms and sat beside Zeus. Licking a front paw clean, she washed her face, shook her head to straighten her whiskers, and shouldered her male companion aside.

I offered coffee. MacPhearson accepted, and we waited in the kitchen while it brewed.

"This is nice." MacPhearson ran his hand over the counter and inspected the stove.

"I like it," I said, watching him look and feel his way around the room.

"How long have you lived here?"

"Almost four years."

MacPhearson stopped in front of the sink and looked through the window into the backyard. From where I stood, I could see both his real self and his reflected self.

"What made you buy a house?" the face in the window asked.

"I didn't buy it, I inherited it."

MacPhearson turned away from the window, and I refocused on the real man.

"My parents were killed in an automobile accident twenty years ago," I said. "Four of us were in the car, me, my mom and dad, Uncle David's wife, Aunt Susan . . . everyone but Uncle David. We were going for ice cream. He didn't want any. Of the four of us, I was the only one who survived."

I was babbling, offering more information than was necessary, but my tongue had a mind of its own. I yanked a pair of mugs from the cabinet, hoping to stop the flow, to block old memories with current activity. It didn't. The mountain was there, and the drop-off to the lake. The car was out of control. Everyone was screaming, me, Mama, Daddy, Aunt Susan.

I kept my back to the man I knew was watching, not wanting him to see the pain the years had not erased or, worse still, the more recent pain of Uncle David's betrayal.

"Did your Uncle David raise you?"

I felt MacPhearson's eyes on me, gentle yet probing, a touch without hands.

"After the accident, I mean," he said.

I reshuffled the mugs, hiding my emotions behind the improvised shell game. "He helped, but I lived with my grandmother before moving here. We rented this house out until I was ready to live in it."

The coffee maker signaled ready, and I filled the mugs.

"Sugar or cream?"

"Straight," MacPhearson answered, then asked, "Your Uncle David—this is the same David Arthur from Arthur & Arthur Security?"

"The same Uncle David," I said. I pulled a bottle of Christian Brothers from an adjoining cupboard and offered the brandy for MacPhearson's inspection. He nodded appreciatively, and I added a generous dollop to each cup of the steaming brew. "Uncle David had the Michigan Street apartment and I spent a lot of time there when I was growing up."

I handed a mug to MacPhearson. He breathed in the pleasant aroma, took a sip and smiled appreciatively. "The apartment belonged to your Uncle David, to David Arthur?" he asked.

"The same," I said. I waited for MacPhearson to ask about David Arthur's notorious past, present or future. He didn't, but then, why should he? He probably knew more than I did about David Arthur's exploits.

We carried the mugs into the living room. The Siamese pair, finished with their late-night supper, joined us. I curled up on the couch. Hera settled on my lap, tucked her head between her front paws, and promptly fell asleep.

MacPhearson roamed restlessly. Stopping occasionally to sip coffee or pick up a book, he surveyed the room and its contents. A curious Zeus tailed behind, dogging his every step.

"Does it meet with your approval?" I asked.

"Reminds me of the house I grew up in."

"You and the sister with the broken arm?"

MacPhearson nodded. "And a younger brother and a dog, Spot. Not too original, but it fitted him."

He stopped before an end table. "You have a lot of medical books and journals."

It wasn't a question, and I didn't answer.

MacPhearson finished his prowling and sat beside me on the couch. "Were you scared?" he asked.

"While we were inside the Sandcastle?"

He nodded.

I considered the question. "A little, more nervous really. I didn't know where you were going with your questions." I swirled my mug and watched what was left of the brandy and coffee slosh in circles.

"And later?"

"I was afraid."

MacPhearson covered my hand with his and laced his fingers with mine. "I'm sorry."

"Don't be. You did what you had to do." I gave his hand a squeeze. "And I was warned."

He smiled. "That's right. You were warned." He set his empty mug on the end table.

"Know what?" I asked.

He looked at me, a question in his sapphire eyes.

"You enjoyed it. You liked baiting Maxwell, playing footsies with gangsters, and outwitting the truck."

I finished my coffee and set the mug on the opposite end table. Hera began another round of purring, and Zeus, finished with his after-dinner stroll, sat sphinx-like on the arm of the couch.

"Are you saying I like to live dangerously?" MacPhearson asked.

"That's what I'm saying," I said.

"I could say the same about you."

"I'll admit I like a little excitement, but I wouldn't want a steady diet of what we had tonight."

MacPhearson stretched his legs into the middle of the room, tightened his grip on my hand. "Maxwell asked if you were important to me."

"I heard him." I studied what I could see of MacPhearson's face.

"You are, Ginny." He turned and faced me, reached for me and pulled me slowly to him.

I bent forward, placing my hand on his shoulder.

His mustache tickled my nose. Neither stiff nor scratchy as I had expected, it deepened the pleasure of his kiss.

He pulled me tighter against him, moved his lips over my cheeks, my closed eyes. "I'd like to spend the night with you."

His words warmed my parted lips, tasted of brandy and coffee. Simple and direct like the man himself, they lay between us. Feeling their weight, I shifted away.

He smoothed my cheek with his thumb. "May I?"

I shook my head.

"The doctor?"

"Yes." The one word said it all.

MacPhearson's hand dropped from my face, leaving my cheek cold. He stood up. Zeus stood with him.

"I'll call for that ride."

I waited while he called and accepted more coffee when he brought the pot back with him.

"Fifteen, twenty minutes," he said.

"We still haven't looked at Parker's office," I said, needing to fill the silence, the uncomfortable silence that had invaded the room.

"I'm sure it's been tossed like the apartment." MacPhearson prowled the room, stopping and touching, but not sitting.

"Are you saying you don't want to see it?" I asked.

"No."

"Do you still want me to go with you?"

"I can get a warrant."

"I thought you had one."

He shook his head. "Just an empty envelope."

"I see."

"Do you, Ginny? Do you really see?"

I shrugged my shoulders.

"If you change your mind . . . Will you, Ginny? Will you change your mind?"

Not trusting my voice, I shook my head.

A rotating red and blue light shone through the parted drapes, coloring the walls and furniture.

"My ride," MacPhearson said unnecessarily. He pulled on his coat and slipped into his shoes. "See you around, Red."

I watched him go then locked the door behind him. "See you around, Mac," I whispered.

The telephone rang. I tripped over the ever-present Hera on my way to the kitchen. She shrieked. It was something I felt like doing but didn't.

"I wanted to know if you made it home . . . if you were all right . . ."

I drew the receiver close and slid down the wall until I was sitting on the floor. Zeus joined Hera in my lap and let her lick him clean.

"The weather's terrible, but I'm here, and everything's fine."

Tall blond men and monster trucks receded from my mind as Steve and I talked of things important to the two of us. We laughed some and finally said goodnight. Lonelier now than before, I kissed the cats.

The matched pair followed me through the house as I turned off lights and checked windows and doors. A surveillance system would have made the task easier, a fact I always pointed out to potential clients. It had been on Uncle David's to-do list for years, and was still on mine. But like the cobbler's children who had no shoes, I had a security business but no security system.

In the bedroom, I pulled off my jeans and added them to the pile of dirty clothes that littered the floor. Feeling guilty, I gathered an armful and headed for the bathroom. The crinkling sound of paper stopped me from stuffing the lot into the hamper.

I searched the pockets and found the receipt the hospital had given me for Leslie Parker's valuables. Except for a torn edge, it had worn well, and I stuffed it into my wallet for safekeeping.

The ringing telephone sent the cats scampering and me hurrying to the bedside table. Steve? MacPhearson?

"Hello?" I asked and waited for the answer.

"Ginny?" A voice, low and sounding strangely muffled, asked.

"This is Ginny." The voice not being readily recognizable, I searched my memory for a clue to the caller's identity.

"Ginny Archer?" the voice asked.

"No," I answered.

"Sorry, I must have the wrong number."

There was a click and the dial tone sounded in my ear. With the disquieting feeling such calls sometimes leave, I replaced the receiver.

My shower was short, and I fell asleep hugging Steve's pillow. A deep and dreamless sleep free of redheaded detectives with soft mustaches and muffled telephone voices, until . . .

Chapter Seventeen

THE RINGING TELEPHONE BROKE THE STILLNESS OF THE NIGHT. HAVING LEARNED FROM experience that middle-of-the-night calls harbingered no good, I answered the ringing phone cautiously.

"Did I wake you?" a voice on the other end asked.

"Pete Titus?" I asked.

"I'm calling about Kevin," Thelma's son-in-law answered. "He's in jail."

I pushed to a sitting position. "Has he been arrested?"

"Hell! I don't know. Mom said the police came to the house and took him to police headquarters. She's with him now, and I'm on my way. Can you meet us there?"

"I'll be there in half an hour."

I pushed away the covers and looked at the clock. The digital face read two a.m. My life was becoming a series of long days and short nights.

As the situation with Pete's brother sounded official, I pulled a pair of corduroy slacks and a matching jacket from the closet. A look in the mirror told me I would also need makeup—a lot of it.

My houseguests watched my one-man show from Steve's side of the waterbed, and stared sleepy-eyed as I slipped into leather ankle boots and a wool car coat. Having been mostly silent, they offered meows when I called good-bye.

MacPhearson's footsteps showed in the moonlight, and I followed them down the walk, passing by the snow angels as I went.

Something I had not seen earlier, though, was all too clear now as I rounded to the driver's side. The Ranger's passenger door and front bumper boasted a deep scrape. The grill was intact, but the bumper, instead of lying straight across, angled sharply upward. I climbed into the cab. Fearing the worst, I tried the ignition. To my delight, the engine coughed into life and settled into a familiar hum. God was good.

The barn-like squad room of police headquarters swarmed with uniformed officers and young men between fifteen and twenty whose faces wore fright, flight, and I-don't-give-a-damn looks. A number of older others whose expressions said otherwise completed the picture. Another visual sweep located my late-night caller along with his hand-wringing mother, Pearl, and a sullen-faced Kevin. The absence of Rhodes and MacPhearson told me that neither robbery nor homicide was the reason for the turmoil.

I breathed a sigh of relief and excused my way through the crowd, interrupting several conversational "I don't know why I'm here . . . It's like this, man . . . You know the cops . . ." as I passed.

"We still don't know what this is all about," Pete greeted.

"Kevin says he didn't do anything wrong," the mother said.

Taller by several inches than his six-foot-two brother, Kevin shifted uneasily from foot to foot.

"And you have no idea why you're here?" I asked the lanky teenager.

Kevin shook his head.

"Answer when you're spoken to, young man." Pearl Titus switched from hand wringing to finger pointing. "Miss Arthur's here to help you."

"I know, Mom . . ." Kevin ran a bony hand through his close-cropped hair. "When the police came to the house, they said I had to go downtown with them. They said they wanted to talk to me, but they didn't say what about."

"Have they talked to you yet?"

Kevin shook his head, a gesture that, with a look from his mother, became an audible, "No."

"Good," I answered, "and keep it that way until I get back." I turned to Pete. "I'll see what I can find out."

Pearl grabbed my arm. "Can you help my son?"

"I'm going to try."

I gave her arm a reassuring pat and left them with what I hoped was an encouraging smile.

Sharp elbows and angry stares impeded my progress as I threaded my way through the crowd. I looked for someone, anyone I could call by name. My search was futile, still, some faces seemed more familiar than others. I chose one that did and headed in his direction. Middle-aged and balding, he sat behind a cluttered desk and instead of a uniform wore a suit coat over an open-necked sport shirt.

"What's going on here?" I grabbed a chair still warm from its last occupant and sat down.

He readjusted horn-rimmed glasses on a face that, upon closer inspection, was one I didn't know, and gave me an appraising look. "You on the videotape?" he asked.

So that was it. MacPhearson's photographs had netted a record number of fish. Being the principal photographer, however, I didn't think I'd been swimming in this particular pond.

"I don't think so, Officer Collins," I answered, reading the name from the ID pinned to his breast pocket. "I represent one of the young men you brought in tonight."

He loosed a long sigh. "Didn't think you looked the type."

I took another, longer look around. The large room with its wall of tall windows and rows of gray metal desks was peopled with mostly blacks who were mostly young and predominantly male.

"The videotape?" I prodded. "Is it the one from the Halloween party at Marfield Park?" I asked, feigning ignorance of what I already knew.

Collins nodded, then glowered. "What do you know about it?"

I shrugged. "Just the scuttlebutt that's going around." I didn't think it necessary to say anything about me having been the cameraman and instead asked, "Were all of these kids on the tape?"

"Which one's your client?" Caught once, Collins became evasive.

"His name is Kevin Titus. When and if you decide to talk to him, let me know."

I left the mostly bald man and his gray metal desk and, having become an expert at dodging elbows, reached the corner unscathed.

Pete moved forward to meet me. "What did you find out?" he asked.

"I'll tell you later. Right now I need to talk to Kevin." But not in this fish bowl, I thought.

Looking decidedly unhappy, the three followed me through the squad room and into the hall. Rhodes's office was open and the darkness beckoned, but I wanted a more secluded place.

MacPhearson's cubbyhole offered the same invitation as had Rhodes's, and I motioned Kevin inside.

"You two wait here." I looked from Pete to Mrs. Titus. Tears pooled in the corners of her eyes. I reached out and touched her arm, lending her my strength and borrowing her love.

I closed the door and walked behind the desk. MacPhearson's swivel chair, though somewhat roomy, fit me just fine. Kevin, whose sullen look had been replaced by uncertainty and fear, sat in the straight-backed wooden one I had so recently occupied.

"How old are you now, Kevin?"

He answered, "Sixteen."

I followed with questions about school, family and special interests, before starting on the questions that had to be asked.

"Where were you on Halloween night?"

"I went to the party at Marfield Park."

"How long were you there?"

"From about seven to ten or eleven. The police sent us home when everyone started getting sick."

"Just sent you home? No questions asked?" I asked.

Kevin took in a deep breath. "They took our names, addresses, telephone numbers, things like that."

I settled deeper into the chair, took a deep breath of my own and started down another track. "Did you get sick?"

Kevin shook his head and slouched lower in the chair, his bravado reasserting itself.

I leaned forward. "Did you know what was safe to eat? What wasn't?"

Kevin stiffened. "No . . . no."

I rocked backwards in MacPhearson's chair. Was Kevin telling me the truth? And if he was, why did the police want to question him?

I mentally replayed the video with its assorted merrymakers, saw a red-nosed clown and a gimpy pirate. "Did you wear a costume?"

Kevin shifted from side to side, rubbed his hands over his pant legs. "I went as a clown."

"Describe your costume," I said quietly.

"I had on a black beanie and a red nose—"

"A false nose?" My fingers found and traced the ribs in my corduroy slacks.

"I used poster paint."

"What else did you have on?"

"It was one piece, red and green mostly and some black, with one of those ruffled collars. I got it at K-Mart."

"The beanie was black?"

"Mostly black," Kevin corrected.

A knock sounded on the door. Without waiting for an invitation, Collins pushed into the room.

"Come in," I said coldly.

"I've been looking for you two," he said. He shoved the room's other chair to the side of MacPhearson's desk.

"And have a seat," I invited.

"I have something I'd like to show you," Collins said flatly, ignoring my sarcasm. He opened a folder, shuffled through several pictures that lay inside, selected one and pushed it forward.

I looked at the picture and then at Kevin, whose eyes darted from the picture, to the policeman, to me.

Collins pulled another picture from the folder and laid it beside the first. He looked at Kevin. "Have you anything to say?"

"He has nothing to say," I said.

Collins shrugged. "No matter. The pictures tell me all I need to know."

He picked up the folder and slid the damning evidence inside. "I have to book him."

Kevin's eyes grew large as the policeman read, "You have the right to remain silent . . ."

Collins finished and took out his cuffs.

"Will you give us a few minutes?" I asked.

Collins nodded. "I'll send someone along after him."

The balding policeman slipped the cuffs into a carrying case fastened to the back of his belt, then opened the door and banged it shut behind him. We were alone.

"I bought the stuff. Crack."

Kevin's pathetically young face stared into mine. "It was the first time ever, and I didn't smoke it. I swear I didn't."

"If you didn't smoke it, what did you do with it?"

"I flushed it down the toilet." Kevin grew visibly limp, sagged against the chair.

Did I believe him? Hell . . .

Could I believe him?

A uniformed policeman came. He cuffed Kevin and led the frightened boy away. A teary-eyed Pearl Titus and a grim-faced Pete stared helplessly after them.

"He's been accused of buying drugs at the Halloween party last Thursday," I said.

"Not Kevin," Pearl argued.

"They have it on tape," I said, "and I'm the one who filmed it."

Pete groaned. "And I gave it to the police."

Chapter Eighteen

Justice ground slowly, taking several hours to loosen its hold on Kevin. The waiting had not been easy. Pete's shoulders sagged, and Pearl's motherly face had acquired a new crop of wrinkles. Kevin's attitude spoke of despair. Me? I was bone-weary, foot-dragging, dog-eared tired.

The four of us came to a stop behind a silver Buick. The halogen lamps looked dim in the morning light, and the parking lot had cleared considerably since my two a.m. arrival.

"I need to see you later today, Kevin," I said.

"When?" Pete asked.

I looked from brother to brother, one a man and the other a lanky teenager who, despite his height, was still a child.

"Go home," I said. "Get some sleep and meet me in my office tonight about six." Kevin nodded.

"We'll be there," Pete said.

The mother leaned heavily against the silver car. The night had been the hardest on her. "I'll be there, too," she said wearily.

"There's no need for you to come, Mrs. Titus," I said. "It's Kevin I need to talk to."

She dabbed her tear-filled eyes with a shredded tissue.

"Stay home," I urged. "I'll call you as soon as I hear anything."

Pearl's pain was palpable, her despair complete. I had to get away. With a "See you later," I did.

Zeus and Hera welcomed me home. Salmon and water satisfied their immediate needs, and sleep would have helped mine. Only it was not to be. It was Sunday, and that meant eleven o'clock Mass at Saint Paul's with Grandma Norwicki. It was a ritual established before the death of my parents, and I could still remember being escorted up the aisle by the three of them. Though two of the group were gone and I was no longer a little girl, it was a habit I had no intention of breaking.

Last night's storm would have brought the average city to a standstill, but Marion was not your average city. When I set out at mid-morning to drive the few blocks that separated me and my grandmother, both the main roads and the side roads had already been plowed clear of snow. The sidewalk leading to her two-story brick and frame house, the same house I had lived in after the accident, had received similar attention doubtlessly from its owner.

Wicki, a shortened version of her name I'd used since childhood, waited inside, her face pressed against one of a pair of long, narrow windows that framed her front door. She raised her gloved hand in greeting, and was hurrying down the front walk before I could park the Ranger.

"I had time to shovel the front walk," she announced as she climbed in beside me. "But I'm afraid my Escort's still buried in the garage. We'll have to use your truck this morning, Regina."

She leaned close and placed a warm kiss on my cheek. "You do look a mess, dear."

She straightened in her seat and fastened her seat belt. I returned her kiss but remained silent, better to learn what she knew than to offer contradictory information.

"Thelma told me you'd been sick, but I didn't expect to see you looking so banged up." She tightened her grasp on her handbag. "And I'm certain she never mentioned your truck."

I offered a lame excuse about snow, traffic, and hitting my head on a table.

"No need to explain. Thelma told me all about the Halloween party and about David's apartment being broken into, but she assured me you would soon be just fine." Wicki patted my leg and smiled encouragingly.

I took in a deeper breath than usual. Thank God Thelma didn't know about the visit to the Sandcastle.

"May I assume your young man will not be joining us for Mass this morning?" Wicki's question interrupted my thoughts.

"Your assumption is right. Steve won't be here." I checked the rearview mirror and pulled away from the curb. "He's on call this weekend."

"Dr. Brock is a fine young man, Regina. You'll not do better than him, you know."

Though she refused to sanction our living arrangements—Grandma Norwicki was a stickler for old ways and old rules—she thought highly of Steve and rarely missed an opportunity to champion his cause.

I glanced in her direction, only to see her looking in mine. Our eyes, both green and tilted upwards at the corners, met and held.

"Have I said something wrong?" she asked.

"No," I answered. "You're right. I can't do any better than Steve." A redheaded man insinuated his way into my thoughts, the prick of conscience as real as his remembered kiss. "I can't do any better than Steve," I repeated.

We were nearing Saint Paul's, and despite last night's snow, the congregation along with its cars were out in force. Gratefully, I gave them my full attention. At least I tried to.

I was still trying to rid my thoughts of dead men, gangsters, and, yes, police detectives when Mass started. Father Kolenda's homily on God's bounty—did he mean the snow, I wondered—helped. So, too, did our regular after-Mass visit to the social hall where we coffeed with the usual mix of parishioners.

"Your grandmother said you were in an accident, Regina," a stoop-shouldered older woman I recognized from past Sundays said as we sipped coffee.

I said I had and was saved from having to say more by Wicki's welcome voice. "Time we got on home, Regina. I'm sure you have a busy day planned."

I knew I loved her, this woman who had been a mother to a little girl who had lost hers, and this latest rescue told me why. Sunday morning coffee was best taken in small sips.

The telephone rang as I came through the door of my Valley Avenue bungalow. I answered without shedding either coat or gloves. It was Thelma.

"Carol told me about last night. Will Kevin have to go to jail?" Concern edged her voice.

"Too soon to say," I said.

"I know all about the videotape and those pictures the police lifted from it." Her tone of voice said it was the police who had committed a crime, and in my mind I saw the frown lines around her mouth deepen. She heaved a heavy sigh. "Have you been to church?"

"I've talked to Wicki," I said, answering Thelma's real question. I wasn't angry—the woman had proven her loyalty too many times for this—but I was irritated.

I voiced my feelings, only to have them ignored. The office oracle was off and running and, as usual, was determined to drag me along.

"What's going to happen to Leslie when she's discharged?" she asked.

"I don't know when that will be." I dug in my heels, determined to stay put.

"Steve can tell you that, Ginny," she said impatiently. "It's the apartment that concerns me. When will the police release it?"

"Rhodes can tell you that," I said slowly, sensing a trap.

"And if they don't, then what?"

"There's always the residents' quarters."

"Won't do." Thelma reminded me of Steve's description of the house staffs' off-duty living quarters—"the pits." Her voice slowed. "You know, Ginny, Leslie shouldn't be left alone—"

"You're probably right," I said and walked open-mouthed into Thelma's trap. "I suppose she could stay here for a few days."

"That's a good idea, Ginny. The poor girl needs somebody, and you're close enough in age to be a real comfort."

The beep of an incoming call saved me from further comment. This time it was Steve, and the conversation much more to my liking.

"He's free for dinner," I told an inquisitive Zeus when I hung up. From his perch on the kitchen table, the sleek Siamese tipped his head and twitched his ears. "And better still, he'll be home tomorrow night." Hera jumped into my lap, fixed me with an adoring look, and began to purr.

I fed and watered them again, cleaned their litter, and checked myself out in the bedroom mirror.

The green wool slacks and the lighter green long-sleeved pullover sweater I had put on for church would do, but the intervening hours had done little for my face. The brown and yellow bruise made a concealing layer of eye shadow mandatory. A light touch of blush and lipstick completed my makeover.

I thought of Kevin with his painted nose as I spread the bright color over my lips. A circus clown who probably wished he'd never heard of poster paint.

I gave myself another critical appraisal, then sought an unbiased opinion. Ever the diplomat, Hera refused to comment.

Sunday's sparse traffic shortened the drive downtown. When I pulled into the parking ramp across from the hospital, I checked my watch. Mickey Mouse's gloved hands told me I had time to finish some unfinished business.

An air of weekend emptiness permeated the lobby of the Professional Office Building. I walked into the elevator and heard the doors swoosh shut behind me. I didn't stay alone for long. Sammy Maxwell, a bad dream I couldn't shake, rode up with me. With him were nightmarish images of dead men and monster trucks.

The tenth floor was also empty, and the frosted pane still read UPCHURCH CHEMICALS Bryan Parker Regional Director. My eyes moved downwards. I saw only darkness. Today no wavering beam of light crept from beneath the closed door. I fitted the key into the lock and braced myself for what MacPhearson had suspected we would find. He was right.

Memories of having been stalked through Uncle David's apartment flooded over me. To guard against imagined ghosts, I left the door wide, looked around then roamed through the office.

There were two rooms and a small half-bath. All three were in total chaos. Overturned chairs, ripped upholstery, dumped desk drawers whose contents littered the floor, a broken towel dispenser, and an upended toilet tank cover spoke of an all-out assault.

I bumped a sad looking computer keyboard that cried, "Pick me up."

I stooped, then straightened. My eyes gave the room another sweep. This time I saw the greasy fingerprint powder that was part of the decor. MacPhearson hadn't wasted any time.

I slammed the door behind me, gave the key a quick turn and ran, rather than walked, to the elevator.

A gentle breeze and warm sun met me as I pushed through the plate glass doors. "The world isn't all bad," the wind whispered. I smiled. If the weather held until next weekend, we would have a good day for the parade.

I allowed another bigger, brighter smile. A visit to Santa Claus would fit nicely into tomorrow's schedule.

The hospital lobby overflowed with Sunday visitors. I worked my way through the crowd and stopped by the switchboard. The operator, a male today, paged Steve. Much younger than the others, I guessed him as a college student working a part-time job.

Steve answered his page and suggested we meet in the cafeteria. Like many institutions that regularly feed large crowds, Mercy Hospital tried to make Sunday dinner special. Today, they'd succeeded. The menu featured roast beef and grilled chicken. Steve took both. I had the chicken.

"How's Leslie?" I asked when we were seated.

"Her temp's down, so we'll probably send her home in a day or two."

"And if she doesn't have a home to go to?" I explained about the apartment.

"Any suggestions?" he asked.

"I was thinking of asking her to stay with us for a few days."

"Fine with me." He picked up a chicken leg. "How about telling me about last night?"

I stopped a forkful of green beans in mid air. "Thelma?"

Steve nodded, and I told him about the videotape, Kevin, and my trip to police headquarters.

Steve did not ask about my date with MacPhearson or about the visit to Bryan Parker's office. Had I even told him about it? I couldn't remember, but since Steve hadn't asked, I didn't tell him about Sammy Maxwell, my visit to the Sandcastle, the monster truck, or MacPhearson. How did that quote about tangled webs go?

A candy striper offered coffee, and we accepted.

"I stopped by Bryan's office on the way over," I said. Not hearing an I-thought-you-went-there-last-night response, I breathed a sigh of relief and added, "Whoever trashed the apartment had a go at the office, too."

"Do the police know?"

"They've already been there."

Steve slid a slice of chocolate cake in front of him, and I helped myself to a forkful.

"Should I tell Leslie?"

"She has to know sometime, and sooner is usually better."

My conscience cringed at Steve's words, but as this was becoming more usual than unusual, as usual I did nothing.

Leslie was sitting in a chair by the window, the sunlight lending color to her pale face.

"You're looking better," I greeted.

"Tell him that." The dark-haired surgeon pointed to Steve. "He won't let me go home."

I settled on the end of Leslie's bed. "That's one of the things I'd like to talk about."

Leslie's welcoming smile fled.

I laughed. "It's not that bad. It's about the apartment. The police haven't released it, so even if Steve were to discharge you, you would have nowhere to go."

"And what's the good news?" She crossed her arms over her breasts and pulled her elbows tight against her.

"Someone broke into Bryan's office," I said reluctantly.

Leslie crumbled, a fortress whose defenses had been breeched. "The same person who broke into the apartment?" she asked.

"The police haven't said," I said, and no need in telling her what MacPhearson thinks, I thought.

"I've got the feeling someone out there doesn't like me," Leslie said softly.

"Not you, Bryan," I corrected. I left the bed and knelt beside the troubled girl and took one of her slender hands in mine.

She shook her head. "I'm the one with no place to go."

"We'd like you to stay with us until the apartment's ready." I looked at Steve, including him in the "we."

"Oh, Ginny, I couldn't do that."

Steve rested his arms on the over-bed table. "You don't have a lot of options, Leslie. Besides which, I don't think you should be alone."

I squeezed the hand I still held. "Let me play nurse," I urged.

"I'm a bad patient," Leslie said.

"I'll chance it," I said.

We left Leslie and detoured by Steve's office for a goodnight kiss and some minor surgery. The kiss came first. Soft and delicious and tasting of chocolate cake rather than brandy and coffee, it ended too soon.

"I saw Dr. Canfield today," Steve said as he dabbed my stitches with antiseptic solution.

"And?"

"He wanted to know how you were doing and to remind me I had to take half of your stitches out today."

I felt the pressure of tweezers, heard scissors snip. Steve tilted his head to one side and studied his handiwork. "Another kiss should just about do it," he said and added action to his words.

It was still visiting hours when I left Steve's office, and the lobby was filled with people. I dug into my shoulder bag for the Ranger's keys. My hand bumped against my wallet, a reminder that I hadn't yet retrieved Leslie's valuables.

The switchboard operator, as willing to share information as his female counterparts, directed me to the admitting office. "They take care of releasing valuables on weekends," he explained.

As promised, they did and, upon obtaining my receipt and my signature, handed me an oversized padded envelope.

Mickey Mouse said six when I walked through the back door of 100 Michigan Street. Oscar, the building's long-time security guard, waved me into his office. Old now—his hair was gray and his skin wrinkled—he'd been around since my grade school days.

"I put the two who said they have an appointment with you in the lobby," he said. He scratched his head. "That older one looks like Thelma Riggs's son-in-law."

I laughed. Though he might be old and gray, Oscar still had a special way of wheedling information from people. "You're right. His name's Pete Titus. The other one is his brother, Kevin."

"He's a tall drink of water." Oscar lifted his chin and looked upwards as if scanning Kevin's long frame. But his curiosity was satisfied, and he waved me away with an added, "Give me a call when you want I should let you out."

I took the stairs to the lobby, and as Oscar had said, Pete and Kevin were there.

"Been waiting long?" I called.

A loud bang-bang drowned out their answer.

Chapter Nineteen

A RED-FACED OSCAR BARRELED INTO THE LOBBY AND HUFFED HIS WAY TO THE FRONT DOOR. Another bang sent Pete charging after him.

"Let me in," a voice from outside shouted.

"Whoever it is, I've got him covered, Miss Arthur." Oscar's shaky hand waved a long-barreled gun.

Another bang and another shouted demand to be let in followed.

"Stand back!" Oscar cried. "I've got a gun and I damn well know how to use it."

"Let him in," I said.

Oscar shot me a questioning look.

"I know him," I said.

Reluctantly, the gray-haired security guard lowered his gun and unlocked the door.

MacPhearson, his wide grin in place, walked into the lobby. "Hello, Red." The detective's grin grew even wider. "I thought you would never answer the door."

"What are you doing here?" I demanded. I wasn't grinning, our shared intimacy forgotten.

"Following him." MacPhearson pointed at Kevin Titus.

The gangling youth stumbled back, away from the pointing finger.

Pete grabbed his brother's arm. "Take it easy, Kev."

"What do you want with him?" I positioned myself between the predator and his prey.

MacPhearson looked past me to Kevin. "I want to ask him a few questions."

"Nothing doing." I jabbed the UP button on the elevator. Pete, with Kevin in tow, crowded close beside me.

"You going up or out?" Oscar asked MacPhearson. "I've got to lock this door."

"Ginny." MacPhearson ignored the night watchman. "If I can't talk to Titus, how about letting me talk to you?"

He wore a look of expectancy, one that expected yes. I wanted to say no, but—

"Okay, but not here, upstairs."

"You've got a deal."

The elevator door opened, and the three of us stepped inside. MacPhearson hurried forward. The closing door bounced hard against his shoulder. It was a nice touch.

We rode up in silence and remained so until we were inside the offices of the Arthur & Arthur Security Agency.

"You two can wait here," I told Pete and Kevin, pointing to the couch that marked the reception area. "And you," I looked at MacPhearson, "can come with me."

I flipped on the lights in the inner office and claimed the swivel chair behind the desk, which as usual protested being sat on. The legal pad and a pair of sharpened pencils, things on the desktop that didn't need arranging, I rearranged.

"Okay," I said, "I'm here and you're here, so talk."

MacPhearson, comfortable in the wood and leather client's chair, extended his legs in front of him. "Got a bug up your ass?" he asked quietly.

Bug? The thought niggled. He wouldn't. Would he?

"No bugs anywhere." My face felt hot, but I matched his casual tone.

A smile tugged the corners of his mouth. "Have it your way, Red."

"You requested this conversation."

"So I did." His mustache sagged and his smile faded. "I want to talk to the Titus kid about Williams."

"My client and that subject are off limits."

MacPhearson rested his elbow on the desk. "Be reasonable, Red. That kid's Williams's only known contact."

I enjoyed a silent chuckle. So, MacPhearson wasn't having as easy a time as he thought he would.

"It's important that I speak to him, Ginny, important that I find out what he knows."

"Important to you or to him?"

MacPhearson slammed his fist against the desk. "Okay, you've made your point." I scrambled to catch the rolling pencils. "Banging the desk won't make me change my mind."

MacPhearson raised his hands. "Then how about you asking him for me? Find out what he knows about Williams."

I quirked an eyebrow. "You can't be serious."

"Maybe we can make a deal." MacPhearson persisted.

"You haven't got the authority to make any deals, Mac. You know it and I know it."

We looked at each other, stared until it became a contest.

"I went by Bryan Parker's office this afternoon," I said finally.

"So?"

"You might be right about Maxwell trashing both places."

"Could be." MacPhearson recrossed his ankles. "I'm still waiting for your answer."

"I can't help you," I said.

"Then I guess there's no reason for me to stay."

"No reason at all," I said.

Kevin sat where MacPhearson had sat. He didn't fit the chair as well, nor did he look as comfortable.

"Relax," I said.

He didn't.

"Tell me again what you did Thursday night."

"I went to the Halloween party with my friend, Johnny Martinez. We were supposed to meet some girls, but they didn't show." Kevin's eyes found a spot over my head and settled on it.

"Go on." I gave him an encouraging smile.

"These guys came along, and . . ." Kevin rubbed his arm, looked at me, then looked away. "I don't know their names. They're just some guys I'd see around."

"Around where?"

Kevin named two of the more popular high school hangouts.

"They weren't classmates of yours?"

Kevin shook his head. "They go to South Side. I go to North Side." He relaxed some, softening the lines on his face that told what he would look like when he grew older.

"How did you come to know them, Kevin?"

"Johnny introduced us."

"They were his friends?"

"I don't know. It wasn't something we talked about."

"Whose decision was it that you get together on Thursday night? Yours? Johnny's?"

"Nobody decided. We just, like, ran into them." Kevin fell silent, as if sorting his thoughts. "I liked being with them," he said finally. "I felt important."

"Are they important?"

Kevin shifted restlessly. "They always had lots of money to throw around, fancy cars, girls."

"Do you know where they got their money?" I didn't expect an answer, was in fact hoping—

"Drugs."

Hope fled. I felt cold.

"Sold them or used them?" I spoke slowly, easing the tension inside me. This boy was sixteen, only sixteen!

"Some pushed, some used, and some did both."

"What did you do? Push or use?" Sixteen no longer seemed young.

Kevin gave me a startled look. "You . . . You don't think—"

"Push or use?"

"I didn't do either."

"I saw the pictures, Kevin."

"I explained that last night."

"Tell me again." I couldn't let loose of my anger, my frustration.

Kevin gave me a belligerent stare. "I bought some crack."

Our eyes caught and held. "And what did you plan to do with it?"

His knuckles whitened over the arms of the chair. "I didn't know what I was going to do with it."

"Get off it, Kevin." I hit the desk. The pencils flew almost as high as they had for MacPhearson. "You bought the damn stuff. So tell me. What were you going to do with it?"

"Smoke it," he cried and, like the child he was, knuckled away a tear that threatened his cheek.

"Tell me about the man you bought the drugs from."

Kevin gave me a confused look. The change in subject was too abrupt.

"The man you bought the drugs from?" I repeated.

"What's to know about him? He was just someone I'd see around, usually with those guys from South Side."

MacPhearson's question had been asked and answered. I could drop the subject of Tim Williams.

"What did you do after you made the drug buy?"

"Johnny and me went in the fun house, and then danced some. When everyone got sick, I tried to find Carol and the kids." Kevin took a deep breath. "People were running everywhere. The police were there. It was a mess."

"You didn't get sick?"

Kevin shook his head.

I hesitated but decided to move on, unwilling to paint him guilty of both buying crack and adding ipecac to the food.

"You said the police sent you home?"

Kevin nodded. Squirmed in his seat. "They were all over the place."

"Did you go home?"

"Johnny wanted to smoke the crack. We went to his house."

I waited.

"I chickened out," he said.

"Did Johnny chicken out?"

Kevin did more squirming. "I—"

"Did Johnny smoke the crack, Kevin?"

The nod was slight, almost imperceptible.

"You just stood there and watched?"

Kevin slumped lower in the chair. "I was afraid," his voice broke.

"Afraid? A big guy like you who likes feeling important?"

Kevin's voice grew louder. "I was afraid of what my mom would say if she found out, afraid of what Pete would do . . . Hell! I was afraid of what the damn stuff would do to me."

"So you just took it home and flushed it down the toilet?"

"I took it home and flushed it down the toilet."

"Why didn't you sell it? Drugs are expensive and you paid good money for it."

He looked startled, as if the idea had really never occurred to him. "I just wanted to get rid of it before anyone knew I had it."

"Johnny knew, and the man you bought it from, and the guys from South Side." I snorted disgustedly. "How did you expect to keep something secret that never was secret?"

Kevin looked defeated. "I guess I wasn't thinking."

I wanted to believe him. It was the same story he had told before, nothing added, nothing changed. I pushed back my chair and stretched my legs. The action reminded me of MacPhearson, and I heard myself say, "About the man who sold you the drugs—"

Kevin sat up straighter. "I already told you, I don't know anything about him."

"Let's give it another go." I leaned forward, inviting a confidence. "Do you know his name?"

Kevin's sigh suggested defeat. "I think Johnny called him Jim, Ben, Tim . . . something like that."

"How about his last name?"

Kevin shook his head. "If Johnny mentioned it, I don't remember ever hearing it."

"Is there anything you can tell me about him? Anything at all?"

Kevin wet his lips. "I saw him a few times with that guy who was killed at the motel last week."

"Bryan Parker?" Whatever I'd expected to learn, this was not it.

Kevin nodded. "Johnny remembers seeing them together, too."

"Did you know Mr. Parker?"

"Mrs. Riggs introduced us. He came in to collect his mail a couple of times when I was here with Pete."

I picked up a pencil and doodled on the legal pad that lay in front of me. "Can you remember where you saw them?"

"No place special, just around."

"Around where?" I paused my pencil over the pad.

"I saw them in the mall once."

I doodled a line of question marks.

"And once I saw them driving around in a car." A smile touched Kevin's face. "It was a midnight-blue Jaguar."

I doodled faster. Was this another nail in Williams's coffin, another piece of evidence that linked him to Bryan Parker's and Nancy Webber's murders? More importantly, how could I use this information to help Kevin?

I started slowly, framing sentences as I went. "The man you bought the crack from went by the name of Tim Williams, Kevin, and he was shot to death Friday night in Bryan Parker's apartment."

Kevin's jaw dropped and his eyes widened.

"I might want you to tell the police about you and Johnny seeing the two of them, Parker and Williams, together." I paused then, wanting his full attention. "Would you be willing to do this?"

Kevin's head moved slowly from side to side, and his words when they came were difficult to hear. "Not if it means dissing Johnny."

Chapter Twenty

"NOT IF IT MEANS DISSING JOHNNY," KEVIN REPEATED. I laid the pencil on my desk and folded my hands over the legal pad. Though I admired his loyalty, his not wanting to show disrespect to his friend, I questioned his motive.

"If it was just me . . ." the youth argued.

The discussion was going nowhere. What I needed was reinforcements. "How about discussing this with Pete?" I suggested. "Maybe the three of us can resolve the issue."

"There's nothing to resolve," Kevin said stubbornly.

"How about giving it a try?"

"It won't do any good," Kevin warned.

Despite Kevin's prediction, or maybe in spite of it, I called Pete into the office. He took the mate to Kevin's chair, but like his brother, did not settle in easily.

"What's the problem?" he asked, seeing Kevin's grim expression.

"She wants me to dis Johnny," Kevin blurted.

"Kevin has some information I think he should share with the police," I said.

"Will it help Kevin?" Pete mirrored his brother's grim expression.

"Nothing's absolute, but I think it will." I thought of MacPhearson's eagerness to question the tall, lanky youth and reaffirmed my statement.

Pete laid a reassuring hand on his brother's arm. "Let's hear her out, Kev." Pete turned to me. "Okay, let's hear it."

I told Pete about Kevin's having seen Parker and Tim Williams together. "This is the information I want to take to the District Attorney," I said. "The two of us talk. Then we," I nodded to include the three of us, "wait and see if the DA's willing to deal."

The brothers looked at each other, Pete hopeful, Kevin more resigned.

"If I say yes, and you talk to the District Attorney, what will he do for me?" Kevin asked.

"He can reduce the charges or maybe drop them altogether." I rested my elbows on the desk and worked my facial muscles to resist a yawn. It was turning into another long night.

"Do you really think you can get them to drop the charges?" Pete blinked hard, tried to hide the emotion that showed in his eyes.

"I can't answer that, at least not yet." Slim though it might be, I had to offer them a glimmer of hope.

"Kev's never done anything like this before. He's a good kid, Ginny. He studies hard, gets good grades, plays first-string basketball . . ." Pete's voice wavered. "Surely that should count for something."

"I'm sure it will." I moved in my chair, sending creaking noises through a room grown suddenly quiet.

"Is there anything I, we," Pete motioned to his brother, "can do in the meantime?"

The older brother sounded as tired as I felt.

"Go home and get some sleep," I advised, "both of you."

"Do you think you can keep Johnny out of it?" Kevin asked.

"I'll see what I can do," I hedged.

"I just want things to be like they were," Kevin mumbled, but they never would. He had traded his innocence for a bag of crack cocaine.

Oscar met us in the hall. "Calling it a night, Miss Arthur?"

"I sure am," I said. Matching action to words, I left the building.

Along with a ringing telephone, Thelma's smiling face met me when I returned to the office the next morning. Both promised a normal Monday.

Gabenski and Son were among the first callers. They had picked up Bryan's body but needed another signature on the cremation request.

Euro-Imports called next, quoted a price and wanted to know if they should go ahead with the repairs on the Jaguar. I said "yes" and, given the amount I'd just heard, wondered what they would charge to fix the Ranger. I didn't ask.

Several other calls, some potential clients, kept the lines busy, and it was mid-morning before Thelma managed a call to police headquarters. The crime lab said they would release the apartment that afternoon. Another call, this one to the building's maintenance department, secured a promise from them to start the cleanup the next morning.

It was nearly noon before the lights stopped blinking on the telephone console, indicating a clear line. I picked up the handset and with an anticipatory thrill punched in a familiar number, one I saved for special occasions. A softly modulated woman's voice answered on the second ring.

"This is Ginny Arthur," I said. "Is Judge Marfield there?" I used the short wait to glance through my notes. Not that I needed to, as I'd learned long ago the necessity of being prepared for any encounter with the judge and had already committed the material to memory.

"How nice to hear from you, Ginny." I warmed at the greeting. Judge Marfield's voice was as pleasing to the ear as the first, but hers had an added note of pleasure.

I pictured the Tudor house where she lived located near the park of the same name, the land having been donated by her grandfather, and saw her behind the large desk in the library. It was the place she referred to as her office since retiring from the bench six months earlier. Seventy-plus now, Marsha Marfield still had a runner's long legs and slender body. Her hair, mostly silver, was worn in a wedge cut. An informal style, it softened the features of her square face.

"How have you been?" she asked.

I answered with equal pleasure what to most people was a routine question. But Marsha Marfield was not given to asking routine questions. I'd suspected this was so when we'd first met as runners on Marion State's track while I was still an undergraduate, and had come to appreciate its value when she became one of my law school professors. Alone and on my own now, it was not just her knowledge I sought, but her honesty and sincerity.

"I have a drug case I'd like to discuss with you." I waited, hoping for a yes and a let's-do-it-now response.

Judge Marfield, M&M to her friends, said yes to both, and I wasted no time in the telling.

"Should I go for a deal, try to get the charges dropped?" I asked when finished.

"Dropped would be best," M&M said, "and given it's a murder case, the District Attorney should be willing to deal."

"Then I'll go for that," I said without hesitation.

"Be sure it's you who sets the terms, Ginny," she cautioned. "Make them want what you have. Don't give anything away."

With a thank you and a promise to let her know the outcome, I hung up.

I shifted the legal pad to the center of my desk. With a little luck, my glimmer would become a sunbeam.

It was after noon when Thelma set a cup of coffee on my desk. Appointment book tucked under her arm, she pulled up a client chair. Before she could settle, however, the phone rang again.

"Ginny?" Rhodes boomed.

I moved the receiver away from my ear, letting his voice carry into the room.

"Your gun came in this morning."

"I didn't order a gun," I said.

"We talked about it." Rhodes sounded offended.

"You—" I stopped. What was the point in arguing? I'd already lost.

"I enrolled you in a gun safety class. They're hour-long sessions, and the first one starts today at two. Come early and bring the papers I sent you. We can get the gun registered while you're in class. That way you'll be able to take it home with you."

I'd been had, trapped like a rabbit in a snare.

"Rhodes bought me a gun," I said when I hung up. It was a needless comment, seeing as how Thelma had heard as much of the conversation as I had. Still, I had to complain to someone.

"After being shot at, I'd think you'd be glad he did." She opened the appointment book. "Two o'clock's free," she said.

I nodded. Arguing with her was like arguing with Rhodes. Useless.

Lunch was a one o'clock quickie at my desk, after which I set off for police headquarters. Rhodes was waiting in his office. On his desk lay a bluish colored revolver. It had a short barrel and a wooden grip. A box of ammunition lay beside it, and beside that another box.

"Cleaning kit," Rhodes explained, nudging the box.

Reluctantly, I lifted the gun. Its bulk was an unwelcome weight in my hand.

"It's yours," he said proudly. "I picked it out myself."

Rhodes sounded as if he had given me the crown jewels. I suppressed a grimace.

"It's a good gun for a woman," he continued. "Easy to use, not too heavy, and safe to carry either in a purse or holstered."

Only if you want one, I thought.

He patted the gun. "Take it to class. The instructor there will tell you all about it."

Rhodes placed the gun in a leather pouch. "You can decide later how you'll want to carry it." He started for the door. "You did bring the papers?"

I pulled the envelope from my shoulder bag, and followed the police lieutenant out the door.

We walked for what seemed forever, farther even than the pathologist's office, coming at last to the firing range. It smelled of cordite and sounded like the percussion section of a bad rock band.

A police sergeant greeted Rhodes by name. He indicated a room adjacent to the range. It turned out to be a classroom where supposedly I would learn the intricacies of loading, firing, and cleaning what the instructor explained was a thirty-eight, single-action revolver.

I nodded to let the gray-haired, ramrod-straight policeman know I was listening.

"You can throw it across the room and it won't go off," he said. "Which means you can carry it however you choose without worrying."

Should I tell him my only worry was whether I should keep it in the kitchen or the dining room? I didn't. Instead, I accepted the chair he offered and set the gun—excuse me, the thirty-eight-caliber, single-action Smith & Wesson revolver—on the table in front of me, and beside it the box of ammunition and the cleaning kit.

Sixty minutes later the instructor opened the door to the classroom, freeing me and five others, the others looking decidedly more pleased to be there than I. Instead of visions of sugarplums, did images of stepping up to a firing line, adjusting a set of oversized ear protectors, extending their arms in a two-handed grip and squeezing, not pulling the trigger, dance in their heads?

"Same time next week," the instructor called after us.

Rhodes was waiting for me, his grin as wide as the Cheshire cat's. Hell! I was even mixing simile, borrowing from *Alice in Wonderland* and *The Night Before Christmas*.

The clerk had the registration ready. Everything was legal. Under Rhodes's watchful eye, I tucked the revolver, along with the ammunition, into my shoulder bag and shoved the cleaning kit under my arm. I couldn't wait to get home and find a more suitable spot. Maybe the bottom drawer of my dresser?

I left police headquarters and headed across town. Guns be damned. It was time for the special treat, the sugarplum vision I'd promised myself yesterday.

The sleigh and reindeer were in the front yard, waiting for Christmas Eve and its load of toys. Lighted evergreens and wooden elves with wooden soldiers, dolls, and drums told of the preparations for the big night. I ran a practiced eye over the manger scene and the snow couple who peeked over a shared broom, looking for wires and electric eyes. As mostly pressure-sensitive devices with audible alarms were used, I didn't expect to find any, and I didn't. Except for a discreet sign in the corner of a front window that read PREMISES PROTECTED BY ARTHUR & ARTHUR SECURITY, no one would know an alarm system was in place.

Mrs. Roundtree met me at the foil-covered front door. "I knew you'd be out here one of these days," she greeted.

I grinned a child's grin. The yearly visit, once shared with Uncle David, was one I now made alone. "You couldn't keep me away," I said, pushing away the old memories.

The air filled with carolers' songs and the sweet aroma of baking cookies as the door opened wide. "Come in, come in." The short, rotund woman led me through a room that, like the yard, was a fairyland of decorated pine trees, green wreaths, and a holly-covered mantel.

"Has the crew been out to check the alarms?" I asked.

"They came the very next day after we were in your office, dear," she answered.

Her plump fingers busied themselves pouring milk and arranging a plate full of sugar cookies. "Now, you eat and drink."

I did both and, when I'd finished, was taken on a personally conducted tour of house and yard. Santa, busy in his workshop, stuck his head out and called "hello."

"Are you liking what you see, Miss Arthur?" he asked.

"I sure am," I said, hoping the twinkle in my eye matched the twinkle in his.

"Your crew was here and got us all checked out," he announced. "Just try moving anything around after the alarms are set," he chuckled.

"I've already told her, dear. Now, you get back to work. Remember, all the little boys and girls are depending on you."

His head disappeared inside the workshop, and I waved a reluctant good-bye to Mrs. Roundtree.

"Yes, Ginny, there really is a Santa Claus," I told myself as I climbed into the Ranger. A school bus loaded with another generation of believers on their way to see Santa met me at the end of the driveway.

I picked up a pork loin on the way home. It would taste good with the green beans I knew were in the freezer. Rolls, fresh peaches from some faraway place where the sun always shines, and a variety pack of cat food completed my grocery shopping. The sun had almost disappeared when I reached home, as had the snow from my sidewalks and driveway, blown away by a friendly neighbor with a large snow blower. I had off-street parking again.

Zeus and Hera provided a noisy escort into the kitchen. They watched my every move, and shrieked in protest when I readied the pork loin for broiling before dishing up the Nine Lives.

As if this was his cue, Steve banged through the front door. I opened my arms for a welcoming kiss. It was a kiss I didn't get.

"Are you okay?" His eyes raked me up, then down. "You never told me you were in an accident."

I held up my hand, warding off his anger. "It just happened Saturday night. I haven't had time to tell you."

Steve pulled me close. "When I saw the truck . . ." His hands moved over my body. "God, Ginny!"

"I went with MacPhearson to interview a suspect at the Sandcastle. It was snowing, and a truck hit us in the parking lot." I chose my words carefully, editing the "hit" and "truck" part. Strangely, even with the editing, a few of the tangles in the web I'd woven began to loosen.

Steve abandoned words altogether, and as good luck would have it, only the Siamese pair ate early.

Later, much later, dressed in a sweat suit and bunny slippers, I cooked the vegetables and fixed the salad. Steve carved the pork loin, which, I must add, he had broiled to perfection. Using either hand with equal ease, he made each slice a twin to the other.

We ate hungrily, our earlier activity having whetted our appetites, and enjoyed our after-dinner coffee—without brandy tonight—in companionable silence. Hera, alert to every opportunity, teased the corner of Steve's napkin. I watched, letting the events of the past few days trickle through my mind. One separated from the others.

I left the table, returning with the envelope I'd picked up at the hospital. I undid the flap, reached in, and pulled out a brown leather wallet, followed by a beeper, a cell phone, and a pair of matching gold rings. Both rings were elaborately carved. The smaller of the two bore an inscription inside the band which read LRP FROM WBP.

"WBP FROM LRP," Steve read from the other, larger ring.

Chapter Twenty-One

S TEVE AGAIN HELD THE RING BETWEEN THUMB AND FOREFINGER, HAVING RESCUED IT FROM ITS determined roll to the edge of the table.

"R? W?" I asked, looking up from the smaller of the two rings I held between my own thumb and forefinger.

"Leslie's middle name is Rose," Steve said. "I don't know about the W. Leslie just called him Bryan."

Steve handed me the larger of the matching bands. I watched the overhead light dance across the ring's carved surfaces. Hera, diverted from the napkin, chased the bouncing beams, confusion clouding her triangular face when she failed to catch them.

I checked the contents of the wallet. Left the lone twenty I found there and shoved it and the rings back into the envelope and picked up the beeper. "I wonder if this still works . . ." The words more musings than question.

"The batteries would have worn out by now, but . . . " Steve laid down the beeper and picked up the cell phone, "this might still be working." He looked more closely at the cellular phone. "Only nobody would hear it. It's set to vibrate."

"Why would Leslie do that?"

Steve handed back the small phone. "Most of us do that, especially the house staff. Cuts down on the bells and whistles the patients have to listen to."

I shoved the beeper and cell phone into the envelope with the wallet and rings and fastened the flap. "I'll give this to Leslie when she comes home," I said.

"That will be tomorrow. You can make it a homecoming present."

"Is she well enough to come home already?" The anxious layman in me wanted to know, his words diverting my attention from both the envelope and its contents.

"Well enough." Steve yawned. "Want help with the dishes?"

The dishes waited until the next morning, and had it not been for Leslie's expected arrival, they may have waited even longer. Once a neat freak with a place for everything and everything in its place, my life had undergone many changes since Steve had moved into my heart and home. All welcome changes, and I hummed along with the radio as I checked the spare bedroom.

At the back of the house just off the kitchen, it was separated from the one Steve and I shared by the bathroom. Clean sheets, an extra blanket, hangers in the closet, an empty dresser drawer, and it was ready for Leslie's homecoming.

I grabbed a set of fresh towels and a pile of dirty clothes on my way to the bathroom. The towels settled nicely over the rack, but the hamper refused to accept even one more pair of jeans. A hard push almost solved the problem, leaving a gaping lid to remind me of unfinished domestic chores.

From the security of my wrist, Mickey gave me a wide grin. Time to go, he said.

Leslie was pacing impatiently when I walked into her second floor room. "Did you bring me any clothes?" she demanded in lieu of her usual friendly greeting.

I berated myself for having forgotten the obvious, but was cut off by a "Never mind. I had Steve bring me a set of scrubs and my lab coat."

Leslie's green suit reminded me of last week's Halloween party. Instead of shoe covers though, what were once white but now blood-splattered tennis shoes showed beneath her rolled pant legs.

"My work shoes," she explained, looking where I looked.

"I see you got here." Steve's broad smile and cheery "Hello" helped but could not warm the room's chilly atmosphere.

"Do you have my release?" Leslie demanded.

"Everything's taken care of." Steve handed her the form.

The dark-haired surgeon retrieved her lab coat from where it lay among the discarded sheets and blankets at the foot of her bed. She jammed her arms through the sleeves and headed for the door. "Then let's get out of here," she said.

"Not so fast, Dr. Parker." A white-uniformed nurse with a wheelchair blocked Leslie's escape. "Sit," she ordered.

Steve laughed. "If you want to get out of here, you'll have to do as she says."

In tight-lipped silence, Leslie slid into the seat. Calls of "Good-bye" and "Get well quick" from the staff gathered around the nurses' station were acknowledged with a frown and a hand wave. Not until we reached the Emergency Room did Leslie break her grim-faced silence.

"Did they give you my clothes?" she asked. She looked from the nurse, to Steve, to me.

"The police took them away the night you came in," I explained.

"What about my ring?" Leslie rubbed the naked ring finger on her left hand.

"I have it," I answered. "It's at home with your wallet and your beeper and cell phone." I added the last three without being asked.

Leslie gave a slight nod, slipping back into silence for the wheelchair run across the parking lot.

The nurse settled Leslie into the Ranger, tucking a borrowed hospital blanket over her legs as she did. "All set," she said and slammed the door.

Leslie said nothing, and the nurse laughed. "Discharge jitters," she mouthed to the two of us. "Even doctors get them."

Steve walked me around the truck. "She's still having a lot of pain. I gave her a couple of Percocet earlier this morning, but she'll need some more when she gets home. Try and get her to take a couple, Ginny."

I said I would and dropped the small bottle he gave me into my shoulder bag.

I tried a nice-day-to-be-going-home line of patter as we exited the parking lot, but Leslie wasn't buying. Taking the hint, I concentrated on the traffic. Several blocks passed in what I was beginning to feel was an uncomfortable silence.

"I want to go by the apartment and pick up some clothes," Leslie said at last.

"I don't—"

"I feel fine." She had anticipated my protest, but her pale face and bright eyes belied her words.

Leslie caught me looking at her.

"Please, Ginny, I can't go around in scrubs forever." She fanned her lab coat for emphasis.

I waged a should-I-or-shouldn't-I battle. Should I won.

There was an empty parking place beside the Mazda. Leslie's eyes fixed on the gray sedan, and she was out of the truck before the motor stopped turning.

"Do you have the keys?" she demanded.

I dug through my shoulder bag and dropped them into her outstretched hand.

The odor of ammonia and pine spilled out as Leslie opened the door.

"There was a lot of blood," I explained. "I had it cleaned."

Leslie slammed the door shut and pocketed the keys. "I'll drive it over to your place when we finish here."

"Someone from the office can drive it over," I argued.

"I can do it myself." Jaw set, Leslie headed for the building's rear entrance.

Realizing I'd lost another round, I hurried after her.

The hall outside the apartment looked deceptively normal. Inside, it was a different story, and even though the cleaning crew had been there, I heard Leslie gasp.

"You said the apartment had been broken into, but this?" She stopped beside the gutted couch and ran a shaky hand over a nearby end table. "Where are the lamps?"

"Broken," I said.

Her face was an unreadable mask, and I could only guess as to how much was being absorbed.

"Where was the body?" Her eyes roamed the empty spaces where the furniture had once been.

I pointed to where I had heard the bubble gum pops, where I had seen the two men come together, and where Williams's body had lain.

Leslie moved farther into the room, stopping beside the reddish-brown stain that marked the carpet. She looked at it but said nothing. Shaking her head, she walked into the kitchen.

Her blue-violet eyes, the only color in her chalky face, darted restlessly from side to side. This room had also been swept and straightened. Drawers were in place and cabinet doors shut. Along one wall sat several plastic sacks filled with debris, and the scent of ammonia and pine, though not as strong here as in the Mazda, wrinkled our noses.

Leslie crossed to the counter where the brass candlesticks and sculptured figurines that had once graced the mantel sat crowded together. She swayed, reached for the counter.

"Leslie!" I pushed her into the nearest chair and shoved her head to her knees. Her color was slow to improve, but her breathing sounded less ragged.

"You stay here," I commanded. "I'll get your clothes."

She shook her head, but this was one argument I was not going to lose.

Ordering her to remain seated, I hurried down the hall to the master bedroom. Several closed doors along the way begged to be opened, but I ignored their pleas. Whatever lay behind them could wait until later.

I pulled the smaller of two suitcases from a closet in the mirrored dressing room. The clean-up crew had not been here. Along with the clutter, the black and red Jaguar still graced the glass surface.

I gave my artwork a passing glance, then stopped and took another look. One of the mirrored panels had slipped sideways, separating a headlight from the grill.

I ran my fingers along the edge, attempted to push it into place. To my surprise, the panel moved farther sideways, revealing a safe with its door ajar.

I pulled the door wide. What appeared to be a small charm or maybe a pendant and a crumpled piece of paper lay inside.

I pulled both from the safe. The pendant—it was bigger than a charm—was a silver unicorn with a broken horn. I recognized it immediately, and when I last saw it, it had been on Uncle David's key ring.

I smoothed the paper. Written on it was a Bogotá, Colombia, address. I didn't recognize the address. The writing was Uncle David's.

My mind reeled. How long had the unicorn been here? The paper with the address? Who put it here? Uncle David? Who lived in Colombia? A friend? A business associate? Another thief?

I wrapped the address around the unicorn and shoved both back into the safe, closed the door and pushed the panel into place. I couldn't think about it now. Truth was, I didn't want to think about it at all.

I reined in my runaway emotions and looked around, wondered what if anything I could salvage for Leslie's use. His and hers underwear hung from broken lampshades, and sweaters hid with shirts and blouses in the corners of the room. A pair of slacks tried to hang on a hanger, while jeans lost themselves in a tangle of bedclothes and gutted pillows.

What had Williams or his murderer been looking for? Drugs? Money? Whatever it was, they had been thorough, thorough enough to find a safe I'd known nothing about.

I stuffed what remained of the toiletries and a few needed basics into the suitcase and headed back to the kitchen. Leslie's face had more color, but not enough to make me stop worrying. I wanted to get her home, fast.

She was quiet in the elevator, but found her voice in the parking lot. The words were not to my liking.

"I'm driving the Mazda," she said. She pulled the keys from her pocket and headed towards the gray sedan.

"Leslie, I don't—"

"You lead, and I'll follow," she called over her shoulder.

I studied the slender, frail-looking girl, knowing I could, if I chose, take the keys from her. Instead, I watched as she adjusted the seat to fit her short legs and started the engine.

"Well?" Her voice demanded obedience.

I obeyed.

Zeus and Hera welcomed Leslie with loud purrs and much leg rubbing.

She scooped the pair into her arms and buried her face in a tangle of tails and dark-booted feet. "I'm so glad to see you," she purred in a voice nearly identical to theirs.

"Do you want to lie down?" I asked.

She curled into a corner of the couch and sighed contentedly. "I think I'll just stay here." She repositioned the cats and tucked her legs under her.

"What has Ginny been feeding you? You're fat as little pigs." Leslie ran practiced fingers over the cats' tan bodies.

"Canned cat food," I said, "and I only fed them when they were hungry."

"They're always hungry," Leslie admonished.

I ignored the rebuke and carried her suitcase into the spare bedroom, returning with a glass of water and the bottle of Percocet.

"Steve said to give you a couple of these when you got home."

"Are you playing nurse now?" Leslie smiled, her first real smile of the day.

"No, just concerned friend."

Her eyes met mine as she took the water and the pills. "You really are that, Ginny."

"Take your medicine, or I'll call the doctor," I threatened.

"Gone," she said handing back the glass.

I looked at her hand. "Do you want your ring now?"

She massaged her ring finger with her thumb, a thing I'd seen her do earlier. "I would like it," she said.

I retrieved the envelope and handed it to her. "Your wallet's in there, too, along with your beeper and cell phone and so is Bryan's ring."

"Bryan's ring?" She gave me a questioning look.

"You must have had it with you when you were admitted," I said.

Leslie rummaged through the oversized envelope and pulled out the larger of the two rings. She stared at it for several seconds, then balled her fist around it.

"Bryan—" she moaned the name softly. "He left it in the bathroom. He was always taking it off . . . I was going to give it to him."

The words stopped, only to be replaced by noisy, gut-rending sobs.

Chapter Twenty-Two

I LEFT LESLIE TO HER GRIEF AND WENT INTO THE KITCHEN. I STARED OUT THE WINDOW AT NOTHING FOR several minutes and then, tired of the nothingness, started a pot of coffee. Not that I especially wanted any, but the diversion kept my hands busy and my mind quiet. The Siamese pair had added their cries to Leslie's, but eventually the three quieted.

I chanced a look. Nestled beside Leslie's pale face lay twin brown and tan heads. She stirred once, then settled back. She was asleep. I punched the office number into the telephone. Speaking quietly, I told Thelma we were home.

"How's the patient doing?" she asked.

"Too much," I answered truthfully.

"Poor child, she should be resting."

I could see Thelma's head shake.

"She needs someone to look after her."

"Being alone will be tough," I agreed.

Thelma snorted. "If you're referring to that husband of hers, she's better off without him."

"What do you mean?" I bit my tongue. Why had I asked that question? Now wasn't the time to discuss Bryan's faults.

"I'm talking about his running around. Believe me, Leslie knew all about it."

"She told you?" I believed Thelma. What I didn't believe was that Leslie had told her. The reticent surgeon hadn't struck me as the type to share confidences.

"She told me," Thelma answered in a voice that brooked no argument. "She would stop by the office on her days off. We got to be friends. Being new in town, she didn't have many. When she told me what he was up to, I suggested she get someone to tail the bastard."

"Did she?"

Thelma sighed. "She never said." Papers shuffled in the background. "You only have one appointment this afternoon, and I can change that," Thelma said.

We discussed possible dates and times, said our good-byes and hung up. So, despite Leslie's super-surgeon facade, she had sought out someone to talk to, someone to give her advice. I stole another look into the living room. Had they, Thelma and Leslie, talked about Bryan's cocaine habit, I wondered? I brought an extra blanket from the back bedroom and draped it over the sleeping girl, being careful not to disturb either Zeus or Hera.

Leslie stirred, tucked her hand beneath her cheek. Bryan's ring, too big for the finger that wore it, had slipped over her knuckle.

"Poor girl," I whispered, echoing Thelma's sentiments.

I poured a cup of coffee and debated calling Steve. Knowing he was probably scrubbed or making rounds, I decided against it. Though playing nursemaid made me feel virtuous, I also felt lonely. Reach out and touch someone? Like hell you can, not if he's a surgical resident at Mercy Hospital.

I drank the last of the coffee that, by then, was as cold as I felt and headed for the bathroom. Transferring my emotional energy into productive channels, I emptied the hamper of its load of dirty clothes, carried them to the basement and loaded the washer. I reclimbed the stairs. Back again in the kitchen, I checked the fridge. Leftover pork, some rice and fresh carrots would do for supper.

Next I emptied Leslie's suitcase, hanging and folding as necessary before making another trip to the basement to switch the clothes from washer to dryer. My houseguest and her furry friends were still sleeping when I came back upstairs. My up, down, back and forth had not disturbed them at all.

Domesticity has its charms, especially when you're working off a head of steam, but I'd been charmed enough. I resurrected a legal pad from the hutch in the dining room and found a number two lead pencil in a jar with several others on the kitchen counter beside the telephone. Despite the laptop sitting on my desk in the bedroom, I still preferred pencil and paper to a computer for initial drafts, and so armed, had every intention of settling down to work, but thoughts of the silver unicorn with its broken horn and the crumpled address got in my way.

"Bogotá, Colombia." With the pencil, I jotted down the address that had imprinted itself on my memory earlier that day. I stared at what I had written. As hard as I thought, and I'd been racking my brain since first seeing the address, I had no memory of Uncle David either having mentioned being in Colombia or knowing anyone who lived in Bogotá.

I doodled a unicorn below the address. This was something I did remember. It was a memory from long ago, yet one that came readily to mind.

I was a little girl again, with very red hair and a liberal sprinkle of freckles over my cheeks and nose. The silver unicorn was in my hand, its horn long and sharp. I was standing in front of the window in Uncle David's office, staring at the wide wooden sill, at its smooth, unblemished surface.

Thelma had discovered the misdeed, but Uncle David had delivered the spanking. Though darkened by age now, my initials were still there.

My fingers curled around an imagined unicorn. Among the many memories I had of Uncle David, some, like this one, as painful as this one was, were worth keeping.

I turned to a fresh page. It was time to put the thoughts that had been running through my head since my talk with M&M on paper.

I listed first such items as family and social history, school records, work history, and character witnesses.

Kevin Titus, a sixteen-year-old black male . . . The pages filled rapidly.

The dryer in the basement buzzed. I left the dining room table, returning to my bedroom with an armload of folded clothes.

Unfortunately, the thirty-eight with its box of bullets and cleaning kit had usurped the space previously held by the pile of newly washed sweaters. I balanced the load on the edge of the dresser, reached down and attempted to pick up the gun. The sweaters slipped off the dresser's edge and fell in a heap on the floor. Shaking my head at my ineptness, I stooped to the level of the drawer—it was a bottom drawer—and rearranged the drawer's contents.

"So, you really are a private detective, or do lawyers carry guns?"

"I thought you were sleeping." Unexpected as it was, the sound of Leslie's voice had startled me.

Leslie laughed. "Well, I'm awake now, and would you believe hungry?"

Behind her, the cats added their demands. It was time to switch hats from washwoman to cook.

I went back to work the following day, leaving Leslie alone. Not that Leslie would be alone all day. Wicki was bringing lunch and had promised to stay through the afternoon.

As usual, Thelma was already at her desk.

"Have you seen Kevin?" I asked, handing her yesterday's homework.

"Last night," she said, following me into the inner office.

"How's he doing?"

"Says he's sorry. Wishes he hadn't done it." Thelma shook her head. "Such a damn silly thing to do."

"Speaking of silly things. Do you remember the silver unicorn Uncle David had on his key ring?"

Thelma nodded. "The one you used to carve your initials in that window-sill."

Like metal to a magnet, our eyes were drawn to the sill.

"I found it in a safe in the dressing room." I turned my back on the window. "Must be he didn't want to carry any unnecessary memories with him."

I pointed to the top page of my notes. "That address was in the safe with the unicorn. Do you recognize it?"

"Bogotá, Colombia." Thelma frowned. "The only thing I know about Colombia is that they grow beans, coffee and cocoa."

"The address," I repeated, refusing to be sidetracked. "Do you recognize it?"

"It doesn't look familiar, but I can check through the old files and see if anything pops up."

Thelma squared her shoulders and shuffled through my scrawled notes. "I sure wish you'd use your laptop." Head wagging, she started for her office.

I ignored the computer bit, a smoke screen for her frustrated anger at the world at large, namely Uncle David and Kevin, and picked up the telephone. With a little luck I should be able to improve the Titus family's lot in life.

I punched in a number. The phone rang on the other end.

"This is Regina Arthur," I said when a voice answered. "I'd like to speak to Michael Loeb."

I doodled on the ever-present legal pad while I waited.

"Ginny," a familiar voice said. "What can I do for you?"

"I'm working on a case I think might interest you," I said.

"Oh?" Mickey sounded interested, but as behooved a Marion City District Attorney, not too interested.

"I'm representing Kevin Titus, Mickey." I held my breath, inserting a pause. "My client has some information on a couple of cases you're working on."

"Is this official?"

"Official."

"Hummm . . . Okay, give me a minute to check my calendar."

I'd finished a line of snowmen and had started on a row of snow angels when Mickey came back on the line.

"Are you thinking a deal, Ginny?"

"If the terms are right," I said.

I heard pages turning.

"About four this afternoon?"

"Four is fine." I kept the smile on my face from sounding in my voice. He was hooked.

I left the office at three-thirty, getting a quirked eyebrow from Thelma when she caught me reapplying my makeup. I ignored her. A girl was entitled to use all the ammunition she had.

Once, under the pressure of law school, when he had been in his third year at Marion State and I in my first, Michael Aaron Loeb had been my almost lover, but that was before Steve and a long time ago. Still . . .

I pulled into the lot adjoining the municipal building. With the past in mind, I gave myself a final check. The bruise under my eye looked only slightly yellow today, and as Steve had removed the last of the stitches yesterday morning before leaving for the hospital, the scar above it was but a thin red line. Cover Girl and the medical profession could still work small miracles.

I wiped the frown from my face, teased some curls over the scar near my ear and walked into the building.

Mickey Loeb's office was on the fourth floor, one of a row of offices reserved for Marion City's cadre of assistant district attorneys. A secretary looked up as I entered, and at my request buzzed the unseen Mickey.

"Ginny," His familiar voice called from down the hall.

Deepening the smile I had fixed in place, I walked into the lion's den.

"You look great," he greeted. His arm circled my shoulders and hugged tight. "It's been a long time."

I edged between him and the door and squeezed into his office.

"It's not much, but it's a start." Mickey waved his hand over the desk, a filing cabinet, and three chairs.

"You have a window." I pointed to the status symbol, which in the corporate structure of city government meant nearly as much as a promotion.

He took my hands. "It's been too long, Ginny."

I pulled free. "You're looking good." And he did look good. Slim, an inch or two taller than me, with gray-green eyes and blonde, very curly hair cut establishment short. His gray pin-stripe suit looked expensive, family money no doubt, and his wire-framed glasses from law school days had been replaced with contact lenses. He was a man on his way up.

Mickey walked around the desk and settled into a swivel chair. I settled into one of two straight-backed chairs, wiggled myself comfortable, and sharpened my arguments. I had no intention of being one of his stepping-stones.

"Coffee?" he asked, his finger poised above the intercom.

"Coke?" I asked.

He gave me a whatever-you-want smile and buzzed a waiting secretary. "So, to what do I owe this visit?"

We both knew he knew, but politics demanded we play the game. "I'm representing Kevin Titus," I said.

He frowned. "The name's not familiar. Care to tell me more?"

The door opened behind me, and two Cokes appeared on the desk. I smiled my thanks at the departing secretary and waited for the door to close behind her.

"He was one of the young men charged with possession Sunday morning."

"Oh, yes, the group from the Halloween party."

"He was there, and he has some information about a couple of cases your office is working on. You might be interested in hearing him out."

Mickey pulled a silver ballpoint toward him and rolled it between his fingers.

"And what makes you think I might be interested?"

I took a sip of Coke. "One of your detectives has been nosing around. If he's interested, I'm sure you are."

"You mentioned something on the phone about a deal."

I nodded. "I want you to drop the charges against my client."

"You want me to drop charges against a known user and probable dealer?"

"Hold it, Mickey. Let's not jump the gun. First, you have no proof he's a user, and second, what's this dealer crap?"

Mickey's hands shot up, palms out. "Okay, okay, I'll forget the dealer, but not the user charge."

"My client was charged with only one thing, possession, and you haven't proven that."

"Ginny," he said softly. "We have it on film."

"What you have is a videotape of him accepting something."

"He paid money for it. As you know, that was on the tape, too."

"What was he buying, Mickey?"

"Drugs. The blowups made that obvious." He pointed his ballpoint at me.

"What's obvious is that he gave someone money. What he bought has not and can not be established because you don't have whatever it was you think he bought."

Mickey pushed back and opened the drawer in front of him.

I watched as several pictures of Kevin appeared. It wasn't the only thing Mickey had secreted in his Pandora's box.

"You were saying . . . " Mickey dropped a plastic bag filled with irregularly shaped gray stones on top of Kevin's picture. "No need for you to ask, Ginny. I'll tell you. This was part of what was confiscated at Marfield Park last Thursday night."

I smiled, more for my benefit than his. "That doesn't prove anything."

"Maybe."

I spread my hands wide. "I'm still asking, asking you to drop the charges against Kevin Titus."

"And if I do?"

I laid my forearm on his desk and leaned closer, bit my tongue and repeated, "Kevin gives you the information."

"Possession?"

"Possession," I answered. My eyes locked on his. "I'm not out for blood, Mickey. Kevin has the information, and I guarantee he's neither a user nor a dealer."

"As if you'd say anything different."

"It's not just me. I can produce any number of people, teachers, his basketball coach, his minister. Everyone who knows him will swear Kevin's a decent kid."

"Decent kids don't buy drugs, Ginny."

Preferring to err on the side of too few words, I said nothing.

Mickey Loeb hesitated, as if considering the point. "This is his first offense?" he asked finally.

"And his last." I crossed mental fingers. I was out on a limb, but I was convinced it was a sturdy limb.

"Okay, let's see what we have, first offense, a good kid who comes with a guarantee to sin no more, and some information to trade."

I nodded. "Good summary, counselor."

"I listen well, Ginny." His eyes narrowed, and he pursed his lips. "Well enough to know you haven't said a damn thing about what you're willing to trade. I'm not about to buy the proverbial pig in a poke."

I studied his face. Mickey meant what he said. Well, here goes, M&M, and putting all my eggs in one basket, blurted, "Kevin can place Bryan Parker, the man who was killed at the Riverside Motel last Wednesday night, with Tim Williams, who strangely enough managed to get himself killed in Parker's apartment a couple of nights later."

Mickey toyed with his pen. "Can he give us names, places?"

"Depends on how sweet the deal is."

Mickey drained his can of Coke. "I'll check with higher-ups and get back with you."

He stood and came around the desk. "By the way, you never did say which detective was nosing around."

I stood. We were quite close. "You're right. I didn't say."

Mickey traced the scar over my eye. "Was it Douglas MacPhearson by any chance?"

Chapter Twenty-Three

I FIXED A NONCOMMITTAL SMILE IN PLACE AND GOT THE HELL OUT OF MICKEY LOEB'S OFFICE. The two of them had worked this together, had guessed I would try to make a deal. Hell, MacPhearson had even suggested it. Unable to get what he wanted with a frontal attack—and getting me into bed was probably what that was all about—he'd drafted Mickey and caught me in a pincer movement.

I hit the accelerator. The Ranger jumped forward, beating out another Ford. Kevin and I were pawns, stepping-stones for yet another man on the way up. Through us MacPhearson could get to Williams and Parker, and from there to Maxwell and Sands.

I filled the cab of the truck with a barrage of four-letter words. The how-could-I-have-been-so-stupid variety I saved for me and directed the vilest at the redheaded detective.

The sun had begun to set, and a slight breeze stirred the leafless branches of the trees that lined Valley Avenue. My anger, though, made me impervious to the charms of the balmy November afternoon.

The bungalow beckoned. Home at last, with little realization of how I'd arrived there, I pulled in the driveway behind the Mazda, parked and slammed the Ranger's door. It made a resoundingly loud bang.

Hera wrapped her sleek self around my legs, while Zeus maintained his usual cross-eyed stoicism. Leslie, dressed in civvies today, smiled brightly from the couch.

She must be feeling better. The thought almost registered, but fled quickly.

"I've decided to blackmail you, Ginny." Leslie's smile broadened.

"Blackmail?" I dropped my shoulder bag on the floor and myself into the room's only overstuffed chair, too busy plotting revenge to see the smile or recognize the laughter in her voice.

Leslie's smile became a smirk. "If the number of your male admirers is any indication, you're a prime candidate."

Male admirers? Prime candidate? What was Leslie talking about? In answer to my unasked question, Leslie held up an imaginary list. "Mickey Loeb called and wants you to return his call," she read. "MacPhearson called, ditto the message, and . . ." her voice dropped to a stage whisper, ". . . Steve called and will call back later."

I opened my mouth, but Leslie's raised hand stopped me.

"You haven't heard it all yet. Another man called, a couple of times, in fact. Only he didn't leave a message. Just asked for you. When I told him you weren't home, he hung up."

"If it's important, he'll call back." The answer disappointed Leslie, but I was in no mood for games.

"Is Steve aware of the competition?" Leslie cooed sweetly.

I shook my head, not in denial but total confusion. What was the woman talking about?

"Ah-ha." Brows raised, eyes wide, Leslie crowed gleefully.

Mickey Loeb? Douglas MacPhearson? Some unknown voice on the telephone? Leslie's list of would-be admirers ran through my mind. "Steve doesn't know because there isn't any," I said flatly.

Leslie's mouth drooped. I ignored her. My mind was in turmoil.

MacPhearson? Mickey Loeb? The names repeated in my head. I'd expected one of them to call. Someone had to reel the sucker in, but not both and certainly not this soon. Maybe I wasn't such a sure thing after all. The thought was a much-needed face-saver, and I held onto it.

Leslie cupped her chin in her hand. "You mean I can't blackmail you?"

The telephone interrupted her laughter. Eager to escape the maddening conversation, I answered the phone.

"Ginny. This is Mickey Loeb."

I readied myself to fight or, denied this, to keep him guessing.

"I've talked to John Doran." Mickey named the city's chief prosecutor. "He's willing to drop the possession charge against Kevin Titus if he will talk to MacPhearson."

"He'll talk to him," I said. My hold tightened on the receiver. I'd been right. The two of them were in this hand-and-glove.

"It has to be tonight. Can you arrange it?"

"I can arrange it, but I'll need a fax confirming our agreement before the meeting."

"Done. I'll have MacPhearson call you."

"Good news, Ginny?" Leslie's impish smile was gone, but her color was high and her eyes still sparkled.

"The DA is willing to drop the possession charge against Kevin." I ran shaky fingers through my hair. Victory was sweet. I had tasted it, and I liked it.

"Kevin? Possession?" Leslie asked. Her brow furrowed and confusion sounded in her voice.

I dropped back into the chair. My God, I hadn't told her about Kevin, about Williams, or about Bryan. Where to begin, where to begin?

She leaned forward, waiting. I caught the quick intake of breath, saw the rapid rise and fall of her chest. My God, had I caused a relapse?

Knowing I had to tell her, and tell her quickly, I began at the beginning. "Did MacPhearson show you the videotape I shot at the Halloween party?"

Leslie nodded, and I told her what I knew about clowns, pirates, Kevin Titus and Tim Williams, and about Bryan.

"And the DA's willing to drop the possession charge against Kevin?" Leslie asked. Her breathing had slowed and she stroked Hera's back as she talked.

I nodded my head.

Doubt clouded Leslie's eyes. She stopped stroking, causing a disgruntled "meow" from a discontented cat.

The telephone rang again, interrupting another conversation. It was who I expected it would be.

"Ginny, Mickey Loeb said he talked to you," MacPhearson said.

"He did." I suppressed the "damn you" I very much wanted to add.

"Can you arrange it?"

"My office in an hour."

"I'll be there."

I hit the disconnect, found Kevin's number and punched it in. Pearl Titus answered. I gave her the good news, then told her about the meeting.

"Thank you, God." Her voice quivered. "We'll bring Kevin to your office."

This time I didn't argue. She had a right to be there.

"Do the police know who killed Williams?" Leslie asked.

I was back in the living room, picking up my shoulder bag.

"I don't know," I said.

Leslie stared at the television with unfocused eyes. Her strong surgeon's fingers kneaded Hera's back. Dead husbands. Drugs. Dead pushers. How much more could she take? I left the house vowing to do anything, everything I could to make her world whole again.

"You back?" Oscar asked as he let me in the rear door.

"Another late meeting," I explained. "Has anyone shown up yet?"

"Haven't seen anyone but you, Miss Arthur." His smile rearranged the wrinkles on his face. "Do they know to come around to the back?" The door opened in answer to his question.

"Ginny." Pete circled me with his arms and hugged me tight. "I can't tell you how thankful we are."

Pearl Titus crowded close, her cheeks wet with tears. Kevin stood behind her, his smile tentative but there. He stepped in as his brother stepped back and gave me a nervous hug.

"Hold on," I protested. "This is no done deal. A lot depends on what happens here tonight."

"Hello."

The four of us fell silent as MacPhearson came through the door. The impromptu celebration was over.

We rode the elevator in silence. Upstairs, I directed Kevin into my office and waved the other three into the waiting area.

I checked the fax machine. The agreement was there. Reading as I went, I joined Kevin.

The lighted room repeated itself in the dark window, showing Uncle David's desk, the swivel chair that squeaked, and an unhappy Kevin.

I resisted the impulse to run my finger over the initials carved into the windowsill, a thing I had not done in years. I sighed, both for the little girl I used to be and the teenage boy who now sat in front of me.

"What did your mom tell you about this meeting, Kevin?" I asked.

"She said the District Attorney would drop the possession charge if I talked to the police." He inclined his head towards the closed door. "Is he the one?"

"He's the one, but I want to go over a couple of things first."

I leaned forward, meeting and holding his eyes. "When I talked to the DA, I promised him two things. First, that you would answer any questions the police asked about Williams and Bryan Parker, and second, that you'd stay out of trouble."

Kevin shuffled uneasily, his knuckles white against the arms of the chair.

"Clear?" I asked.

"Clear," he said.

"And if they ask about Johnny?" I asked.

"I'll do what I have to do," Kevin answered.

"Sounds good to me." I gave him an encouraging smile. "Ready?"

"I guess so." Kevin tried a smile. It didn't fit, and he abandoned it.

The smell of freshly brewed coffee met me when I opened the door to the outer office.

"Want a cup?" MacPhearson asked.

I was inclined to refuse anything the detective had to offer, but the happy faces of the mother and son decided me otherwise.

Cup in hand, I resettled myself behind the desk. MacPhearson took the chair next to Kevin and settled in as easily as he had the night before. A notebook appeared from inside his jacket pocket. "Standard procedure," he said, balancing it on his knee.

"You're not going to record this?" It was difficult to hide my surprise, as I was sure he would.

"I'll leave that for the big guns downtown. This is just a get-acquainted session."

I didn't believe a word MacPhearson said, and even suspected he might be wearing a wire under the dark gray-green suit he seemed to favor, but let the matter drop.

With a beginning smile, MacPhearson turned and faced Kevin. "I saw you play basketball last year." The detective's smile broadened. "You were damn good."

"Thanks." Kevin made an effort to return the smile.

"Never was much of a player myself, just wasn't quite fast enough." MacPhearson flipped open his notebook.

Kevin's smile vanished, and he went back to white-knuckling the arms of the chair.

"How about we start with you telling me about Tim Williams."

"You mean the guy who was selling drugs at the Halloween party?"

MacPhearson frowned. "I thought you knew him."

"I didn't know his name until Miss Arthur told me."

The two parried questions back and forth, until MacPhearson was satisfied that Kevin could identify Williams as the pirate drug dealer. I took an easier breath. We were off and running, and Kevin was doing just fine.

"What else do you know about Williams?" MacPhearson prodded.

Kevin shifted, then settled in his chair. "You mean what I told Miss Arthur?"

"I don't know what you told Miss Arthur."

"You mean besides his selling drugs?"

"You tell me."

Kevin wet his lips. "I told her that he knew the guy who was killed at the Riverside Motel last week, that I'd seen the two of them together."

"And what two is that?" MacPhearson asked.

"Mr. Parker and Tim Williams," Kevin said.

"How was it you knew Parker?" MacPhearson scribbled in his notebook, turned the page and picked up his coffee.

"Mrs. Riggs introduced us. I met him a couple of times here in the office. He came in when I was in here with Pete."

Again MacPhearson frowned. "Mrs. Riggs?" He set his coffee cup on the edge of the desk and pushed it away from him.

"My secretary," I explained. "Pete, Kevin's brother, is her son-in-law."

MacPhearson nodded, ran an eye over his notes and then asked, "Were you the only one to see the two of them together?"

Kevin's eyes fastened on mine. I nodded.

"I showed the picture of Parker, the one that was in the paper, to a friend of mine." Kevin paused, licked his lips. "He remembered seeing them together, too."

"Does your friend have a name?"

Kevin studied his hands. "Johnny Martinez."

"Did Martinez introduce you to Williams?"

Again Kevin shifted uneasily. "Johnny and me were together the first time I saw Williams. He was with a bunch of guys. Most of them, the guys, were from South Side."

"Do you know the names of any of the guys from South Side?"

Kevin shook his head. "No," he said. "I don't know any of their names."

"Like it was with Williams?"

Kevin's brows knitted.

"You didn't know his name, either."

Kevin said nothing.

MacPhearson brought his hand to his face, rubbed the sides of his nose. "Let's see. You knew Parker and Williams, and both you and this friend of yours, Johnny Martinez, saw them together."

"I knew Parker, and Johnny and me saw him with Williams."

"How many times did you see them together?"

"Three, four times."

"And Johnny was with you every time?"

"Only a couple of times, I think."

"Where did you see them?"

"No place special, just around."

"You'll have to do better than that, Kevin."

Kevin rubbed his forehead. "Outside here once in the parking lot and another time in the mall near the fountain, and then once or twice riding around in that car of Parker's, a Jaguar. I don't remember where exactly."

MacPhearson slumped further into the chair, catching his notebook on its way to the floor. "And which of these times was Johnny with you?"

"Once when they were in the Jag together. I remember because we talked about the car. Then again in the mall, I think."

"How long have you known Johnny?"

"A long time." Kevin stared at the floor.

"Do you trust him?"

"He's my friend," Kevin answered.

MacPhearson leaned forward. "Then, I guess I'd better find Johnny and have a talk with him."

Kevin's hands shot out. "No! Please, you can't do that. He'll think I dissed him."

MacPhearson shook his head. "I don't think so, Kevin. If you and Johnny saw Parker and Williams together, others did, too."

Kevin dropped his hands, and MacPhearson smiled. "You did good, kid, real good."

The notebook disappeared into MacPhearson's pocket as he headed for the door. "See you around, Red," he called over his shoulder.

I said nothing.

"Did I really do okay?" Kevin asked.

"You did a fine job, Kevin. But it's what you do tomorrow and the next day that counts."

Kevin chewed his lower lip. "Yeah, I know."

Oscar let the four of us out, and the Ranger took me home. Leslie was still on the couch, and the cats still kept her company.

The television showed an aerial dogfight. Though the sound was muted, the sudden bursts of flames and the agonized looks on the faces of the pilots spoke volumes.

Leslie stirred, disturbed no doubt by the sound of my arrival.

"I've been sitting here, thinking," she said.

I started to ask what, but something in her face warned against it.

Chapter Twenty-Four

Leslie squared her shoulders. Her back stiffened, became ramrod straight. "Damn you, Bryan Parker."

It was the explosion I had expected, the one instinct had warned was coming.

Leslie pounded the cushion, each blow sending a puff of dust into the air. "You ruined my life when you were alive, and damn it all, you're still doing it."

Her face turned a blotchy red, her eyes dark pools that roamed restlessly around the room.

"I put up with his whoring, but drugs . . ."

The cats had long since abandoned her, but fool that I was, I held my ground.

"I can't stand it anymore," she wailed. "I just can't stand it." Her chest heaved. Her eyes found mine and locked on. "Williams, or whatever you said his name was, came to the apartment looking for drugs. Bryan probably had a private stash, his maybe, or maybe stolen. It had to be that. What else would a drug dealer be looking for?" Her mouth quivered. "Or maybe he decided to cut himself in for a bigger share of the loot. That sounds like something Bryan would do, become a pusher or a dealer or whatever the hell it is they call themselves. Oh God . . ."

"Leslie." Hand extended, I moved forward.

"No!" She sprang from the couch. "I don't want your sympathy. What I want is the truth." She grew quiet. It was the quiet that precedes a storm. "You knew, didn't you? You've always known," she accused.

"You're right, Leslie. I knew Bryan used drugs," I admitted. "Dr. Beller told me after he did the post."

Leslie's expression changed from anger to vindication.

"I'm sorry," I said.

"Why should you be sorry!" Tears washed from her eyes. "Will it never end? Oh God, will it never end?"

She moved again, and like the cats I sought a place of refuge.

She paced the floor in quick, angry steps. "The police think I know something, or worse, think I'm part of whatever it is Bryan was involved in. That redheaded detective has been driving up and down the street all day." She raised her fists, pounded the air over her head. "Why did I always protect him? Everyone said Bryan was no good."

I had no words to offer.

Sleep eluded the Valley Avenue house that night. Caught in a prison of tangled sheets, I heard the floorboards creak as Leslie paced, heard the meows of feline conversation from the cats who shared her vigil.

Morning came, bringing with it an excuse to leave my bed. I showered, skipped breakfast, and debated leaving Leslie alone.

"I can sleep now, Ginny," she argued, "and Wicki will be here at noon."

I studied the dark-haired girl, decided to believe her, and left the house. I'd check with her later and if it was necessary get Wicki to come early.

Thelma and a box of Dunkin' Donuts met me at the office.

"I felt like celebrating," she said, handing me a chocolate-covered fried cake. "You sure worked a miracle in the happiness department. If there'd been a fatted calf in the Tituses' house, it'd be one dead cow by now."

I laughed at Thelma's effusive compliment and popped in the last of the fried cake. Though satisfied with the outcome of last night's meeting, I was still angry at having been manipulated by a redheaded detective and a smooth talking assistant DA.

I licked chocolate from my fingers and helped myself to a glazed doughnut. "Skipped breakfast this morning," I explained, using the explanation as an excuse for pigging out.

"Leslie had a bad night," I said. I washed down the doughnut with a mouthful of coffee. "I told her about Kevin seeing Bryan with Williams, and it didn't take her long to figure out Bryan was probably using drugs." Or worse, I thought but didn't say. "Everything was downhill after that. Neither of us got much sleep."

Thelma selected a prune Danish. "Bastard. Killing was too good for Bryan Parker." She broke off a corner of the gooey confection, frowning as she did. "Was Williams looking for drugs when he broke into the apartment?"

I shrugged my shoulders. "That or money, but I'm betting on drugs. Bryan had to have a stash somewhere," I argued, borrowing from Leslie's logic. "Dr. Beller said he was a heavy user."

"Speaking of drugs," Thelma wiped her sticky fingers on a napkin. "About that address you wanted me to check out?"

"The one in Bogotá?" I said.

"No luck on the address, but I did find something that might interest you."

"Which is," I prompted, knowing Thelma liked to be prompted.

"Your uncle installed the security system in the Sandcastle."

"The Sandcastle?"

"The Sandcastle. As in Victor Sands, Crime Boss, gambling, prostitution, drugs," Thelma explained.

"But we don't have a contract with Victor Sands," I protested.

"You're right. We don't. It was a one-time deal, installation only."

"Another one of Uncle David's deals?" I asked with a sigh.

"Could be. That man had a lot of hidden agendas."

A ringing telephone ended our coffee break. The rush of business that followed pushed the Parkers, Uncle David, Victor Sands and the Sandcastle to the back of my mind.

Lunch was another desktop quickie, and I played catch-up during the afternoon hours. Thelma left at four. She had promised to help Carol take Scooter and Peanut to the doctor. Quiet followed her leaving. I looked at the phone. It was time to report in.

"I talked to Michael Loeb yesterday," I said when M&M came on the line.

"Did you get what you wanted for your client?" she asked.

"I got what I wanted." I answered slowly, drawing out each word.

"You sound like you're not sure."

Was I or wasn't I? Yes or no?

"Is something bothering you, Ginny?"

"They set me up . . ." I rushed the explanation, filled the telephone line with angry words as I told of how I'd been manipulated.

"Did you get what you wanted for your client, Ginny?" Judge Marfield repeated. Our conversation had come full circle.

I thought of the plea agreement Mickey Loeb had faxed through last night. "The DA is going to drop the possession charge. It was the only thing they had and as far as this incident goes, they won't be looking for anything else."

"So relax and enjoy, Ginny, helping clients is what this game is all about."

We said our good-byes, and I replaced the receiver in its cradle. She was right, this woman who had been my mentor long before mentoring had come into vogue. Sometimes, though, her advice wasn't easy to take.

"Anyone home?" Another voice intruded. It was very loud, very male and very near.

I swung away from the window I'd been staring through since ending the conversation with Marsha Marfield. MacPhearson's large frame filled my doorway.

"How about closing up shop and having a drink with me?" he asked.

"No." I crossed my arms over my chest and rolled back from the desk, adding distance to my refusal. "A drink was not part of the deal."

"You sound angry," he said with nerve-wracking calm.

"Damn right, I am. After the way you and Mickey Loeb set me up, you've got a colossal nerve coming here." It was, I told myself, the understatement of the year.

I pushed the swivel chair aside, turned my back on my unwelcome visitor, and walked to the closet. I yanked at my coat collar, attempting to free the coat from the hanger. The collar caught, and the hanger clattered to the floor. As I bent to retrieve it, I felt a rush of conscience, followed by some unwanted common sense.

I slammed the closet door, tried to thwart the double-edged attack on my runaway emotions. It didn't work.

"Hell!" I turned to face him. "Yes, I'm mad." I relaxed my jaw, which had begun to hurt. "And don't you dare tell me you were just doing your job."

I jammed my arms through the coat sleeves, grabbed my shoulder bag, and started to lock up.

"I know a place on Leonard Street. It's on your way home." He grinned a wide grin, the one that made his lips disappear under his mustache.

I shook my head.

"I talked to Johnny Martinez today." He offered the information without fanfare.

I hesitated, turned it over in my mind.

"Tempted?" he asked.

"You know I am." I fought a go-don't-go battle with myself.

His grin disappeared. "Then have a drink with me."

Go won.

We crossed the Oswago River in tandem and together fought the after-work traffic to a hole-in-the-wall on Leonard Street. A hand-lettered BAR, back-lighted by a neon MILLER TIME, marked the place.

MacPhearson led us to a wooden booth near the rear entrance where an adjoining hall led to a wall-mounted telephone and a pair of johns. It was not quite dark and not quite light, with mingled smells that spoke of heavy-duty cleaning solutions, stale beer, sweaty men, and tobacco smoke.

I ran a hand over the cigarette-scarred tabletop. "How did you find this place?"

"It belongs to an old friend of mine."

"How old?" I looked at the high tin ceiling, its pressed design made indistinct from years of secondhand smoke, and the stained mirror that backed the bar.

His eyes followed mine. "Not that old," he said, "a buddy from my army days."

MacPhearson shrugged off a tan, fleece-lined car coat and tossed it into the booth. "What'll you have?"

"Make it a lite, Bud Lite, in a bottle," I said. "I have a patient at home that needs taking care of."

"So I hear," he said.

I shrugged out of my coat, a twin to MacPhearson's I noticed, and draped it across my shoulders. "She says you've been watching her. That you drove past the house several times today."

MacPhearson shook his head. "Not me."

"Then who?" My heart missed a beat. "One of Maxwell's hoods?"

"Could be. Want me to see what I can find out?"

"I want you to find out. Leslie's upset enough. She doesn't need someone following her around."

Kept company by rock playing several decibels too loud, I watched Mac-Phearson work his way through the crowd. The bartender gave him a welcoming grin and an over-the-shoulder look that included me. I scowled back. Business associates, maybe—a couple, never.

"You've talked to Johnny Martinez," I snapped when he returned.

MacPhearson lifted an eyebrow along with a long-necked Bud. "I did. He confirmed everything Titus said."

MacPhearson fitted his mouth to the opening and swallowed. "And according to Martinez, Parker and Williams spent considerable time together."

"Martinez must have spent considerable time with Williams as well." I kept my voice cool, reminded myself that MacPhearson was the enemy.

"You guessed that one right, Red. Claims he did gopher work for Williams, delivering and picking up."

"Delivering and picking up what?"

"Delivering some packages and picking up other packages, and before you ask, he didn't know what was in either."

"And you believed him?"

"I believed him. Curiosity killed the cat, remember?" He drained his Bud. "And Martinez didn't strike me as being stupid."

MacPhearson shook loose a Winston and lighted it. "I'm not stupid, either, Ginny. I know you don't want to be here, but as long as you are, can't you lighten up just a little?"

I waved away the cloud of smoke that followed his words and tried on a smile. What the hell, I'd made my point.

MacPhearson returned my smile. It was bigger and brighter than mine, and I felt my lips soften.

"You look better when you smile, Red."

I squirmed farther into my seat. "We were talking about Johnny Martinez."

"So we were." MacPhearson shifted sideways in the booth. "I think he's angling to cut himself a deal, something on the order of the one you got for Titus."

"What are his chances?"

Cigarette ash dropped to the table, and MacPhearson brushed it away.

"The kid's been a big help. He's put names to several faces on your video-tape, and we're still looking at other pictures and tapes that have come in." MacPhearson leaned closer. "You know, Ginny, if it hadn't been for Titus, we'd never have known about Martinez."

"Oh?"

MacPhearson laughed. "Yeah. The cameraman didn't do her job. Judging from what else I've seen, she missed quite a few of the partygoers."

"She did her best." I couldn't stop the grin. Sometimes being with him was . . . I shook off the thought.

"Did Martinez have anything else to say about Parker?"

"Said he ran an occasional errand with Williams, too."

"Probably needed the money to support his habit."

MacPhearson arched an eyebrow.

"Don't look so surprised. Beller told me Bryan was a heavy cocaine user."

MacPhearson nodded, stubbing out his cigarette in an already overflowing ashtray. "According to our young informant, though, running errands wasn't the only thing Parker did."

I went for a swallow of my Bud Lite, only to find I had none.

"He says Parker was pushing more drugs than Williams. Of course, that will take a lot of checking. The kid's word alone isn't worth much." MacPhearson picked up my empty. "I'll get us another round."

Bryan, a dealer? Maybe Leslie's guesses were not too far off the mark. I bothered a napkin that lay on the table and mulled the idea over. It wasn't one I particularly liked, but had to admit it fit. MacPhearson's return interrupted the thought.

"Did Martinez have anything to say about the ipecac being in the food?" I asked, switching topics.

"We talked about it. He thinks Williams was involved, but he wasn't sure."

"I was hoping—"

"So were a lot of us, Ginny, but don't give up so easily. Some of the others Martinez identified may know more."

I picked up my Bud Lite. It was cold and tasted good.

"We brought Maxwell downtown today." MacPhearson waved away a cloud of smoke, not his, an intruder's from a nearby table. "His lawyer wouldn't let him do much talking, but I managed to get in a couple of questions."

My mind's eye fixed on the Sandcastle's parking lot. "About that truck of his, I hope?"

MacPhearson shook his head. "About murder."

"Whose?"

"I thought you'd never ask." He grinned another of his lip-hiding-under-mustache grins.

"MacPhearson!" I slammed my beer against the table. Foam gurgled from the open top.

"Tim Williams's for starters, and I hope Bryan Parker's and Nancy Webber's."

"All three?" I couldn't hide my surprise.

"You saw him kill Williams, Ginny—"

"I didn't see Maxwell kill Williams," I corrected.

"You were there."

"Okay, I was there." I would argue the finer points later. "But how can you accuse him of killing Parker and his girlfriend? It was Williams, not Maxwell, who was at the motel. Williams shot Leslie, and she can identify him."

"True, but she didn't see him kill anyone, either." MacPhearson poked at the pile of wet napkins.

"What was Maxwell's motive?" I persisted.

"Money. Sex. Drugs. Take your pick."

I leaned over the table. "Do you think Maxwell supplied Parker with drugs?"

"I'm betting on Victor Sands, Mr. Numero Uno himself."

I sipped my beer, nursed it slowly. "Drugs, pushers, murderers." I heaved a long sigh. "What a mess."

"It's messier than you think, Ginny. Bryan Parker had AIDS."

"No!" I choked on my beer, coughed tears to my eyes.

MacPhearson handed me a fistful of napkins. "It's true. I saw the lab report today."

"I'm going home," I said. I could bear no more.

Leslie was asleep on the couch when I let myself in the front door. Beside her, both cats nestled peacefully. The television screen glared brightly, but as was her habit, she had muted the sound. The kitchen provided a bright oasis. Even though it was late, I started dinner, needing to fix on everyday things like white fish, green beans, potatoes—AIDS.

It wasn't long before Leslie joined me, drawn either by the smell of food cooking or dishes clattering. In this deceptively homey atmosphere, we talked of Hera and Zeus, the apartment, how she felt, but not of Bryan, drugs, Tim Williams, or AIDS.

"Oh, Ginny." Concern sounded in Leslie's voice.

I dropped the plate I was holding and watched it break into pieces.

"I forgot to tell you. Steve called. He wants you to call him."

She looked unhappy.

"It's okay," I said.

I punched in the hospital's number and listened to it ring. "Will you please page Dr. Brock?" I asked when it stopped.

"We don't page after nine," the operator who sounded very much like my henna-haired friend answered.

I looked at Mickey Mouse. Nine-fifteen.

"Will you beep him?"

Another voice, still not Steve's, came on the line. "I'm answering for Dr. Brock," it said. "He's making rounds and can't come to the phone now. May I take a message?"

Chapter Twenty-Five

ILEFT A MESSAGE FOR STEVE ASKING THAT HE CALL BACK AND HUNG UP.
"No luck?" Leslie asked.

"No luck," I admitted. I attempted a laugh. It failed, and I settled for, "Just like a doctor, never there when you want one."

While Leslie talked of nothing in particular, and I waited for Steve to return my call, the two of us picked our way through dinner. We finished finally, and I left the table to load the dishwasher. The familiar task failed to lift my spirits.

Fighting an almost overwhelming depression, I swung around to wipe the counter and knocked another plate into the sink.

"Hell!" I exclaimed. Fearing what my face might show, I concentrated on the broken plate. I had to get a hold of myself.

"Can I help?" Leslie asked.

I added the broken pieces to a rapidly filling wastebasket and shook my head.

Leslie continued to wipe an already dry frying pan. "I'm sorry about last night," she said. "I don't usually act like that."

"Forget it." I took the pan from her. "It takes time to get over what you've been through."

Hard as I tried, the tension continued to mount, and with each swipe of the dishrag, I fought the urge to shout, do you know, Leslie? Do you know?

Leslie yawned. "I think I'll turn in." She smiled a half smile. "I promise to stay in bed tonight."

I watched her go. How can I, anyone, tell you? I asked myself. The telephone saved me from having to answer the question.

It was Steve.

"I have the weekend off," he said, "but I won't be able to get loose until Saturday afternoon."

I said nothing, afraid of hearing more bad news.

"I offered to cover for one of the residents," Steve explained. "He wants to take his kids to the Santa Claus parade."

I laughed. If only all my problems were as simple. "How late will you be?"

"The parade should be over by noon. How does one or two sound?"

"Sounds good to me. Steve . . ." I wanted to tell him about Bryan, but as the news was not of the telephone variety, I hesitated. I pressed the receiver tight against my ear. "I love you," I said.

Sleep didn't come that night, either, and I spent the midnight hours pacing where Leslie had paced the night before. Mercifully her door stayed closed. My defenses were down. Tomorrow would be soon enough for her to learn what I wished she didn't have to know.

It was pushing three before I finally turned off the lights. Wrestling between cold sheets, my mind took over where my feet left off. Now instead of the furniture I had skirted, I dodged between AIDS and Bryan, Williams and Maxwell, Leslie and AIDS.

I plumped the pillows. Hot, I threw off the covers. Cold, I pulled them back. Like yesterday, I welcomed the morning.

True to form, Thelma was in the office when I arrived. Thank God some things never change.

"What, no doughnuts?" I asked.

Thelma lifted her fingers from the computer keyboard. "I'm watching your waistline." She smiled. "Besides, there's no time for frivolities today."

The morning was as busy as Thelma had predicted, and the thoughts that had robbed me of sleep lost themselves in a sea of potential clients wanting to know about the latest in surveillance equipment, tracking errant spouses, and catching industrial spies.

Near the end of the day Mr. Peterson, a long-time client with long-running grandson problems, came into the office. His gray hair and wrinkled skin were the same, but instead of his usual frown, he wore a smile.

"I'm going to California for Christmas," he said.

"Are you going alone?" I asked.

"No," he chortled, "with a plane."

Startled by this unexpected humor, I laughed. Even more startling was Mr. Peterson's loud guffaws.

"How are you going to like staying in a commune?" I asked. I knew it was where his grandson lived.

"I don't intend to find out. I've got myself a hotel room. If I can go all the way to California, he can come to the hotel." The usual frown settled over Mr. Peterson's face as he spoke.

My row of smiley faces stopped their march across the yellow pad. "How can I help you today?" I asked.

"I need to know if my will is good in California."

"Mr. Peterson, your will . . ." I began to explain, and despite his many interruptions, finished an hour later.

"Mind you, Miss Arthur, I'm not planning to die out there, but an old man like me can't take any chances."

Honoring me with another smile, my octogenarian client left the office.

Our last appointment cancelled. Given the free hour, I did some mental hemming and hawing, letting my thoughts wander aimlessly. AIDS was their most frequent stopping point. Telephone calls ran a close second, followed by a too-large ring on a too-small finger.

After a fifth row of yes and no, I tore the page away and wadded it into a ball. My concentration—or rather the lack of it—was broken. I pushed away from my desk.

"I'm out of here," I told a surprised Thelma. Unsure of my destination, I added, "Check with you later."

Her voice followed me out the door, but I was gone. I needed no more input, not hers, not anybody's.

Having no destination in mind, I gave the Ranger its head. It took me to the municipal building. An empty parking place in the last row beckoned. I pulled in and left the battered Ford to lick its wounds.

Propelled by a sudden sense of urgency, I walked up the stairs and down the corridors that led to MacPhearson's office. But the redheaded detective was not there.

As deflated as last week's Halloween balloons, I retraced my steps, rounded a corner and stopped in front of Rhodes's door. The police lieutenant was there, his attention claimed by a folder that lay open on the desk before him.

"Busy?" I asked, angling for an invitation to enter.

"I am," he said, "but come in anyway."

He closed the folder and offered a cup of the ever-present coffee. I refused and asked instead for what I now knew had brought me here.

"I'd like to see Bryan Parker's autopsy report. I know the official copy isn't out, but MacPhearson told me he saw some of the lab reports."

"Why the rush?" Rhodes's frown drew his brows into a straight line. "Didn't Beller cover the highlights with you?"

"He did, but there're a couple of things I want to check."

Rhodes relaxed his frown. "Okay, I'll see what I can do."

He picked up his phone, punched in a number and asked about the report. Whoever was on the other end said something that caused Rhodes to smile.

"Martha said she sent a copy up here. Give me a minute. I'll see if I can track it down."

He left. I waited. Would it be there? Would I find whatever it was my subconscious told me had to be there?

"I have it." Rhodes slid behind his desk and handed me a large envelope.

"Is there someplace—"

"You can stay here." He checked his watch. "I have a meeting in the chief's office. Just leave the report on my desk when you're through."

Rhodes picked up the file he'd been studying and was gone before I could thank him.

I unfastened the clasp on the envelope and pulled out a sheaf of papers. The title, Pathology Department Forensic Report, gave them an important look. I read the first sheet. It listed Bryan's name, age, sex, race, weight, height, and so on. It read like a physical exam and caused me to think how much death mirrored life.

The head wound, listed by Dr. Beller as the primary cause of death, was described in such gory detail I was back again in the motel room, seeing Bryan as I had last seen him.

I rid my mind of the awful scene, which was not an easy thing to do, and lingered over the description of the torso and extremities. Listed were all the visible scars, scrapes and bruises of the skin.

The next page addressed tissue sampling and exams of the internal organs. One paragraph described Bryan's fragile, inflamed nasal tissue and told of a septal perforation. Couched in medicalese, some details taxed my understanding, but Dr. Beller's conclusion, "changes consistent with heavy cocaine use," was easy to understand.

I gave the pages a final check and turned to the post-mortem summary. As before, the cause of death was listed as massive head trauma, and the histological findings of the nasal mucous membranes were attributed to chronic cocaine abuse.

I paused for a deep breath and read on. As MacPhearson had said, the lab tests were also positive for HIV. Heavy-hearted, I returned the report to its envelope and laid it on Rhodes's desk. The summary of a wasted life, left there for anyone to read.

I wrote a note thanking Rhodes for his help and paper-clipped it to the envelope. A late afternoon quiet pervaded the squad room. It fit my somber mood exactly.

Though not quite dark outside, the streetlights were already lighted. The glow, feeble at first, intensified as daylight waned. Traffic, as was usual for this time of day, was stop-and-go. Yet the time it took to drive across town was too short.

I pulled in behind Leslie's Mazda and switched off the Ranger's ignition. A coward, unsure of what lay ahead, I was afraid to go inside. I sat there, wrapped in a cocoon of darkness. Only I could not stay. It was an unreal world. The real world lay outside the Ranger, waiting to claim me. I opened the door and slid into the cold night, and unwilling to announce my presence, closed it gently behind me.

Bright lights drew me to the kitchen, where Leslie hummed a song I did not recognize. Seeing me, she smiled. "I'm making stir fry," she said.

Leslie stood before the counter, slicing a variety of vegetables and a pair of chicken breasts into thin strips. On the stove a heavy cast iron frying pan waited.

"You do like stir fry, don't you?" she asked.

Her words filled what for me was an uncomfortable silence.

"I like stir fry," I said.

I crossed to the table and pulled out a chair. In their corner of the kitchen, Zeus ate steadily, and Hera waited patiently.

"I went shopping today. Your grandmother insisted on driving. Still, it was nice to get out."

Leslie continued slicing as she offered the explanation, bringing the knife up, then down against the cutting board.

"I read Bryan's autopsy report." The chair creaked beneath me, underlining my words.

"Was it interesting reading?" Leslie scraped a pile of mushrooms into a bowl and slid a green pepper under the blade. Switching the knife to her left hand, she continued to raise and lower the knife, feeding the bell pepper forward with her right hand as she did.

"I thought so," I said, watching the moving knife.

"What interested you the most? The head wound?" She stopped cutting and looked at me, her face an expressionless mask.

I shook my head, watched as she slid more green pepper under the blade.

"What did interest you?" She added the sliced peppers to the bowl of mushrooms.

I took a deep breath. "His hands."

Leslie laughed. "His hands?" She laid the knife on the cutting board and moved away from the counter. "What was so interesting about Bryan's hands?"

I sat up straighter, watched Leslie move closer. "He had a scraped knuckle on his left hand."

She stood very still. "Anything else?"

I smoothed an already smooth tabletop. "The serology report." I stilled my moving fingers. "Did you know Bryan had AIDS?"

In the kitchen of the bungalow on Valley Avenue, friends became enemies, and like warring animals, took each other's measure.

"Did he infect you, Leslie? Do you have AIDS?"

She answered with a keening wail that vibrated through the air.

I pulled up from the chair, tried to move away, but caught my foot in the chair leg.

Leslie wrapped her fingers around the handle of the frying pan.

I moved.

She was faster.

Chapter Twenty-Six

MY EYES BLINKED OPEN. I MOANED, BUT STRANGELY FELT NO PAIN. I SAW THE DARK. WAS IT night? Thinking yes, I slept.

Something rough scraped against my cheek. I moved my head, hit out seeking to brush it away, and bumped something soft and furry that meowed a protest.

Hera? Zeus?

I rolled from side to back, expecting the yielding comfort of my waterbed. It was not there. I reached out and found a forest of wooden legs. Grasping the largest, I pulled to a sitting position.

The room blurred. I closed my eyes and reopened them slowly. I gave the leg a careful scrutiny. It most definitely belonged to the kitchen table, and I was under it.

The realization made me dizzy, and I felt nauseated. Hell! Was I doomed to spend the rest of my life puking?

Refusing to accept the fate that it seemed the gods had once again planned for me, I reached for the tabletop and pulled upright. My flesh-and-blood legs threatened collapse, and I dropped into a nearby chair, tripping over a frying pan as I did.

A memory tugged for recognition. Frowning, I raised tentative hands, feeling my face and head. There was no blood, only a large—a very large—bump above my ear on the left side of my head. I cupped my hand over this latest insult to my person and enjoyed a moment of self-indulgence.

The strong smell of onions drew my eyes to the counter. The cutting board was there, a pair of chicken breasts, sliced vegetables, and a broad-bladed chopping knife.

Leslie? Leslie! Adrenaline readied me for fight or flight. I looked around, but did not see the dark-haired surgeon.

A chorus of meows shattered the silence. The Siamese pair, barely visible in the morning gloom, jumped on the table. Hera, her pointed face wearing a solicitous look, licked me with her sandpaper tongue. I buried my face in the cat's tan coat, wincing at the movement. The jackhammers had returned for an encore. Zeus's loud meow echoed my sentiments.

I massaged my pounding head and wall-walked my way into the bathroom. Three Tylenol found their way into my hand. My stomach said no, but despite the warning, I forced water and pills down my throat. A few deep breaths produced a calming effect.

I did then what I should have done earlier. But the silence had not lied, the house was empty. Leslie was gone, and she had taken everything with her.

Everything?

Fear drove me down the hall and into my bedroom. I pulled the dresser drawer open and pushed aside the pile of sweaters. The thirty-eight Smith & Wesson was still there.

Weak with relief, I braced myself against the side of the bed. The phone on the bedside table beckoned. The clock beside it read six.

"Too early," I said.

"To hell with it," I answered, and before I could change my mind, lifted the receiver and punched in MacPhearson's office number.

"Squad Room," a voice too gravelly to be MacPhearson's answered.

I explained who I was and who I wanted, only to find the who I wanted was not there. A lengthy discussion persuaded the gravelly voice to call the absent MacPhearson and have the detective return my call.

The wait was short.

"What's up, Red?" MacPhearson greeted cheerfully.

I shuddered. How could anyone be so cheerful at six o'clock on a Saturday morning?

"Leslie hit me with a frying pan," I cried. The memory was clear. A beggar no longer, it had moved from my subconscious to my conscious mind and demanded it be shared. With it came the irritation MacPhearson always seemed to provoke.

"What the hell—" MacPhearson exchanged cheerful for surprise.

"She's the killer," I said.

"And I'm Santa Claus."

I closed my eyes and counted to ten. "Leslie said she talked to someone who called after nine, and she has Bryan's ring."

"Rings? Telephone calls? You're not making sense, Ginny."

"Just listen. What you were saying last night is true. Williams didn't kill Bryan Parker or Nancy Webber."

"Now just a minute. I—"

"You nothing," I cut off the argument. "I was with Williams when he was killed but didn't kill him and the same is true of Williams."

"You're saying Williams didn't kill Parker and his girlfriend?"

"That's exactly what I'm saying. Williams didn't kill Bryan Parker or Nancy Webber. Leslie did."

"Anything else?" MacPhearson sighed. His cheerfulness was definitely gone, and if I wasn't mistaken, he was fast running out of patience.

"I read the autopsy report yesterday. Bryan's left ring finger had a scraped knuckle. Someone either twisted or yanked his ring off." I took a quick breath. "Leslie has Bryan's ring, Mac."

"Pretty slim, Red."

"What do you want? A signed confession?" I was neither cheerful nor patient.

"It would help," he said calmly.

"Well, forget it. She's not here."

"But I'm sure you know where she is." MacPhearson had moved to sarcasm.

"As a matter of fact, I do," I snapped back. I told him about Leslie's wallet and the single twenty inside it.

"So you think she's gone to get some money."

"What else? She already has clothes and a car."

The line grew quiet.

"Damn it, MacPhearson, say something."

"I need proof, Ginny, not guesses. Hard evidence that I can take to the DA."

I groaned. "She's a surgeon. If she has AIDS, and I'm betting she does, her career is over," I said, fueling my argument with motive.

"Okay . . . okay, I'll buy that. But if she killed Parker and Nancy Webber, who shot her?"

I saw her nimble fingers pleating hospital sheets and shifting knives from hand to hand, saw the bullet hole in the lipstick Jaguar I'd drawn on the mirrored wall of the dressing room, and shoved my left index finger hard against my right side. Trying my damnedest not to shout, I shouted, "Leslie shot herself."

"More guesses, Ginny?"

"I gave you motive and opportunity. What more do you want?"

"How about a murder weapon? We didn't find the gun on her, and Leslie sure as hell didn't take it anywhere."

"Hell! I solved the case. The least you can do is find the damn gun."

"Since you're so sure she's the killer, you find the damn gun." It was Mac-Phearson's turn to shout.

"Okay, I will." I slammed the receiver into its cradle and picked up my shoulder bag. Asshole. If proof was what he wanted, I'd damn well get it for him.

As I reached for my coat, the thirty-eight stared at me from the open dresser drawer. I dropped to my knees. Monday's lesson had taught me how to load a gun. When I left the house, the shoulder bag hung heavier than usual against my hip.

The Ranger I had parked in the driveway last night was now parked in the street. Leslie had moved it to get the Mazda out. I dug into my bag for the keys. They were not there, nor were they inside the truck.

I searched the street and then the driveway, hoping against hope Leslie had simply tossed them aside in her haste to be gone, but found nothing. With the spare key I kept hidden at the base of the Don Juan climber, I retrieved a spare set from the house, making sure the apartment key was on the ring as I did. It was. Despite the delay they'd caused, the missing keys had confirmed another of my suspicions.

The parade, slated to begin at nine, had already snarled traffic. Barred from my usual Monroe Avenue route, I switched to side streets, but police cars, uniformed officers, barricades topped with flashing lights, and a horde of pedestrians rendered even these impassable.

I revised my strategy further and attempted a back alley approach. When this maneuver failed, I abandoned the Ranger and hoofed the final blocks to the Michigan Street building.

The discordant sounds of marching bands, practicing as they waited, grew louder as I neared my destination. I passed by the front entrance. It was open. A departure from the usual weekend procedure, it gave entry to employees wanting to use their offices for viewing stands. I passed by the front of the building and headed for the back lot. Just as I had known it would be, the Mazda was there, parked in its reserved slot. What I didn't expect was the redheaded police detective who stood beside it.

"I thought you'd never get here," MacPhearson said.

I turned on my heel and headed for the building's rear entrance.

"Hold on, Ginny." MacPhearson called. "We have to talk."

"We have nothing to talk about." I pushed through the door and hurried down the hall to the elevator.

MacPhearson caught the door on its back swing and rushed after me. "The gun's not up there, Red. The techs have been all over the apartment."

"Leslie Parker is."

"And what are you going to do if she is? Ask her where she hid it?"

"She's the only one who knows."

"If you think she's the killer, why would you want to be anywhere near her?" MacPhearson made no effort to hide his anger.

"Know! Not think." I shot him a don't-try-and-change-my-mind look.

He raised his hands. "Okay, it's your show, but why are you so sure she's here?"

"Why were you so sure I would be here?" I challenged.

"Ginny . . ." MacPhearson's tone was threatening.

"Her checkbook and credit cards are upstairs," I answered defiantly.

"I still think Maxwell is a better bet."

"You're wrong."

The elevator door opened, and the two of us stepped inside. Pulling my shoulder bag tight against my hip, I punched the tenth floor button.

Chapter Twenty-Seven

I FITTED THE KEY INTO THE LOCK, TURNED IT, AND PUSHED THE APARTMENT DOOR OPEN. THE ANSEL Adams print that hung on the right-hand wall caught my attention. Instead of its usual flush position, it now hung sideways from the wall, revealing the numbered keypad and bank of green and red lights that hid behind it. Seen in the dim light of the hall, the red light glowed a deceptively cheerful greeting.

"This tells us she's either here or she's been here." I shot MacPhearson an I-told-you-so look as I entered the codes that changed the lights from red to green and fixed the Adams print in place.

MacPhearson, Glock in hand, pushed open the kitchen door. "Nobody in here," he said.

Sunlight brightened the living room, fell on the gutted couch and beyond to a pair of end tables sitting side-by-side against the far wall. This room was also empty.

I followed MacPhearson down the hall and watched as he opened each door we passed. Each room received a quick scrutiny, my unasked question answered with a shake of his head.

Unlike the others, the library door stood part way open. Not that it would have done much good to close it as a bullet hole larger than my fist gave visual access whether open or closed.

MacPhearson peered cautiously around the doorjamb. "Nothing," he mouthed. Darkness and silence were the room's only occupants.

I switched on the overhead light and followed MacPhearson inside. The desk was cleared of its usual clutter, including the lamp I'd thrown at the masked intruder. I pushed the swivel chair aside and opened the middle drawer. Leslie's checkbook along with several credit cards was still there.

Had I been wrong? Doubt crept in, partnering the logic that had brought me here.

"Problem?" MacPhearson asked.

"No-o-o." I made the word longer then necessary, still convinced I was right. If Leslie wasn't here, she soon would be. I took another look around the room, half expecting to see the dark-haired girl materialize.

She didn't, and I flipped off the overhead light, plunging the room back into darkness.

I followed MacPhearson into the master bedroom. A light glowed on the bedside table, showing the slashed mattress and open dresser drawers. Mute testimony that the cleanup crew had not been here yet.

MacPhearson picked his way through the debris. "Maxwell and Williams did quite a job."

I let the reference to Maxwell ride and studied the dresser, my eyes, then my fingers opening and closing drawers, making a closer inspection. "It wasn't like this the last time I was here."

"And that was?"

"Tuesday, the day I brought Leslie home from the hospital. We stopped by to pick up some of her clothes."

MacPhearson didn't exactly ignore me, but he didn't say anything, either. He just walked through the door that led to the dressing room.

Here, as in the bedroom, a light had also been left on. Stopping before my hand-drawn Jaguar, he gave a low whistle. Smeared over with additional layers of red lipstick and black eyebrow pencil, it bore little resemblance to Bryan's sports car. The panel that I had lifted back into place had stayed in place, keeping secret the secrets that hid behind it. There being enough to talk about, I didn't mention it.

"Have you been at it again, Red?" MacPhearson looked at me, then back at the defaced artwork.

"You know damn well I haven't. You're looking at some more of Leslie's handiwork."

MacPhearson frowned. "You never did say why you drew it."

"I wanted to see if the bullet that hit Leslie was the same bullet that killed the Jaguar."

"Was it?"

"It was," I said, "And it also proves my other theory."

"Which one?"

"I've already told you." God! Didn't the man ever listen?

"Tell me again. I'm a slow learner."

Deciding to show rather than tell, I turned my back on the disfigured Jaguar and squatted to Leslie's smaller size. My left index finger became a gun, which I jammed into my gut.

"Bang!" I shot an imaginary bullet through my right side straight into the Jaguar's grill.

"She's right-handed," he said.

"Surgeons can work with either hand, and Steve says Leslie's one of the best."

"You're saying she's ambidextrous?"

An ear-splitting electronic alarm drowned my answer.

"What the hell—" MacPhearson reached for his gun.

"It's the alarm." I raced for the hall.

MacPhearson shoved past me, through the open front door. I turned off the alarm, silencing the electronic wail, and hurried to the wall phone in the kitchen. The half-open pantry door swayed as I passed by. A quick look inside told me it was empty—now.

Refusing the lure of spilled milk or missed opportunities, I picked up the handset and punched in a three-digit code. The surveillance room operator answered on the first ring.

"This is Ginny Arthur," I said and gave orders to cancel the alarm.

"Whoever it was is gone," MacPhearson said, joining me in the kitchen. "The elevator's on its way down."

"Leslie," I said flatly. "She was here when we got here. I don't know for sure, but I'm guessing she hid in the kitchen pantry."

I headed for the library, leaving MacPhearson to make the call that would start the search for the missing surgeon. A light shone through the open door. With a sinking heart, I rounded to the back of the desk. Its center drawer stood open, the checkbook and credit cards were gone.

I should have taken them when I had the chance. I slammed the drawer shut and berated myself for being a fool.

"Help's on the way," MacPhearson said from the doorway.

"Who's there?" another louder voice called from the front hall.

MacPhearson flattened himself against a nearby wall, lifted his gun to a firing position, and motioned me behind him.

"Who's there?" The call came again.

"Don't shoot!" I hissed. "It's Jackson Brown, one of our security guards."

His gun leading the way, the uniformed guard peered around the door-jamb.

"It's Ginny Arthur, Jack," I spoke rapidly, "and this is Detective MacPhearson." I moved from behind my would-be protector. "Someone else was here. They triggered the alarm when they left, and then took the elevator down."

Brown showed himself in the doorway. His face, at first suspicious, became friendly when he saw me. "Sorry, Miss Arthur, I didn't know you were up here."

"Did you see anyone on your way up?" MacPhearson holstered his gun as he spoke.

Brown shook his head and, following the detective's lead, holstered his weapon. "I took the stairs. It's faster," he explained. "I was on the seventh floor when the alarm went off. With so many extra people in the building, I've been pretty busy."

"How about Dr. Parker? Did you see her this morning?" I asked.

"Yeah, I did." Jackson Brown beamed like a kid with good news. "She was in the parking lot earlier on. I helped her load a couple of suitcases into her Mazda."

Brown looked from me to MacPhearson. "If I see her, want I should tell her you're looking for her?"

"I think she's already gone," I said ruefully.

Brown left the way he had come, hoofing it down the stairs. The two of us rode the elevator to the ground floor. Outside, the sun, shining in a cloudless sky, danced off the car tops, and a gentle breeze whipped up an occasional gust. It was a perfect day for a parade. Only we were not going to a parade. We were hunting a killer.

The Mazda was still there, parked in its usual spot. I moved closer and looked through the driver's window. The driver's seat was positioned far back, too far back for Leslie's short legs, and the carpet in front of the driver's seat was pulled away from the floorboards.

"It will be a while before the back-up gets here, but I guess we should consider ourselves lucky. If you couldn't get in, she can't get—"

"Mac." I cut off his words, words I had not heard. "Look at this." I pointed inside the car.

"I'll be damned." MacPhearson reached past me and opened the driver's door, exposing a small compartment set into the undercarriage of the Mazda.

"Is the gun there?" I asked.

MacPhearson bent for a closer look. "Just some rubber gloves and a plastic bag full of what I'm guessing is probably cocaine."

I wiggled nearer for a closer look. "I'll bet the gun was there."

MacPhearson slammed the door shut. "Stay here," he commanded.

I started to protest, my usual response when ordered to do anything, but MacPhearson was back, pulling on a pair of latex gloves. Reopening the car door, he reached inside and lifted the bag of white powder and settled it inside an evidence bag.

"No sense in inviting more trouble," he said. He engaged the Mazda's locks and slammed the door shut.

"We Wish You a Merry Christmas" played in brass echoed around the parked cars as MacPhearson deposited the bag and its contents in a strongbox in the trunk of his police car.

"Do you know what bank Leslie uses?" he shouted in my ear.

"First National," I shouted back, naming a local bank located midway on the Monroe Street Mall.

"Wait here while I let headquarters know what we've got, and where we're going."

He opened the driver's door of his unmarked car and side-saddled the front seat.

I watched MacPhearson key the mike, then pressed my face against the Mazda's window, and stared at the small compartment. It was a box really with a hinged cover that when closed was undetectable. "And to think I was sitting right on top of the damn thing," I said.

"Sitting on top of what?" MacPhearson asked from behind me.

"The gun." I turned away from the car and shook my head in disgust.

MacPhearson caught my arm and pulled me after him. "If you're right about the gun, Ginny," he tightened his grip, fitted his pace to mine, "she probably has it with her."

I clutched my shoulder bag tighter. "I already thought of that," I said.

We left the parking lot and entered a world of make-believe. A grossly inflated Mickey Mouse, Donald Duck, assorted elves, and even Tinker Bell bobbed over our heads. Brass trumpets, tubas, and baritones passed us at eye level, and large drums filled the air with a boom-boom beat.

"Stay close," MacPhearson cautioned. "I don't want to lose you." Only brightly uniformed band members, calling the names of friends, forced us apart.

I skirted a float with a bevy of snow princesses and scanned the crowd. MacPhearson, red head swiveling to and fro, was trapped by Bo Peep and a pair of bleating sheep. Unable to get to him, I fought my way to the next corner, and searched the crowd for Leslie's familiar figure. Several dark heads caught my eye. I elbowed forward, but though their shapes were right, their faces were wrong. MacPhearson, too, had vanished from sight.

I side-stepped a group of teenage boys chasing the snow princesses and took to the less crowded street, only to have a policeman motion me back to the sidewalk. Once again I found myself bucking the pedestrian traffic, moving up Monroe as they moved down.

A red head popped up ahead of me. I rushed forward and called MacPhearson's name. A clean-shaven face turned toward me. Another, farther away, had a mustache, but didn't stop when I called.

A hole opened. I darted through. A slender girl, her dark hair brushing her shoulders, moved across the periphery of my vision. Like me, she was headed up instead of down Monroe.

A passing band announced "Here Comes Santa Claus." The crowd surged forward and hid the girl from view.

A daddy, piggy-backing a small boy, blocked my way.

"Excuse me, please . . . please excuse me."

I pushed past, but the dark-haired girl was gone.

A hand gripped my shoulder. I struggled, but couldn't break free.

"Hold on, Ginny. It's me."

I pulled MacPhearson close. "I saw Leslie. She's in the bank." This last was a guess, but she'd been in front of the bank building, and my mind labeled it fact.

A rousing cheer announced Santa's arrival, and a rush of admirers pulled us away from the bank's entrance. It was useless to struggle, and we went with the crowd. Half a block later, MacPhearson broke us free.

"Are you sure it was her?" he asked.

In the window behind him a trio of store mannequins dressed in multicolored ski parkas smiled encouragement.

"It was Leslie," I said, "and she went into the bank."

"How long ago?"

"Just before you grabbed me."

We retraced our steps and reached the bank just as Leslie came through the door.

"Leslie Parker," MacPhearson called.

Recognition showed on her face, and she moved back inside.

MacPhearson broke into a run. Third in line, I made it inside in time to see the redheaded detective follow Leslie through a side door.

I bumped a startled bank guard out of my way and followed MacPhearson's rapidly disappearing back.

I dodged a couple pushing twins in a double stroller, and rounded a corner, saw Leslie stumble and saw MacPhearson reach for her.

Leslie balanced against the front of a building. Her arm came up. It straightened. Sunlight glinted off the barrel. I screamed a warning. The gun fired.

Chapter Twenty-Eight

MacPhearson was down. My warning had come too late. Heart racing, hands shaking, I knelt beside him.

"Get help!" I cried.

The crowd, some curious, others reluctant, pressed in on us.

"Get help," I repeated. My fingers, sticky with blood, searched frantically for a pulse I could not find.

"Let me through. Stand back," an authoritative voice barked.

A pair of policemen broke through the crowd. The female half spoke into a walkie-talkie. Almost immediately, sirens sounded over the din.

Despite my tears, I got to my feet and left MacPhearson to his fellow officers.

"Is he dead? Do you know him?" The questions followed me, but I did not answer.

"You were with him." The couple with the twins was there, staring at me with rounded eyes.

"Is he dead?" the daddy persisted.

"He's dead! MacPhearson's dead, and Leslie Parker killed him," I screamed silently. In the midst of this horror, the babies laughed. Seeing their happy faces, I ran.

The crowds slowed my flight. Forced to a walk, I replayed MacPhearson's final minutes, but the memory was too painful, and I struggled to break the mental tie. I could not.

I neared the parade's end. The crowd's pace quickened. I broke into a run, running as I now knew Leslie had run, not from that bloody scene but to the Mazda.

The gray sedan was still there, parked behind the building. I looked for Leslie but did not see her. Fearing the gun she carried, I slowed my steps. I might be crazy, but I was not a fool.

The sun still shone, and a gentle breeze still blew. Except for a now almost empty parking lot, the crowd from the parade having begun to disperse, things looked the same as before. Only things were not the same, nor would they ever be again.

A door opened and footsteps sounded on the asphalt. My senses on full alert, I hid behind the corner of the building. It was Leslie, and she was shoving another suitcase into the Mazda's already crowded trunk.

My shoulder bag nudged my hip. I reached inside and freed the thirty-eight from its hiding place. Fighting off the revulsion I felt as my blood-stained fingers curled over the barrel, I fitted the loathsome thing into the palm of my hand.

The trunk lid on the Mazda slammed shut, and the driver's door opened.

"Stop!" I called from the safety of my hiding place. "It's Ginny Arthur, Leslie, and I have a gun."

Leslie froze, half in and half out of the gray sedan.

"Move away from the car!" I yelled over the mingled parade and crowd noises that sounded in the distance.

A bullet slammed into the corner of the building, showering my head with shards of brick. It was a thing I had anticipated, intellectually if not emotionally.

Wiping my dry lips with an equally dry tongue, I crouched low and chanced another look. She was still there, hiding behind the open car door. I steadied my hands and pulled the trigger. The bullet ricocheted off metal, hitting Leslie's car I hoped.

Leslie retreated behind the Mazda. I moved when she moved, finding shelter behind a green Chevy as another of her bullets hit where I had been.

Leslie's back was to me. She had not discovered my new hiding place. I moved closer and readied myself for another shot.

"Drop the gun, Leslie."

She whirled, firing as she did. I heard the blast, felt the pain, and pulled the trigger of my thirty-eight. Once, twice, three more times, the sound of each gunshot echoing loudly in my ears.

A distant drum boomed . . . boomed . . . boomed. Overhead white clouds scudded across a blue sky. I couldn't breathe. I couldn't . . .

The ground was hard beneath me, the air around me cold. A blurry figure leaned over me, murmured nonsense in my ear and stroked my face with gentle fingers.

"Ginny . . . Ginny," he whispered.

Wanting the comfort the voice offered, I tried to answer, but had no voice. Tried to focus, but had no eyes.

"Miss Arthur? Miss Arthur?" Jackson Brown called my name. The police came after him, and after them an ambulance.

"Ginny." Another voice, Steve's voice, called to me. "Everything's all right. You're going to be fine." But as it was with most doctors, I knew he didn't always tell the whole truth.

Time passed, stood still. Pain came and went, came and—

Beside me something, no, someone, stirred.

"It's me, Regina." A lined face with green eyes, as green as my own green eyes, leaned over me.

"Wicki." A flood of memories washed over me, love, hate, hurt . . . hate . . . hurt . . . . I reached out to touch her. "Leslie shot me."

Wicki nodded. "I know."

I moved, tried to escape the pain.

"Don't," she cautioned.

A nurse came and stuck a needle into the tubing that led into my arm. The pain went away, and I slept.

Steve came back.

"Leslie shot me," I said, still needing to validate the memory.

Steve nodded. It was a reassuring nod. "The bullet hit the bone in your shoulder. We had to take you to surgery."

I pushed aside the pain that said he spoke the truth and steeled myself for what I feared would be a greater hurt. "Is Leslie dead?"

In wordless confirmation, his fingers tightened over mine. We talked of Mac then, and I cried for him and her.

The nurse with the needle came again. The pain left, but not the memory. The thirty-eight was in my hand, and a voice inside my head commanded me to shoot.

Leslie was dead. I had killed her, and nothing or no one could take this pain away.

Later, much later, I heard the curtains move apart. Sunlight warmed my face and invited me to open my eyes.

"It's about time you woke up." Fists riding her hips, Thelma smiled her familiar smile.

"I'm hungry," I said.

"Sounds like things are back to normal." She laughed, filling the room with much needed merriment.

As if from nowhere, a tray of red gelatin, variety unknown, chicken broth and hot tea appeared before me.

"You call this breakfast?" I asked. Knowing neither the time of day nor which meal was being offered, it was only a guess.

"It's what your doctor ordered." She rolled up the bed and plumped the pillow behind my head. "So eat."

I ate.

"Feel better?" she asked when the tray was gone.

"Not really," I said, the meal's aftertaste still lingering on my tongue. I began an exploration of the bandages that covered my shoulder.

"You're lucky it's your left shoulder," Thelma said watching me.

"Feel up to having company?" Rhodes called from the doorway. He wore a broad smile and carried a large bouquet of tissue-wrapped roses. "These are from Marianne. She sends her love."

Thelma took the flowers. "I'll get a vase and give you two a chance to talk." She left the room, closing the door behind her.

"What are they saying downtown?" Starved for information, I wasted no time.

Rhodes pulled an uncomfortable looking ladder-back chair closer to the bed, eyeing it suspiciously before sitting in it. "They're saying Leslie Parker killed her husband and Nancy Webber."

"Do they agree she shot herself?"

"The powder burns on the clothes she was wearing when she was shot seem to confirm it." He raised a precautionary hand. "And before you ask, the bullet in the Jaguar came from the same gun."

"The one she used to shoot me?" The question was out of sync, but I had to know.

Rhodes nodded.

Satisfied, I switched back to the original topic. "Was Williams in the motel room that night, or did Leslie just say he was?"

Used to my conversational high jinks, Rhodes grinned. "They picked up a couple of other dealers who said Williams was with them all night."

"But how? And why?"

"How is easy," Rhodes cut in. "Leslie hired a private dick, a damn good one, too, a PI by the name of Baxter. He not only told her about Parker's girlfriends, he told Leslie about Parker's other late-night roaming and provided her with an album of pictures. We found the album and a written report in her locker at the hospital."

"But why Williams?"

"She needed a convenient shooter, and Williams, scar and all, figured prominently in a couple of the pictures Baxter provided. Probably figured if there was any question, it would be his word against hers."

"And who would believe a drug dealer?"

"And who would believe a drug dealer," Rhodes agreed. He shifted in his chair. "She was pretty damned clever, Ginny. What made you suspect her?"

"The ring, Bryan's skinned knuckle, the telephone call, the way she handled the knife . . ." I listed the parts, then fitted the pieces into a whole. "She found out where Bryan was meeting his latest girlfriend, went there, and shot them." The grisly scene replayed itself as I talked. "I think the ring was an afterthought. She saw it, got mad and yanked it off his finger."

"Then shot herself on the way out and stashed the gun in that hidden compartment in the car," Rhodes finished.

I nodded agreement. "She knew just how and where to shoot herself for maximum effect on the outside and little damage on the insides." I leaned into the pillows and closed my eyes. "I should have known the gun was in the car," I said, shaking my head. I massaged my bandaged shoulder, easing the ache.

"Don't be too hard on yourself, Ginny. The techs also missed it. It was her father who told us about it. Had the box fitted before he gave her the car. Said he had one just like it in his car. Used it to carry his medical bag, drugs, whatever he wanted to keep out of sight." Rhodes stretched his legs in front of him, crossing them at the ankles.

"Have you seen Leslie's autopsy report?" I asked.

"It hasn't come across my desk. Robbery isn't primary on this one. The case belongs to homicide."

I looked away, plucked at the sheet that covered me. "What about Maxwell? MacPhearson—" I paused, my heart growing heavy as I spoke his name. "He thought Maxwell killed Bryan and the girl."

"Those are a couple of charges Sammy-boy won't have to face, but they stuck him with the other."

"Williams?"

Rhodes nodded. "And you should have been there. When Maxwell heard he was being charged with three murders, he told his lawyer to get lost and started singing—names, dates and places."

"Enough to implicate Victor Sands?"

"Don't I wish." Rhodes smiled ruefully. "I'm not sure yet if there's anything we can hang on Victor Sands, but Maxwell did name several of his lieutenants, and Bryan Parker was one of them."

"MacPhearson was hoping for bigger things." I sank back against the pillows, suddenly very tired.

Rhodes laughed. "It isn't all bad news. Before he was through, Maxwell confessed to having engineered the ipecac fiasco. It was in the baked beans, a donation from the Sandcastle's kitchen to the ghosts and goblins of Marion City. It was a diversion tactic, set up to cover what he claims was a million dollar drug deal."

"Bastards," I said.

Rhodes did another leg shuffle. "Do you remember the last scene on that videotape you shot?"

"The one showing Williams talking to a ghost?"

"That's the one, and it's another case where a ring, an onyx pinky ring with diamond initials to be exact, helped nab a killer."

"The ghost was Sammy Maxwell?" I asked, remembering a diamond-studded pinky ring, the Sandcastle, and a dimly lighted booth.

"You got it."

"It couldn't have happened to a nicer guy." I leaned deeper into my pillows. "But why pick a citywide Halloween party? You'd think all the people, especially the kids, would get in their way."

"Think it through, Ginny. Noise, confusion, costumes, and masks to hide behind? What better place could they find?"

Rhodes laid his hand over mine, and I laced my fingers through his.

"Did Maxwell say why he killed Williams?"

"Not really, but he probably thought either Parker or Williams was holding out on him. Then when Parker got himself killed, he figured it had to be Williams and went after him."

"Ironic, isn't it, that Leslie should be the one to find the drugs?" I frowned. "It was cocaine, wasn't it?"

"It was, almost one hundred percent pure, as a matter of fact, and worth a king's ransom on the street."

"Or a man's life," I said.

"Several lives," Rhodes corrected. He leaned closer. "Do you remember that friend of Kevin Titus's, Johnny Martinez?"

"I remember him."

"He's given us several names. The going's slow, but we've been able to tie up some loose ends."

Rhodes gave my hand another squeeze. "Speaking of loose ends, can you tell me what happened in the parking lot?"

"Is this official?" I stared at the ceiling, not wanting him to read my face.

"Semi-official. Homicide will be around in a day or two to make it official."

I freed my hand from Rhodes and pleated the bed sheet much the same as Leslie had done when a patient. "It was either her or me, and you always said I'd shoot if I had to."

Rhodes frowned, pulling his brows together.

I avoided his eyes. God! Could he read my mind? Did he know I had wished Leslie dead? That I had named myself her judge, jury, and executioner?

"I'm waiting," Rhodes said.

I fisted my hands around the edge of the sheets. "What is there to tell? Leslie shot me. I shot her."

"I'm still waiting," Rhodes said patiently.

"Waiting for what?" I demanded.

"For you to tell me about the other shooter."

"What other shooter?" Was I hearing what I was hearing?

"The one who shot Leslie," Rhodes answered.

"I shot Leslie."

Rhodes shook his head. "You had a thirty-eight, Ginny. Leslie was killed with a forty-five."

"But there wasn't anyone else, only me."

Rhodes continued to shake his head.

"Who then? Maxwell?" I was grabbing the wind, looking for straws.

Thelma backed into the room, her hands holding the vase of roses. "Aren't they beautiful?" She looked at the two of us. "Did I interrupt something?"

"Nothing that didn't need interrupting." Rhodes abandoned his chair and edged his way to the door. "I'll be back," he said. "We can finish this up later."

Thelma watched the door swing shut. "Finish what up later?"

"I didn't kill Leslie." My face began to crumble.

"Nobody said you did." Thelma centered the roses on the bedside table, and then turned to look at me. She saw the tears. "My God! You didn't think—"

I couldn't stop crying. What else was buried inside my head? Once an ally, my mind had become an enemy.

Thelma's arms encircled me. "We thought you knew."

I slept when Thelma left. It was a dreamless sleep, and I awoke feeling better, much better. The knowledge that I had wanted to kill Leslie Parker was still there, and I would have to live with that, but knowing I was not her killer would make it easier—not easy, just easier.

The scent of the roses filled the room. I turned to look at them. The yellow long-stemmed blooms were as beautiful as Thelma had said they were. It was not the flowers though that held my attention. It was the blue velvet jeweler's box that sat beside them. A gift from Steve? The thought lifted my spirits. I reached for the box. Inside, a silver unicorn with a broken horn hung from a silver chain.

My eyes fastened on the broken horn. It was the same unicorn I had left in the safe, hidden behind the mirrored wall of the dressing room.

A nurse stuck her head into the room. "Just checking to see if you found your present." She smiled. "A good-looking redheaded man left it for you at the nurses' station. He asked how you were, but said he couldn't stay."

My hand cupped the velvet box. Who? I knew it wasn't MacPhearson. Leslie had seen a redheaded man driving past the house. Another police officer maybe? Only MacPhearson had denied this. One of Maxwell's men? MacPhearson had suggested . . . I shook my head. Thinking of the detective was too painful, thinking of redheaded men too confusing.

I slid the velvet box into the drawer of the table. Out of sight, out of mind, I hoped, but it was not to be. The questions continued. Did the redheaded man have a forty-five? Did he have gentle fingers? Did he put the unicorn in the safe? Leave it there for me to find? Was he David Arthur? The man was an enigma. I sighed, a thing I seemed to do whenever I thought of the uncle who, God help me, I still loved.

Steve came into the room, leaving my questions unanswered. "Who's sending my girl roses?" he asked.

We shared a kiss, and Steve sat where Rhodes had sat.

"The roses are from a secret admirer," I teased.

Steve laughed. "I met your secret admirer in the hall a couple of hours ago." Steve claimed my hand. "John Walters showed us Leslie's autopsy report this morning."

The room grew cold, the scent of the roses overpowering. John Walters was Mercy Hospital's Chief of Surgery, and for him to share an autopsy report with his staff had to mean bad news.

"Was she—?"

Steve nodded.

I sighed. "Poor Leslie. All those years of hard work for nothing."

"It means a lot of hard work for us, too. Walters is setting up a task force to track her patients." He massaged the palm of my hand with his thumb. "It won't be pleasant, but it's got to be done."

I curled my fingers tighter around his.

"Feel up to taking a ride?" he asked.

I said I was, and he helped me into the wheelchair.

We made the trip in silence and, except for inquiries about my health from those we met on the way, remained so.

The rubber wheels on my chair squealed against the tiled floor as we passed through the doors marked NEUROLOGICAL INTENSIVE CARE. Like me, they protested being in this place. I took a deep breath and braced myself for what I knew was to come.

The white-faced figure with a red mustache and a turban of even whiter bandages lay motionless on the bed. Wires sneaked from under the covers and led to monitors showing spiked patterns, but the respirator, which only yesterday had been attached to a tube in his mouth, no longer whooshed its rhythmic song.

Did this mean he was better?

I followed the tubes that led from veins in his arms to bags that hung over his head to Steve's face. Tell me he's okay. Tell me he's going to be fine. It was a silent plea, and Steve did not answer.

I wheeled closer to the bed and took hold of the still hand. "Hello, Mac, it's me, Red."

About the Author

Called Barb as often as Barbara, Mrs. Kiger was born in Michigan but moved south with her husband and most of their six children in 1979. A nurse by profession, she began writing seriously after losing her sight in 1985. Her work has appeared in magazines and anthologies, the most recent being William B. Toulouse's *Amazingly Simple Lessons Learned After Fifty*. "Beginnings," a short story, received Honorable Mention in the Tallahassee Writers' Association 2002 Seven Hills Contest, and appeared in that year's *Fiction Review*. This is her first published novel.

Other Books Published by

Cy**P**ress
ublications

For Children/Families

Orion the Skateboard Kid, **by Juanita S. Raymond and Leland F. Raymond. ISBN 0-9672585-0-2, 63 pages, $9.95**
 —*Enthusiastically recommended for school and community library collec-tions* Orion The Skateboard Kid *is entertaining, engaging reading for 4th and 5th grade level students.* —Midwest Book Review, "Children's Bookwatch," December 2001

Sarah and the Sand Dollar. **by Kathie L. Underwood, ISBN 0-9672585-7-X, 36 pages, $11.95**
 This book, *Sarah and the Sand Dollar,* is based on a true story. While fishing in the Apalachicola Bay, off the coast of Florida, Kathie Underwood experienced the miracle of the sand dollar. Now, inspired by God, she has written her story for children, so they may learn of His abundant love for us.

The Smallest Toy Store, **by Regina N. Lewis, illustrated by P.M. Moore. ISBN 0-9672585-8-8, 44 pages, $12.95**
 —*The holiday is Christmas, the day children dream about all year as they imagine gifts with their names on them. In her charmingly illustrated new book,* The Smallest Toy Store, *Regina Lewis gently reminds her readers that there are children who face the holiday, and every day, without a place to call home, much less a tree or presents. Join the magical Ms. MerryWood and celebrate the true meaning of Christmas."* —*Adrian Fogelin, author* Crossing Jordan, Anna Casey's Place in the World, My Brother's Hero, Sister Spider Knows All, *and* The Big Nothing

Visit our website for ordering information and news of upcoming titles.
http://cypress-starpublications.com